The Hunt for E
By
Christopher Cartwright

Prologue

Minamisōma Harbor, Japan – Friday, 11, March, 2011

The *Hoshi Maru* rode the sea off the north-eastern coastal waters of Japan with arrogant indifference. At a hundred and eighty feet in length, a beam of fifty, and a double layered hull of steel, it was difficult to imagine anything that would disturb the fishing trawler.

Captain Itaru Katsuzō grinned as his eyes swept the horizon. The dark swells shifted against one another like giant shards of shale, forming an impenetrable layer of a puzzle, as it mirrored the velvet black of the night's sky. The conditions made for good fishing. They would pull in their last net shortly and be home within another twelve hours.

At three-thirty a.m. the diesel motors stopped and the final haul of yellowfin tuna was dropped into one of the ship's two live-holds. One of his men noted that the second hold was now full. The captain nodded, his lips curling upward with pleasure. They would be home a full week ahead of schedule. It was a good omen. The best he could have asked for. After nearly ten years working for the fishing company, he had been given command of a trawler of his own – and not just any trawler – the *Hoshi Maru* was the company's newest addition to the fleet. His success would go a long way to validating the executive's decision to promote him.

Katsuzō pushed the twin throttles forward until the powerful Akasaka diesels ran at approximately eighty percent of their maximum RPM and the *Hoshi Maru* headed toward her home port at nine knots. At five-foot ten inches, he was considered tall and good looking. Katsuzō thought about his fiancé. They had been secretly engaged for nearly two years. But as the fifth son of a fisherman, he had little to offer her and her family. His recent promotion had changed all that. When his appointment was ratified, he would go to her parents and formally ask permission to marry her.

Yes, tonight's catch was a very good omen.

The *Hoshi Maru* motored on through the night, until the inky black sky turned into the gray of predawn – when he first heard the strange sound.

It was a firm knocking sound from the internal hull, like the sound one makes when they rapped their knuckles against a door. Only in this case, it was the quarter inch thick steel of the internal hull. His eyes darted across the ship's instruments, confirming that the diesels were running smoothly, that nothing was overheating, and that the impeller was still drawing seawater to cool the engine.

He breathed out gently. Whatever it was, it wasn't affecting the vital parts of the ship's propulsion. That meant they could still reach the harbor early. Let the maintenance workers and engineers resolve the problem. It was most likely something simple. A teething problem with a new ship.

He closed his eyes and listened, trying to imagine what could be the cause of such a strange sound. Captain Itaru Katsuzō's face hardened as he listened to it.

The knocking sound came from somewhere inside one of the live fish holding tanks.

It was quite persistent.

He imagined some strange creature of the deep being accidentally pulled up along with the yellowfin tuna in his net. Fishermen were traditionally superstitious, but he didn't believe any of that. He'd heard stories of sharks being brought up and dropped into the live hold, decimating the dense population of live fish. But he'd never believed stories about secret monsters from below, being dragged to the surface.

One persistent story was that of the chimera.

A chimera is a single organism that is composed of two or more different populations of genetically distinct cells. Most frightening of all, the Nue – described in the Japanese folklore of the Heike Monogatari, the creature was said to have the face of a monkey, the legs of a tiger, the body of a tanuki dog, and the front half of a snake for a tail.

Captain Itaru Katsuzō had heard stories of fishermen who claimed that they had had the misfortune to bring up a Nue inside their fishing nets. The Japanese chimera, a creature that formed the basis of many nightmares, then destroyed the crew and ship with menacing efficiency. Those few survivors who have told the stories, had only ever done so after being rescued from the sea after their vessels had become shipwrecked.

As far as Captain Itaru Katsuzō believed, they were nothing more than the ravings of half-starved, dehydrated, and near-death sailors, and nothing more.

A moment later the knocking stopped.

He exhaled a sigh of relief.

Hyoo, hyoo

The sound changed to a terribly eerie bird cry. It resembled that of a scaly thrush, a nocturnal Japanese bird.

And also, the call sound of a mythical Nue.

Yuki Tono, a short and wiry fisherman, turned to face the captain, his dark brown eyes wide with fear. "It's the call of a Nue!"

Captain Itaru Katsuzō looked Yuki Tono directly in the eye. "The Nue is a myth, made to frighten little boys."

Hyoo, hyoo

The creature cooed again.

Yuki Tono's lips twisted into a hardened grimace. "Does that sound like the imaginings of folklore to you?"

"Control yourself!" Captain Itaru Katsuzō commanded. "We have thousands of yellowfin tuna in our hold. You and I both know that such a large group can make strange sounds. It could be anything. Not just some sort of stupid mythical creature to tell children as bedtime tales."

The knocking on the internal hull started again.

Both men turned their heads toward the bow of the ship.

This time it was clear where the sound was coming from. It was the forward live fish hold. And the knocking was coming from directly inside the hatch. Of that there was no dispute between the two men. Something, or someone, wanted to be let out.

Captain Itaru Katsuzō set his jaw firm and walked toward the hatch.

"What are you doing!" Yuki Tono asked, his face set with abject horror.

"I'm going to find out exactly what is turning you into a frightened child."

"How?"

Itaru Katsuzō grinned. "I'm going to open that damned hatch and have a look."

"No! You can't."

"What else do you suggest I do?"

Yuki Tono said, "We should wake Patrick!"

"Patrick!" Captain Itaru Katsuzō shook his head in disgust. "Patrick can't protect us. He's still running from whatever past he left behind in Ireland. You think he's a real tough man? A murderer? A paid enforcer?"

Yuki Tono nodded. "Yes. You can see it in his eyes. He's a cold-blooded killer. You've seen him with a knife. That's not normal. Whatever past life he left behind, he was trained to kill. A scar like that never leaves a person, no matter how much he runs from it."

"Yeah. Well, whatever Patrick is, we don't need for him to tell us what's making a spooky sound deep inside the hold." Itaru Katsuzō shook his head. "I'm going to go find out now."

Yuki Tono gripped his shoulder. "Please, Captain…"

Itaru Katsuzō shrugged the hand off his shoulder, his eyes filled with defiance. "Leave this to me."

Captain Itaru Katsuzō stepped right up to the forward hatch. Paused for a second. Slid the bolts all the way out, and then opened the hatch. It wasn't the same hatch where the fish were dropped into the hold. This one was smaller, a square, roughly four feet wide. The door was secured by two bolts on one side and thick steel hinges on the other.

He opened the hatch up until it folded back on itself, lying flat on the deck of the *Hoshi Maru* and peered in.

It was entirely dark inside the hold.

Itaru Katsuzō switched on his GENTOS flashlight, sending a thousand lumens into the dark hold, turning it to daylight. Kneeling beside the hatch, with his left hand firmly locked on the side of the deck, while his right gripped the flashlight, his eyes swept the forward compartment of the live fishing hold.

His dark, straight eyebrows narrowed. "What is that?"

He fixed the flashlight on a razor-sharp line in the middle of the fish hold. It was like an imaginary line had been drawn and none of the fish dared to cross it. The damned thing looked as though someone had taken a solid glass divider and cut the hold in two. Itaru Katsuzō knew there was no such thing in his live fish hold. He should know, he'd been inside it when it was dry only three weeks earlier before the *Hoshi Maru* left its dock at Minamisōma harbor.

Even so, it was extraordinary to watch the fish.

He'd seen something similar, although not to the same extent, just one time previously, when they'd somehow dragged a great white shark into the hold. The predator had eaten as many fish as it could manage and then drowned in the narrow confines of the hull. But in the process, the remaining fish had compressed into the narrowest of corners in an attempt to leave space between the predator and themselves.

Even then, it was nothing like the vision he had now. That time, it was more like the shark maintained a small spherical bubble around its teeth-filled mouth, while the fish compressed into the rest of the compartment. In this case, there was no shark, and the dividing line was very specific. What's more, it divided the hold into port and starboard sides, splitting the hatchway in two, with the fish on the starboard side.

His taut jaw muscles flexed.

There was something mythical, if not magical, about the way the line was straight, as though the fish knew that to cross it would be to their certain peril. But there was nothing obviously dangerous to be seen.

Yet still, the fish seemed to keep away from it.

Itaru Katsuzō stared at the dividing line down the middle of the hold. He shined a flashlight into the empty section. The beam flashed through the empty line.

He squinted his eyes.

Nothing.

What the hell had gotten the fish so spooked?

The captain reached in and touched the invisible dividing wall. His hands reached through, penetrating the imaginary divider.

Captain Itaru Katsuzō shook his head. He must be going crazy. For a moment he was almost certain that he would find someone had installed a new glass partition in his hold.

"Find anything?" came the voice of Yuki Tono from a distance.

Captain Itaru Katsuzō turned around to greet him. "Nothing."

He touched the imaginary partition and laughed.

There was nothing there.

He turned and tried to remove his hand, but something forcibly gripped it. Itaru Katsuzō shifted his position, using his other hand to gain leverage.

Itaru Katsuzō felt a surge of adrenaline rush through his body. His heart pounded in his chest. He thrashed, trying to escape whatever had gripped him on his left wrist. Whatever it was, it hadn't hurt him – yet. Instead, it simply held on. He twisted his wrist trying to slip free, but the invisible force that held him seemed to simply tighten.

"Help!" he shouted. "I'm stuck! Something's got me!"

Yuki Tono moved toward him.

But he was too late.

The creature pulled hard with one sudden movement and Captain Itaru Katsuzō was dragged into the live fish hold. His head dipped under the cool water. He kicked with his feet fighting to reach the surface again. His head broke the surface and a moment later he was swimming toward the hatchway.

He nearly made it too.

Yuki Tono reached in.

Itaru Katsuzō gripped his hand thankfully.

But something yanked on his right leg. It was the same sort of vice-like grip of something far from human.

He tried to kick it free, but it was impossible.

Above him Yuki Tono's eyes widened in terror. "A Chimera from the deep!"

Itaru Katsuzō kicked harder.

While confusion, fear, and horror reigned.

A moment later he was dead.

*

Patrick opened his eyes with a jolt.

He stood up from his bunk and listened. The fishermen were all yelling something. In the past two years his Japanese had become pretty good, but they were speaking too fast for him to get any real comprehension.

He glanced out of the porthole, taking in the calm waters. The *Hoshi Maru* appeared steady in the water. It wasn't listing or riding low in the water, which meant they weren't in any immediate danger.

Yuki Tono burst into his quarters. "Patrick! Help there's a Nue!"

He blinked. Patrick was tall by comparison, nearly six feet, with the well-defined and muscular build of a soldier. At thirty-eight years of age, his posture was still ram-rod straight, and his body bore the marks of multiple injuries from a lifetime on an unknown battlefield.

He picked up his shirt and casually pulled it over his head.

"Patrick!" Yuki Tono said, holding him by his shoulders. "Are you listening to me? We're in serious trouble. We're going to die!"

Patrick nodded. "Start again… what's going on?"

"Captain Itaru Katsuzō has been killed by a Nue."

Patrick tried to blink away the haze of confusion. "Sorry, what's a Nue?"

"It comes from ancient Japanese folklore. But it's real. I just saw it kill the captain!"

"Wait…" Patrick met Yuki Tono's gaze. "Itaru Katsuzō's dead?"

"Yes."

Patrick asked, "How did he die?"

"A Nue killed him!"

"Right." He took a deep breath. "You want to tell me exactly what a Nue is?"

"It's a chimera with the face of a monkey, the legs of a tiger…"

Patrick felt a sudden rush of fear rise in his throat. "What did you say?"

"It's a chimera… a type of animal…"

"I know what a goddamned chimera is!"

Patrick reached for his duffel bag. It contained what few possessions he still owned. He unzipped it and foraged into a secret compartment at the bottom, withdrawing a Sig Sauer P226. Despite not being fired in nearly two years, the Swiss-made pistol had been well serviced, its parts regularly stripped and oiled, and loaded with .357 SIG pistol cartridges.

Yuki Tono frowned. "Where did you get a handgun?"

Patrick ignored the question. "Where is it?"

"Where's what?"

"The chimera! That damned killing machine!"

"The Nue?" Yuki Tono cocked his head. "It's in the hold."

"Right." Patrick chambered the first round of his Sig Sauer P226. "The hatches are locked. It might hold it for a few minutes."

"A few minutes?" Yuki Tono's face was ashen gray. "That's all we have?"

"It's all we have. We'll have to scuttle the ship before it escapes."

"Scuttle the ship?" Yuki Tono asked, his voice incredulous. "Why would we scuttle the ship?"

"It might just be the only way to kill it for good. Maybe we can drown it."

"What about your handgun?"

Patrick glanced at the Sig Sauer P226. "This... are you kidding me? This won't even scratch it."

"Then why do you have it?"

"This..." Patrick held up the weapon again. "This is to shoot myself before it can get its hands on me."

"What will the Nue do to us?"

"Anything it wants. It's pure evil. Only it's not called a Nue. Its name is Excalibur – and it was a genetically engineered weapon built in secret by a team from the British Secret Intelligence Service – MI-6."

Yuki Tono turned gray as the overcast sky. "Why would you tell me this?"

"Because when the program was shut down, and the weapon ordered to be destroyed. Excalibur didn't take too kindly to the concept of being broken into little pieces. Instead, he went about systematically hunting down each of the seven-man group who worked on the project. Of which, four are already dead. That's why I have been in hiding. But now he's come for me."

"Stop. I don't want to know anymore. Why are you telling me this?"

"Don't you see?" Patrick's lips curled into a sardonic grin. "Some weapons can't ever be broken. Excalibur will systematically hunt down every one of us, until we're all dead."

He stepped out onto the deck.

The *Hoshi Maru* motored through the second break wall of Minamisōma Harbor. Patrick looked up. "Holy shit! You didn't tell me we were almost on land!"

"Yes. I thought you knew. We just need to keep that...
thing locked within the hold until we reach land and then
we'll be all right!"

"No, we won't!" Patrick's words were emphatic. "We'll
never be all right. Not until that creature is destroyed."

He turned and raced toward the raised pilothouse.

"Where are you going?" Yuki Tono asked.

"To change the course of the future."

*

Dr. Jim Patterson stared through the binoculars at the
fishing trawler that was motoring into the Minamisōma
Harbor. He focused the binoculars on the name on the side of
the ship – *Hoshi Maru*.

He shook his head. From this distance there was nothing
to show that the vessel was in any sort of trouble.

He turned to Dexter Walsh. "Are you sure he's on the
Hoshi Maru?"

"Certain," Dexter replied. "I heard the skipper's mayday
call, saying that they had pulled up a Nue and needed police
to meet them at harbor. It has already killed their captain."

Dr. Patterson looked blank. "What the hell's a Nue?"

"Some sort of Japanese Chimera described in folklore,"
Dexter explained. "It has the face of a monkey, the legs of a
tiger, the body of a tanuki dog, and the front half of a snake
for a tail."

Dr. Patterson grinned. "That's got to be Excalibur!"

"If it is, he's a hell of a swimmer."

"To reach three miles off shore, he'd have to be."

"It's got to be him. No other description fits. Besides, the
coincidence is too much for it to be anything else."

Dr. Patterson nodded in agreement. "Well, that just
proves it."

"What?"

"You were right, Dexter. After we were tipped off that Patrick was hiding onboard the *Hoshi Maru*, Excalibur came after him. That proves it; he's hunting every one of us. He's lashing out all right, but his kills aren't the random attacks of an animal, he's systematically taking out each member of the original team – everyone that knew the truth – until there's no one left."

Dr. Patterson scanned the vessel from left to right. Nothing appeared to be wrong on board. "Where's Excalibur now?"

"Locked inside a fish hold," Dexter replied.

"That won't keep him very long."

"No way in the world." Dexter asked, "Should we get on the radio and tell them what they're facing?"

"Why would we do that?"

"I don't know. Maybe to give the police a fighting chance?"

"There aren't enough police in Minamisōma to give them a fighting chance. No. We're better off leaving. It's time we get on an international flight."

"Where are you going to go?"

"I don't know. I can't imagine there is anywhere on Earth that can keep me safe from Excalibur."

Dr. Patterson lowered his binoculars.

A moment later a siren filled the entire harbor. It sounded like one of those old air raid warning sirens from World War II.

Dexter asked, "What is that?"

Dr. Patterson swallowed. "That's the tsunami warning."

*

Patrick stepped into the wheelhouse and grabbed the wheel, trying to turn the *Hoshi Maru* around until it was heading out to sea.

Sojuro Ishiyama, the skipper, gripped the wheel and fought to hold the course. "What are you doing?"

"We have to get back out to sea!" Patrick yelled. "That creature in our hold can't be allowed to survive!"

The skipper met his eyes. "We can't go back out to sea!"

"Why the hell not?"

"There's been an earthquake off the Pacific coast of Tōhoku. The harbor master says it was big. The harbor's in the process of closing in case there's a tsunami."

Patrick shook his head. "Trust me. With that creature on board, a tsunami's the least of our worries."

"You can't seriously be thinking of taking us out of the harbor channel. It's too long. We'll never make it before the tsunami reaches us."

Patrick pulled out his Sig Sauer pistol and pointed it at the skipper. The weapon didn't have a safety. It could be fired immediately out of its holster. "I'm afraid I'm deadly serious, Sojuro Ishiyama."

The skipper glanced at him, considered fighting, and then, thinking better of it, said, "Okay. If we're going to try and beat this thing, we need to hurry."

"Right."

Patrick took hold of the wheel and shoved the twin throttles all the way forward. The Akasaka diesel engines made a deep, resonant, gravelly rumble. The twin screws found their perch in the water, and the *Hoshi Maru* lurched forward.

Minamisōma Harbor was designed with two long, narrow, shipping lanes surrounded by a large break wall. They were heading out along the inner shipping lane now. It continued for another quarter of a mile, before opening into the outer harbor, which held a large upside-down U-shaped break wall that was twenty feet high.

All they needed to do was get outside that wall, and they would be free. There would be enough water beneath their keel to ride out the tsunami.

Not that it would help them much. If Excalibur was indeed on board, their lives were already over. The real question was, if they reached the deep waters outside of Minamisōma Harbor, what was he going to do about it? He might not be able to shoot Excalibur, but nothing prevented him from drowning. That was it! He would need to open the sea-cocks and sink the *Hoshi Maru* as soon as they were in deep waters far off the coast of Japan.

But first, they needed to get out of Minamisōma Harbor.

Patrick glanced at their speed. They were doing six knots through the water, but sixteen over land, meaning there was a ten knot outward going tide.

He'd never seen anything like it.

Patrick turned to Sojuro Ishiyama. "What's going on?"

"That's water feeding the tsunami. We don't have long."

"Will we make it?" Patrick asked.

Sojuro Ishiyama shrugged. "I don't know. But there's no point turning around now. It's too late. Our best chance is to reach the outer harbor. Depending on how big the tsunami is when it reaches the harbor, we might be able to ride it out in the outer harbor."

"And if it's really big?"

"Then we make sure to hit it head on. Then hope like hell that we survive, because there will be nothing else we can do."

Patrick nodded.

He put the pistol into the side pocket of his cargo pants, and gripped the wheel so tight that he felt it in the tendons and muscles of his forearms.

The *Hoshi Maru* came around the first break wall and into the outer harbor. In the distance, beyond the outer break wall, something caught Patrick's eye. It looked like the white crest of a wave rising in the distance.

It was moving so slowly, he asked Sojuro Ishiyama, "What is that?"

Sojuro Ishiyama's face was set with the hard resolve of a man who knew he'd gambled and lost. His life was over. There was no way to avoid a direct collision with one of the largest tsunamis to ever reach Minamisōma Harbor. "That is your tsunami."

The muscles around Patrick's jaw went taut. "It doesn't look that dangerous."

"None of them do until they reach shallow water. That's where they start to rise."

Patrick turned to port into the outer harbor. He pulled the twin throttles back to idle. There was no question of being able to round the outer break wall before the tsunami struck. Staring at the incoming wave, he waited, trying to judge the moment it would collide with the outer break wall.

That was their only chance.

He needed to hit the wave just as its force had been weakened by the thirty-foot high wall of concrete designed to protect the harbor.

The wave approached slowly.

So slowly, that for a moment, he thought it might not be powerful enough to penetrate the outer break wall.

The receding water finally stopped.

For a moment all was still. It was the calm before the storm. A slack tide. Where the water had reached its equilibrium.

But that was all about to change.

Small ripples approached through the narrow entrance to the harbor. They were now more than six feet tall and far from threatening to the ninety-foot fishing trawler.

Then the wave hit the rising seabed, sending its crest upward like a giant monster rising from the sea. It was a monster all right. And so powerful that it would easily engulf the entire harbor city.

Next to him, Sojuro Ishiyama shouted, "Go! Go!"

Patrick pushed the twin throttles all the way forward and turned the wheel so that the *Hoshi Maru* raced to meet the oncoming wave head on.

The wave struck the outer break wall, rising over the top of the concrete barrier in a torrent of white, turbid water.

Patrick cursed, and held his left hand hard on the twin throttles, praying that they would carry his momentum forward.

A couple seconds later, the bow struck the first wave.

The *Hoshi Maru* jolted as it slammed into it. For a moment, Patrick thought the force alone was going to rip the hull apart.

But the trawler proudly kept her position.

Whitewash flowed across the deck until the pilothouse was temporarily submerged. It only lasted for a split second, before bursting out the other side, riding proudly in the discombobulated water between the outer break wall and the first wave.

Patrick looked up to see that the second wave was approaching fast.

He pushed the throttle forward, but nothing happened.

The first wave must have fully submerged the engine room, flooding the Akasaka diesel engines. There was nothing they could do about it. They were now sitting ducks, at the mercy of whatever waves the tsunami would throw at them.

Patrick turned to watch the wave approach.

Above the thirty-foot outer break wall, white, turbid, and angry water flowed over as though the wall had never existed.

The sight was so unbelievable that it took Patrick a moment to realize what it was.

In that instant, he knew that this was no ordinary tsunami. This was the worst tsunami in Japan's living history.

He didn't bother to hold on.

There was nothing that he could do. He accepted that his life was over.

The wave struck the *Hoshi Maru* on its starboard side and his world turned to darkness – forever…

*

Dr. Patterson stared out at the water.

The *Hoshi Maru* took the first wave head on. The turbid water had washed over her, swamping her diesels, and leaving her dead in the water.

By the time the second wave struck they were listing nearly perpendicular to the approaching thirty-foot wave.

Without propulsion, there was nothing they could do.

The wave struck their starboard side, causing them to broach instantly.

The *Hoshi Maru* went under the turbid froth of buildings, water, and rubble – and never came back up again.

Dexter turned to him and breathed out. "What do you think?"

"I think it's finally over." Dr. Patterson closed his eyes as though considering the possibility. "Nothing could have survived that hit."

"You're certain?"

"After two years of hunting for Excalibur, we finally tracked him down to the far ends of the Earth, cornered him, and then God himself, angered by his very creation, sent this horrible wave in his wrath to destroy him."

Dexter glanced at the turmoil below. Many people would die that day. He grimaced, unsure that even an angry God could do so much harm out of vengeance.

Dr. Patterson said, "Excalibur's finally been destroyed."

Chapter One

Tillamook State Forest, Oregon – Present Day

The yellow 1956 Ford Thunderbird cruised north along US Route 101.

Sam Reilly glanced at the temperature gauge. It had started to shift all the way to the right into the danger zone. He'd been nursing the old car all the way up from San Francisco along US Route 101. It was an old car and he'd been taking his time. But now it looked like he was going to have to stop and do something about it.

At the Devil's Lake Fork, he turned right, following a sign for the nearest garage along the Wilson River inside the Tillamook State Forest. The car was a collector's item, once owned by his grandfather and maintained with love. But over the last few years, Sam Reilly's schedule meant that it was a distant love. And the car was starting to feel it.

It was a yellow convertible, with the hard-top removed. After complaints with the 1955 Ford Thunderbird's cockpit floor area being too hot, the 1956 version added vents in front of the doors to help improve interior air flow and thereby reduce the interior heat. Despite this, the entire floor panel felt hot to the touch.

Sam leaned back in the T-bird's bench seat and shifted the three-speed Ford-O-Matic floor shifter down a gear, as he took another turn-off heading down deeper into the Tillamook State Park. He crossed the Wilson River along a rickety wooden bridge, and took off along the winding roadway that hugged the river.

He eased his foot down on the accelerator and the T-bird's dual four-barrel carbureted 312 cubic inch V8 roared proudly, as though it might one day be in a position to produce its full advertised 260 horsepower.

Up ahead he spotted the small gas station and garage. It was a combination of a gas station with a single bowser for gas and diesel, an old pit-styled mechanic's workshop, and a general store – which looked like it doubled up as the owner's home.

Sam pulled in beside the workshop, switched off the engine, and pulled up the handbrake.

An older man in overalls greeted him with an oily rag and a kind smile. "Hello. Do you want fuel?"

"No thank you, sir," Sam replied as he stepped out of the car. His eyes met the man's and he said, "I was hoping to find a mechanic."

"I'm the only mechanic around here. What do you need?"

"The engine keeps overheating. At first, I thought it was a fault with the gauge, which is prone to getting stuck, but now that it's moving again, it shows the car's overheating. The radiator's got coolant, but I'm guessing there's a blockage somewhere."

The mechanic's face crunched up in an apologetic grimace. "I'll have a look at her for you, but it's unlikely she will be fixed today."

"That's a bummer. I was keen to reach Portland by tonight."

"It's the parts, you see. If it's something simple, I might be able to tinker a replacement, but if something's broken, I'll need to send away for it, and that might take the better part of a week."

Sam shrugged. "If there's nothing you can do, so be it."

The mechanic smiled, relieved that Sam wasn't going to be demanding services that he couldn't provide. "Okay, unlock the hood and I'll see what we've got."

Sam pulled the latch to the hood and the mechanic lifted it forward.

He glanced at the radiator. Using his oily rag, he carefully released the radiator cap, until steam escaped out the sides.

The mechanic said, "Well, we know it's not a fault with your gauge. The engine's definitely overheating."

"Do you think you can fix it?"

"Oh, there's no doubt I can fix it. The question is more a matter of when and that depends entirely on what's wrong." The mechanic met Sam's worried glance. "Look. Everything appears intact. There's no doubt about it that this car's been otherwise maintained beautifully. The radiator might just need a clean out."

Sam's eyes narrowed. "If that's the case?"

"Give me a couple hours and you'll be back on the road."

"All right thanks."

"You're welcome. If you want to wait inside, I've got some magazines but not much else for you to do to pass the time."

Sam ran his eyes across a path behind the garage that led into a dense forest of Douglas-fir trees toward the Wilson River. "I might just go for a walk. Beautiful part of the world you've got here."

"That it is," the mechanic agreed. "There's a nice swimming spot along the river about a klick and a half down that path."

Sam wiped the beads of sweat off his forehead. "That sounds perfect. Thanks."

The mechanic's face hardened. "Have you got a weapon?"

Sam said, "Excuse me?"

"Have you got a weapon? Something big, preferably."

Sam nodded and made a coy grin. "Sure. A hunting rifle in the trunk. Why?"

The man sighed. "Look. It's probably not a problem this far down the river or this time of day for that matter, but we've been having some trouble with a cougar in the park. It's attacked three people in the past week. Better to be safe while you're out here on your own."

"Really?" Sam asked. "Does that happen often?"

"No. It's almost unheard of. Mountain lions, despite their name, number less than five hundred in all of Oregon, and rarely come into the touristy parts of the state."

Sam held his gaze. "But something's changed?"

"Yeah. It appears something's got the taste of people. In the past two weeks something's made a few attacks."

"Was it definitely a cougar?"

"Hard to say. The hard answer is no. Trackers say that the damage looks like it was done by a large predator cat, but..."

"What?"

"There were no cougar tracks to be found."

"What did the survivors say?"

"That's just it. No one survived. Of the three people taken, no one was found alive."

"Really?" Sam made a slight grimace. "They were all on their own?"

"No." The mechanic crossed his arms. "That's just it. The truth is, one of them was hiking by himself, but the other two were in a group."

Sam raised his eyebrows. "And no one saw anything?"

"That's right. Whatever it was, came in quick, snatched its target, and ran off before anyone could get a look at it."

Sam leaned in past the Thunderbird's spare tire, which was mounted onto the rear bumper and unlatched the trunk. It was another style change in the 1956 Ford Thunderbird, and was commonly known as the "Continental" style, after the Lincoln Continental cars.

Inside, in a purpose-built armorer's safe he withdrew a Remington 12-gauge shotgun. "All right. I'll take your advice and bring a weapon."

The mechanic's jaw opened. "Good God, son, what were you planning on hunting?"

Sam smiled. "Honestly. I wasn't planning on hunting at all. I'm supposed to be having a couple days off."

"Okay. Well, I'm sure you won't have any trouble with cougars carrying a weapon like that. If you give me a couple hours, I'll try my best to have the car ready for you when you get back."

"Thank you, sir."

"You're welcome."

Sam secured his shotgun to his backpack and headed into the woods.

The trail quickly turned dark under the canopy of giant Douglas-fir trees. He followed it for a little over a mile, before the trail opened into a clearing beside the Wilson River. A crepuscular beam fixed on the large bend in the Wilson River, turning the water emerald green, as it nestled beneath a wall of jagged shards of white dolomite.

The swimming hole looked divine.

Sam glanced around the area and listened. Birds chirped away in the trees, while squirrels played on their branches, but there were no other people and no large animals he could see. He picked up a perfectly smooth piece of river stone and skimmed it across the calm swimming hole's surface. It skipped twice and sank.

He picked up another one and tried again. It hit the water and dug in first go.

On the third attempt, the stone skipped right across the large bend in the river, skipping all the way out onto the stone beach on the opposite side.

Confident that he was all alone, he put down his backpack, removed his shirt and dived into the crystal-clear water.

It was refreshingly cool.

His head broke free of the surface.

A moment later, he heard the downwash of two military helicopters as they raced low overhead.

Chapter Two

Jordan Creek, Tillamook State Forest

The tiny log cabin appeared diminutive, almost unassuming at the center of the small clearing. It was surrounded by a dense forest of spruce-fir trees, which jutted upward like an impenetrable barrier as though protecting its occupants from an unknown predator.

Inside, a golden retriever woke up from its almost permanent state of dozing on the cool pine floor with a jolt, the dog's ears perked and the fur on its back suddenly spiked.

Dr. Jim Patterson spoke with a soothing voice, his eyes turning to meet the dog's. "What is it Caliburn?"

The dog nuzzled him, before cowering at Dr. Patterson's knees.

Jim persisted, "What is it, old boy?"

The dog's eyes widened with terror, locking with the doctor's, its gaze penetrating his soul. No words were spoken, but Dr. Patterson knew without a doubt what was on the dog's mind. It wasn't the first time the poor dog had woken up with the same nightmare. It was always the same thing. He sighed. Humans developed PTSD, no reason an animal as smart as Caliburn couldn't suffer with the same affliction.

He smiled patiently, his voice taking a gentle approach, similar to how a parent might speak to a child who'd had a nightmare. "It's okay, Caliburn, he's dead. The tsunami killed him. It's been years."

The dog maintained his gaze. His eyes large and glassy. Jim noticed that the eyes weren't just filled with fear. There was fatigue there, too. More like the weight of their shared burden had finally overcome the old dog.

Jim gave him a pat beneath his chin. "It's all right. I've buried Excalibur, too."

Caliburn gave a defiant groan.

Jim nodded. "Yes. I know. Some weapons can't be broken. But I've buried it in a way no one will ever find it. I've put it back, back where it belonged, where nobody knows about the wretched tool and its evil purpose."

Dr. Patterson patted the dog for a few minutes until fear finally gave way to comfort, and he nuzzled his chin down onto the pine floor and resumed his position of rest.

An hour later, the golden retriever stretched lazily, enjoying the coolness the log house's pine floors provided. He tilted his head and sat upright with a jolt, his ears cocked, as he listened to the almost imperceptible sound of a newspaper being thrown onto the porch by a young boy who made the weekly hike to deliver his master's mail.

Caliburn's head tilted to his master, the dog's big brown, doe eyes, pleading.

Dr. Jim Patterson leaned back in his leather armchair, reading an email on his laptop. It was late in the day. Unusual time for the paper's delivery, but then, that was one of the many oddities that came with living out in the woods.

He met his dog's gaze with a slight nod. "Go on, Caliburn, you can go get the paper if you like."

Caliburn made an appreciative bark, scrambled to his feet, and ran off through the large doggie door, and outside.

Patterson laughed. He was always amazed by how such a seemingly intelligent creature could achieve so much pleasure out of collecting a damned newspaper.

Caliburn returned thirty seconds later, obediently delivering it to his feet.

He patted the dog beneath his chin. "Thanks, Caliburn."

His tail started to wag happily at the praise. Caliburn nudged the newspaper again, as though encouraging him to open it.

Patterson finished what he was doing on his laptop, closed it, and put it aside. The golden retriever was staring at him.

He smiled. "What?"

Caliburn barked once and nudged the newspaper again.

"Really?" he asked. "You want me to read it to you now?"

Caliburn wagged his entire body – if such a thing could be done – and made another short bark. It was playful, like any other dog might do while trying to encourage his master to play fetch.

Patterson nodded, and ran his right hand through Caliburn's thick, straw colored mane. "Okay, okay… I'll read to you. But just the prime news."

The dog placed a single paw on his lap, keeping his eyes fixed on him in a piercing, albeit adorable, gaze.

Patterson broke. "All right, maybe a couple classifieds and that's it."

Caliburn nudged him with his cold wet nose in appreciation. Patterson pulled his arm back, looking at the mixture of dog slobber and who knows what, he had left. "All right, all right. Enough of that. I said I'll read you the damned paper."

Patterson opened the Tillamook Headlight Herald.

It was a locally run community-based newspaper, with a subscription of just 7,486. It was delivered once a week and for reasons he would never understand, his dog liked to listen to the classifieds.

Patterson removed the rubber band and opened the front page. There was a picture of a family and the tease of a good news story of the family, who had set up a self-sufficient community capable of going off the grid.

Jim smiled. It wasn't that hard to do, live off the grid. Unfortunately, it just cost more money to set up and was generally less sustainable, less environmentally friendly than working with society as a whole entity. He smiled and turned the page of his newspaper.

The sight of the next page turned his blood to ice.

Color quickly drained from his face as he stared at the picture on the second page. Caliburn started to bark wildly. His entire body went taut and the hair on his back pointed upward.

Patterson dropped the paper on the floor, recoiling his hand as though it was poison – but his eyes remained locked on the picture.

It was an image of Cannon Beach, Oregon. The photo was taken in the early morning, with a thick fog of sea mist rising eerily over Haystack Rock, the distinctive 235-foot high sea-stack, and its surrounding smaller intertidal rocks known as The Needles.

Positioned at the forefront of the image was a shipwreck.

The boat was heavily encrusted with barnacles, but the remains of a boom-arm, typical of trawling vessels, was still present.

On the bottom right hand corner, the Tillamook Headlight Herald had enlarged an image of a brass fitting, on which appeared to be the vessel's name.

Jim's eyes narrowed as he read it out loud.

Hoshi Maru

Dr. Patterson patted his dog's thick, golden mane, reassuringly.

"It's going to be all right, Caliburn."

He barked and nudged him.

Jim took his dog into his arms and cradled him. "It's all right old boy. Nothing could have survived that hit. Excalibur's dead."

When his dog had settled, he stood up.

It was impossible to think that Excalibur could have escaped, but now he knew with certainty that he had survived.

He locked the cabin's only door and went to retrieve his shotgun.

Chapter Three

Dr. Jim Patterson opened the safe and removed the Benelli M4 Super 90 shotgun. The Italian semi-automatic shotgun was designed for the military, the ultimate hunting weapon, capable of taking out the world's most deadly animal – humans.

He loaded a single 2.75-inch shell into the chamber and then attached a magazine carrying another seven rounds. It was a military version, designed to work with the weapon's gas-operated rotating bolt, to fire each round in rapid succession.

Under normal circumstances, nothing was going to be getting up after being struck by the first round, but this was anything but an ordinary circumstance. If he was even given the chance to spot Excalibur, it might just take every shot he had to drop the monster.

That was, assuming that he could be killed.

Jim considered that for a moment. Seven or eight years ago, he doubted any projectile could kill him, but after all this time, there might just be a chance that Excalibur had been weakened. He would be far from defenseless, but there was no doubt about it, he needed the same thing the ancient relic of his namesake required to go on.

That's why Excalibur would come for him.

The monster needed him. It wanted revenge. And it would have it, that was for sure. Nothing Jim could do about that. It was like an infantry soldier armed with a knife going up against a Sherman Tank. There was no question regarding the inevitable outcome. But first, Excalibur needed information that only he could deliver.

Dr. Patterson felt the thrum of his heart pounding in his chest, and mentally chided himself for not taking better precautions with the information. It was vanity, nothing more, that had allowed him to keep possession of his lifetime's work. After all, it was his life that he had traded to locate the truth. But now, how many other lives would suffer as a result of that act of narcissism?

In front of him, Caliburn tilted his nose upward as though picking up a new scent. The dog bared its teeth and gave a low, guttural snarl.

Jim's eyes flashed with fear. "Excalibur's here already?"

Caliburn let out a couple sharp barks in reply.

The dog's growl suddenly snapped him out of his thoughts regarding the faults of his past. Instead, it sharpened his focus on the future, and what must be done.

He turned to his laptop and removed the single secure USB flash drive. It was shaped like a dog's tag and had Caliburn's name engraved on it.

"Come here, Caliburn."

The golden retriever approached him with his head low, his eyes somber, as though they both knew there was only one outcome available.

The dog whined softly.

Jim stroked his back and behind his ears soothingly. "It's all right, Caliburn. I've had a good life. Better than most, and far better than I could have asked for or expected."

Caliburn barked. There was no doubting its meaning. The dog wasn't going to listen to him give up. Excalibur wasn't inside the log cabin yet. There was still time. There was always a chance while there was still life.

But Dr. Patterson knew that was a flawed argument. He was merely on borrowed time. There was no way he could hide, outrun, or defeat Excalibur. His death was as much a certainty as that of an inmate on death row. The question was, what could he do with the few minutes he had left to change the outcome of the future?

Patterson stroked the dog. "No. You and I both know I'm not getting out of here alive. So stop thinking that way."

Caliburn gave a conciliatory whine. It was the sort of familiar and appealing sound that all dogs make when they express their natural desire to be loved by their masters.

He scratched the dog behind his ears and attached the encrypted USB flash drive onto his collar. "Now, I need you to do something for me. Can you do that?"

Caliburn met his gaze, and Jim was almost certain he could see understanding in the canine's intelligent face as the dog acknowledged him.

"Good. I need you to run. Only you can escape Excalibur. And only you may one day prove capable of defeating him." He gave his dog one last embrace and then said, "Now run!"

The dog gave a defiant bark. He wouldn't leave his master to certain death.

Jim turned to face his dog. "Bless you, Caliburn... you have been a dear friend. But now you must leave. You're too valuable. Remember, you carry the only solution... you have to escape."

Caliburn made a somber whimper, and nudged him affectionately one last time. Their eyes locked. Jim reached down with his left hand and patted him.

The door burst open.

Jim turned and said, "Caliburn... run!"

Chapter Four

The purple martin was the first to catch his attention.

Sam Reilly, relaxed on his back in the water, and stared up at the unique bird. It was the largest of the North American swallows. Known for its speed and agility in flight, it appeared dazzling as it raced from the sky at speed, weaving through the branches of the thick forest of spruce-fir trees with its wings tucked backward. It was quickly followed by a pair of great blue herons, which were in turn followed by green herons. By the time he spotted the horned grebe fly by overhead, Sam's eyes narrowed at the mystery.

Something nearby had gotten all the birds spooked.

He squinted as he made out the shape of a large white-tailed kite flying high above the tree line. He shrugged. The North American raptor might very well explain what had upset the nearby birds. A moment later, the entire forest erupted in a cacophony of distressed birdlife. Horned grebe, northern pintail, peregrine falcon, red phalarope, snowy egret, and tundra swans flocked in such dense numbers that they shielded the sun from the forest, turning daylight into night. The wall of trees, which had previously looked spectacular at more than a hundred and fifty feet, now appeared like the uninviting ramparts of a sinister castle in a medieval wood.

Sam meandered back to the edge of the river, dried his face and hands and casually retrieved his shotgun. A wry smile creased his lips as he wondered, more out of curiosity than any real fear, what had spooked the birds.

What the hell are you all afraid of?

There was no reason a coyote, cougar, or a bear should instill such terror in a flock of birds that could fly.

He leveled the shotgun, aiming the same direction from which the birds had approached, and where the forest had somehow turned evil.

He felt the drum of his heartbeat, and dismissed the rising fear with incredulity.

He was holding a Remington 12-gauge shotgun. The same weapon was used by militaries and police forces throughout the world. It was designed to kill bad things.

Sam's lips curled upward into a smile. There was no doubt in his mind, at this very moment, he was the most dangerous animal within the Tillamook State Forest.

A moment later, he heard the sound of multiple gunshots echoing through the forest.

The flock of birds overhead dissipated into an outward direction, leaving an ominous opening from where the gunshot reports had originated.

Sam stared at the opening.

He took up a defensive position and called out, "Hey! Are you all right?"

But was greeted only by the growing silence, as all wildlife appeared to scatter.

Sam shouted again, but was met by the hiss of silence.

He finished drying himself and got dressed.

Concerned that someone had been shot or was injured, he followed a well-worn deer path deeper into the forest. Sam wondered who had fired the shots. If it was a hunter, the person would have most likely answered him by now. More likely, it was a hiker, who had been attacked by a wild animal, and had hurriedly attempted to fire his or her weapon in defense.

There had been four shots fired.

No production weapons were designed to hold just four shots. Either the magazine wasn't full, or the person had stopped midway through their magazine.

The question was why?

Had they just run out of shot? Did they hit their target? An alternative explanation, and this was the most likely, the unknown predator had already reached the person, preventing them from releasing any further shots.

Sam moved quickly.

He considered dialing 911 on his cell phone. But what would he say? He heard rifle shots in a forest? There was no reason to think someone had been injured or killed. There could be any number of logical explanations for why a person should shoot four rounds and then stop. Likewise, just as many reasons why a hunter might not answer his calls – perhaps he or she was deaf, or wearing ear protection.

No, all he had to go on right now was a gut feeling.

And right now, it just felt wrong. Worse than wrong. The previously sun-filled forest imbued with the chatter of birds, squirrels, and other wild animals, now appeared dangerously quiet, as though some sort of hidden evil seeped out of its shadows.

Sam climbed the ravine at a brisk pace. He reached the top of the first ridgeline and was stopped by a dog.

It was a golden retriever. Docile and friendly by nature. This one appeared to have missed the memo, because right now, it was facing him, with bared teeth, and growled low in its throat.

Sam frowned. "What is it boy?"

The dog paused, as though suddenly brought out of its trance. A confusion set across its intelligent face. The dog picked up Sam's scent, and began to wag its tail. It was panting heavily as though it had been running hard.

Sam said, "It's okay. I'm not going to hurt you."

The dog tentatively moved toward him, dipping its head to smell Sam's outstretched hand. A moment later the golden retriever gave a relaxed whine.

Sam stroked the dog behind its ears. "You're okay now."

He looked up toward the log cabin on the peak of the next mountain up ahead.

The two Sikorsky UH-60 Black Hawk helicopters he'd seen flying low over the forest canopy a few minutes earlier were now hovering low above it. A team of soldiers were sliding down ropes, and setting up a defensive perimeter around the cabin.

Sam's eyes darted between the helicopters and the dog. "Is that your home?"

The dog barked.

It was a subdued bark, somehow somber, but clearly affirmative.

Sam said, "Something bad happened up there, didn't it?"

The dog's large brown eyes became hooded and somehow darkened. It made a slight whimper.

"I heard gunshots." Sam spoke soothingly, as he gave the dog a gentle pat. "Was that your master?"

The dog nudged him.

He couldn't be sure, but the dog almost seemed to be answering him, trying to tell him about some sort of hidden hardship.

Sam said, "I'd better go see what this was about. Someone's going to want to know what happened to you, I'd bet."

He stepped around the dog to continue up the trail, but the retriever bolted in front of him on the deer trail and bared its teeth.

Sam said, "Hey, I thought we were friends."

The dog's tail started to wag again, as it continued to pant.

Sam gave it a quick pat. "That's better. Now I have to go up there. I might be able to offer some help if someone's hurt."

The dog didn't give an inch.

It shifted the weight of its front paws to the back, and jumped ahead of Sam, turning around to meet him viciously.

Sam's eyes narrowed. "Hey, what's got into you?"

The dog's eyes turned toward the forest up ahead. It had been reforested with spruce-fir saplings. No more than five or six feet in height.

Sam stared at the lush forest with its blue-green foliage so dense it formed an impenetrable carpet of leaves.

He took a deep breath, settled into a defensive stance, and lifted the Remington shotgun up ready to take fire, aiming it toward the new saplings.

He stood still and listened, while his eyes swept the surroundings. The forest was silent. Much too silent to be natural. There were no birds, no insects, no chatter from squirrels playing on the branches of nearby trees. Even the omnipresent hum of the Oregon Cicadas had turned deathly quiet.

Nothing at all.

Sam felt it before he saw it. Whatever *it* was. If he didn't know better, he would say he simply felt an evil presence approaching beneath the canopy of new foliage offered by the spruce-fir saplings, as though it were an ancient predator, stalking its prey.

And in this case, its prey was Sam Reilly.

Sam spotted the first flicker of movement in the woods. Nothing more than a glimmer, mostly concealed by the dense foliage of young conifer leaves.

He traced it with the Remington's iron crosshairs until it stopped.

Sam yelled out, "Stop right there. I can see you."

He didn't receive a reply.

Not that he was expecting to. At this stage, he still assumed that the predator that was stalking him must have been a coyote or a mountain lion, although he'd never heard of one being so bold that it was willing to take on a fully-grown man. Besides, if it was just a wild beast, that didn't answer the question as to why two teams of American soldiers would be scrambling from a pair of Sikorsky UH-60 Black Hawks.

He mentally filed that question for something to work out after he was safe. Preferably after he'd killed whatever it was lurking in the woods.

The dog growled, voicing Sam's sentiment. It was soft, but none-the-less menacing. Sam's eyes darted between the dog and blanket of juvenile spruce-fir. The golden retriever's lips skinned back from its teeth, and the dog released a guttural growl.

Sam waited. He listened. And looked. But nothing moved.

His heart pounded in the back of his ears. Sam could literally feel the evil. It was something he'd never felt before. It wasn't fear. It was the creature itself.

Whatever it was.

Hyoo, hyoo

A mysterious sound filled the forest.

"What is that?" Sam asked.

The dog barked. If he could have talked, Sam was certain the dog was yelling, run!

Sam started to back away tentatively.

In front of him, the dense foliage of the short spruce-fir trees started to bend, and move, toward him. Whatever it was, it was running straight for him. Too fast to be human. Too confident to be a wild animal.

Sam lifted the barrel of his shotgun and fired a warning shot.

The beast continued.

Sam leveled the shotgun, took aim at the monster, whose shape he could see filtered between the branches and the undergrowth.

And fired.

Chapter Five

Sam looked at the dog. "What do you think, old boy… did I hit it?"

The dog tilted its head curiously. Its big brown eyes darting between him and the hidden section of forest. It started to growl. The fur on its ridge spiked upward.

Sam took a step forward, into the hidden section of the wood.

The dog moved in front of him, preventing Sam from moving any closer. He stepped to the left, around the dog, but the golden retriever moved with an immediateness, to block him.

Sam met the dog's gaze. "It's okay. I just want to see what it was."

He took one step forward.

The dog shifted forward to prevent him from taking a second one, giving a small growl that left no confusion about its intention.

Sam swallowed. His heart thrummed and his chest burned. It was the sight of the frightened dog that infected him with fear. His eyes drifted toward the thick section of young pine trees, no more than six feet tall, where whatever had tried to attack him had been silenced.

What was the dog trying to do?

It was trying to protect him. From what though?

He said, "It's okay, boy. Whatever it was, it can't hurt you anymore."

The dog just looked at him, his doe eyes, silently pleading with him not to go any farther.

Sam took one more step forward. He could almost feel the evil rising from the forest ahead of him. Again, it was a gut feeling, based on nothing more than superstitious stories of a dangerous coyote that had taken upon itself to start stalking humans in the Tillamook State Forest.

He glanced at the log house up ahead, back to the dog. "I have to go there, buddy. I need to see what happened. Someone might be hurt. They will need my help."

The dog regarded him beseechingly and gave a soft whimper.

There was no mistaking the message. Whoever lived inside that building was beyond all help. Sam's own fear was amplified every time he saw the dog's fear manifest.

"I have to try," Sam persisted. His eyes turned toward the sapling forest. "It's okay. You don't understand. With this weapon, I can defend us. Whatever it is, it's no match for me."

The dog dipped down on its front paws in a show of submission and concern.

Sam grinned. "It's okay boy."

He stepped to the side. The trees started to sway in the distance. Something was moving again. Sam felt that indescribable evil racing to get him.

Sam took aim at the drifting branches. His eyes narrowed through the cross-hairs at the invisible darkness that sprinted toward them, and he squeezed the trigger.

Three successive shots.

The forest went quiet once more.

Sam stepped forward.

The dog gave a baritone bark.

It was sharp, and confident, but there was no mistaking its message – something evil was in there, and I'm not letting you in to find out what!

Sam nodded.

Fear now thoroughly rising in his throat, he forced himself to smile. "You might be right, boy. Come on, let's get out of here."

The dog didn't need to be told twice. It barked and then ran at full speed down the trail on which Sam had first arrived.

Sam swept the forest one last time for signs of a predator. His eyes squinted, searching for the eyes of a danger that lay concealed and hidden, staring back at him. Again, the pure evil was palpable. He'd never felt anything like it, and his work had introduced him to plenty of evil over the years. No, this was different.

Somehow, this was less human, less animal, pure evil.

He turned and ran.

Chapter Six

Sometimes he led, and sometimes the dog led.

It picked up Sam's scent, following the invisible trail alongside the Wilson River along which he had arrived, as easily as though it had made the journey with Sam the first time round. Neither of them stopped until they were out of the forest and back at the mechanic's garage.

Sam breathed hard. His chest burned, and the muscles in his calves and thighs pounded with lactic acid after their exertion. He turned his head, looking back over his shoulder, up at the rising forest in the distance. Everything looked still. The forest, no longer dark, somehow no longer evil.

The dog approached him, its eyes somehow somber, as it nudged him with its nose. The gesture was unmistakable. The damned dog was thanking him.

Sam grinned. "You're welcome."

The dog gave an appreciative bark.

Sam laughed. "It's all right. I said, not a problem."

The dog lifted its nose in the air, as though taking in a deep sniff of the scent, and then barked again. It was a short, crisp, bark. There was no urgency in it like before. Instead, this one seemed to be an acknowledgement that they were out of danger for the time being.

Sam asked, "What was that thing?"

The dog put its paws forward, and lowered its head, as though cowering from a distant memory by covering its eyes.

Sam patted it behind his ears. "It's all right. Whatever it was, it won't hurt you now."

The dog moved one of its paws. His single visible eye, glanced up at him, in a gesture one might see a child perform with a blanket, staring out after a monster interrupted their dreams. There was more than fear behind the dog's eyes. There was a deep hurt. A loss and a pain that could never be fully healed.

"That thing…" Sam said, looking back at the forest. "It killed your master, didn't it?"

The dog whimpered.

Sam said, "I'm sorry. We'll find out what happened here. Whatever it was, won't get away."

The dog ignored him for a moment. Either it didn't believe him, or it didn't want to ever go back to the forest to see what had happened to his master.

Sam changed the subject. "I'm Sam by the way. Don't suppose you want to tell me your name?"

The dog perked up, rubbing its thick, golden mane across Sam's hips.

Sam gave him a good pat under his chin. "You're a good dog."

He stopped at the dog's collar.

A smile creased his lips. He turned the nylon collar around until it revealed a thick nametag.

"Well. I'll be…" Sam said. "You were showing me your name, weren't you? You're a smart dog…" Sam stared at the thick nametag. "Caliburn."

The golden retriever barked once in confirmation.

"Caliburn," Sam tried it out again. "Nice name."

The dog set its dark brown eyes on him again. They were somehow distant, more lost than confused, as if to say, now what?

Sam said, "Now we find out if my car's been repaired."

Chapter Seven

Sam looked at his yellow 1956 Ford Thunderbird.

The hood was down and the keys were in the ignition. A handwritten note was left on the steering wheel.

It read, *I fixed the radiator, but you have some other issues with the car that you'll need to get addressed before you want to drive it.*

Sam sighed.

That was the last thing he needed. Some vacation this was turning out to be. First the radiator, then an evil creature in the woods, and now this.

His eyes set on the keys in the ignition with a half-grin. Only in the country are folks so trusting. The Thunderbird was a collector's item, originally purchased new by his grandfather, and lovingly maintained. It was worth a mint.

Caliburn barked, snapping Sam out of his thoughts.

He turned to face the dog, who was now growling at the resident's section of the garage and general store.

"What is it, boy?" Sam asked.

The dog made a low-pitched growl.

Sam raised the Remington shotgun, taking aim toward the door.

Everything felt different than in the forest. Whatever it was, it didn't seem to have the same sense of evil that the forest was projecting. The situation, including the missing mechanic and growling dog, was wrong, but not overtly evil.

In a loud, clear voice, he said, "Excuse me, sir. Are you all right?"

He was greeted with the hiss of silence.

"Hello. Is anyone there?"

Still no response.

Sam stepped toward the door.

The door itself was made of wood and had been wedged open with part of an old engine block, but a screen of beads designed to keep the flies out, drifted in the wind. He glanced at Caliburn, half expecting the dog to prevent him from entering the mechanic's home.

He glanced at the dog. "Are you coming?"

Caliburn turned his head toward the forest, as though taking a protective stance as a guard. His blank face looked outward, his tongue resting out the side of his mouth, still catching his breath after the hard run through the forest.

Sam stared at the dog.

There was something else in its face. Was it disinterest? No, not disinterest. Instead, something else entirely. Resignation. As though the dog accepted that he'd already made his warning to Sam, and no longer cared what the mere human decided to do with the information.

"Some help you are," Sam said. "All right, I'll go check it out myself. You just stay here and let me know if we have company."

Caliburn made a single bark, stretched his paws out, shuffled his belly across the ground until he was comfortable, and stared out into the forest.

Sam used the barrel of the Remington shotgun to part the beads that draped down from the doorway. It looked like the mechanic lived on his own. Sam ran his eyes across the room. It was little more than a single room log cabin. A bachelor pad for an old man with the need for very few possessions. There was a fireplace with an iron pot and a couple of cooking utensils hanging above. On the opposite end of the room was a single bed and a leather chair overlooking the flicker of an untuned TV with its volume switched off.

The mechanic appeared to be sitting in the chair. Sam could just make out the view of his leather boots as they stuck out, relaxed from the base of the chair.

"Are you okay, sir?" Sam asked, lowering his shotgun.

The man didn't flinch.

Sam stepped forward, and swore.

The mechanic was dead.

His head had been sliced clean off, and someone had gone to the trouble of setting it upright in his lap, staring straight at the TV.

Sam stepped outside.

The dog looked up at him with somber brown eyes, as if to say, "I told you you wouldn't like what you saw in there."

Sam picked up his cell phone and dialed 911.

Chapter Eight

The sky turned to pre-dusk gray and the garage became shrouded in darkness as the last of the sun disappeared behind the mountains.

A gentle breeze caused the distant trees to whistle as it made its way through their branches, and rustled the leaves. Sam stared outward at the woods. His eyes narrowed, as though searching for the somehow hidden evil that lurked.

The whistle turned to a mysterious and somehow sinister, *hyoo, hyoo…*

The dog lifted his nose upward and took in the scent which blew with the wind. His ears pricked up, the hair on his back spiked, and the dog released a low pitched, guttural snarl.

Sam said, "You hear it too, don't you boy?"

The dog met his eye, and mewled unhappily.

"It's crazy. But I think you're right. There's something out there that's pure evil. It's still coming for us, isn't it?"

The dog made a soft bark. Something about it made him think the dog was saying no.

Talking to himself, more than the dog, Sam said, "Not me?" His eyes widened with realization. "It's coming after you?"

The dog shuddered violently.

His fear was somehow infecting Sam.

Sam looked at his cell phone. It was impossible for him to try and explain to a dog that he'd called 911 and that help was on its way. Besides, the Sheriff's department said someone would be there as soon as possible, but how long would that be in the middle of the Tillamook State Forest? Somehow, Sam just couldn't shake the unmistakable and uniquely palpable sensation of evil stalking him. Stranger yet, was the fact that despite holding a Remington 12-gauge shotgun, he still felt the fear creep in too.

He said, "You think we should keep going?"

The dog stood up, barked immediately, his eyes pleading.

"We've traveled nearly three miles. You think it's followed us here?"

The dog tilted his head to the left, his eyes drifted toward the door to the mechanic's place.

Sam swallowed. He turned around so that he could face the door, before completing a three hundred and sixty degree sweep of their defensive perimeter. "You think it beat us here?"

The retriever growled.

Sam said, "Where is it now, boy?"

The dog cocked his head to the right and fixed his eyes into the darkest section of the forest across the road, at a place shrouded in the shadows of the nearby mountain crest.

Sam aimed the shotgun at the darkness.

He could feel its presence.

Sam said, "It's there, isn't it?"

The dog gave a quiet bark.

"What's it doing? What's it waiting for?"

The retriever remained silent, but its head drifted to the right. Sam followed its gaze out to the middle of the roadway. A large shadow slowly crept toward them from the opposite side of the road.

Understanding dawned on him in an instant.

"It's waiting for the darkness to come to us." Sam said, "That's it, isn't it?"

The dog barked.

Sam looked at the T-Bird and then back at the dog. "Come on, let's get the hell out of here."

He didn't have to give the golden retriever any more of a suggestion than that. The dog jumped up, over the low door, and into the Thunderbird's bench seat. For a split second, Sam wondered what his grandfather might have thought about a stray dog going for a ride in his pristine collector's car... but what other choice did he have? The dog was being hunted by whatever it was that was waiting out there for him. It wasn't like he could leave it there.

Sam opened the door, climbed in behind the wheel of the classic Ford Thunderbird, and turned the ignition key. It started with a roar. He ran his eyes across the gauges. Everything appeared to be in order.

He lowered the handbrake, and slowly turned the wheel, until he faced south, along the road out of the Tillamook State Forest.

A strange figure of a man appeared in the shadow behind his headlight. It was so fleeting that he couldn't be certain he had the right shape at all. Then, the brush up ahead moved faster than any human could have possibly run, as the creature raced toward them.

Sam gunned the engine.

The dual, four-barrel carbureted 312 cubic inch V8 roared, and the T-bird took flight. Three hundred feet down the road, and still picking up speed, Sam glanced in the rear-view mirror.

The specter of a man could just be seen disappearing once more into the shadows.

At fifty miles an hour, Sam settled onto the main road, starting to feel the strain and tension of the past few hours rapidly dwindle.

In the passenger seat next to him, Caliburn looked nearly ten years younger, as the wind swept across the dog's head.

Sam said, "It's all going to be all right now. What do you think, Caliburn?"

The dog gave a sharp bark.

"Yeah..." Sam grinned. "I know. We had a rough start, but it's all okay now."

Caliburn began to bark uncontrollably.

Sam jammed on the brakes and the antique T-Bird slid to a jolting stop.

Because, there, in the middle of the road, lit up in the Thunderbird's high beams, was a woman waving her arms frantically at him to stop.

Chapter Nine

The woman ran around to Sam's side of the car.

"Please," she said, "Let me in… something's chasing me! I need help."

Sam reached over and opened the passenger door. Caliburn obediently shuffled into the middle space along the bench seat, making room for another human passenger.

She climbed in a second later and said, "Quick! We have to go…"

Sam happily pushed the three-speed Ford-O-Matic floor shifter into gear, and accelerated again, feeling better as the heavy old car picked up speed once more.

"Thank you. You just saved my life," she said, her accent revealing a slight trace of British ancestry.

Sam kept his eyes focused on the road. "What happened?"

"I was being chased by…" she stopped speaking.

"What was it?" he persisted.

"I don't know. It's going to sound crazy. I never saw it. But I…"

"Felt it?" Sam suggested.

"Yeah, and it felt like pure evil. Does that sound crazy?"

Sam took a deep breath. "Yeah it does, but I believe you."

"Why?"

"Because I felt it too – and the farther we get away from it the better I feel."

She took that in for a moment and said, "I think you're right. I can feel the evil presence being somehow left behind."

Sam drove on in silence, taking care to put miles between them and whatever evil might still lay in wait.

After a few minutes, Sam turned his gaze and glanced at his new passenger.

She had wild, dark red hair, full of curly ringlets that spread across a striking face of porcelain. Her complexion was smooth and pale, with an array of fine freckles. It was a handsome face, straight out of a medieval painting of an Irish princess. She had a curved nose, strong, dark eyebrows. Liquid jade eyes with golden flakes, and a straight, thin-lipped mouth set in a dangerous smile. She was neither tall, nor short. Neither voluptuous nor skinny.

She was entirely bewitching.

Sam said, "Are you hurt, ma'am?"

"No." She met his eyes, locking them for a moment, as though to prove it. "I'm okay. I'm alive."

Sam turned his focus ahead, focusing on the curving road. "I'm Sam Reilly by the way."

"Guinevere Jenkins," she said, offering her hand.

He glanced at her. A street light caught her regal face, emphasizing her wild hair, a key marker of her Welsh heritage. In that moment, Sam thought that she looked every bit like the legendary queen of her namesake

He took it. Her handshake was firm. Her grip strong. Small calluses on her hand suggested that despite her appearance, she was physically active. She squeezed his hand, holding it slightly longer than was normal. It wasn't flirting or sexual. Instead, it was more a form of human touch, and the embrace of two people who had survived a near death experience. Sam, suddenly aware of holding her hand, let go of it, feeling the slightest disappointment with the loss.

Guinevere smiled, revealing a set of evenly spaced, white teeth. "What's your dog's name?"

"Caliburn. But he's not my dog. I… um… offered him a lift out of here, too."

"Caliburn…" she said the name out loud. "Like the sword."

Sam grinned. "Sorry?"

She turned her palms upward. "The sword imbued with magical powers once given to King Arthur."

"Wasn't that Excalibur?"

"No. King Arthur was given Excalibur by Merlin after his prized sword, Caliburn, was fractured into two pieces and lost during a battle fighting the crusades in the Middle East."

"I thought he pulled Excalibur from the stone in the lake?" Sam said, a slight upward curl in his lips, teasing her.

"The sword in the stone?" She laughed. "That was all just a legend. Nothing but a story made to entertain kids in medieval Britain. How could a sword get into a stone in the first place? And what power would any man have to retrieve it over another one? Certainly not a boy named Arthur. Caliburn was the first sword. The most powerful of the two."

Sam thought about that for a moment. "Okay, so Arthur had two magical swords?"

She smiled. "Apparently. Hey, I didn't make up the story. I'm just telling you what I know about the legend."

Sam said, "But the crusades didn't start until somewhere in the middle of the eleventh century."

Her lips formed a half-grin. She turned to meet his eyes directly. "So?"

"So, the fictional Saxon king of Camelot died while fighting off Roman invaders during the seventh century."

She lifted her hands in the air in acceptance. "Hey, like I said, I didn't make up the legend. I'm just telling you what I heard. Besides, what makes you think the legend isn't true?"

It was Sam's turn to laugh. "Probably the fact that there's no written historical evidence of the legendary king, let alone Camelot, or its band of chivalrous knights."

"You know the Dark Ages were named that for a reason, right?"

"Touché." Sam changed down a gear, slowing the old T-Bird so that he could steer round an upcoming snake-like bend. "So maybe King Arthur lived much later, somewhere around the late 10th century?"

"Beats me. I just liked the stories. But you know what I'd like to imagine?"

"No. What?"

"What if King Arthur and his legends of honor, duty, and chivalry, were like a flaming torch, passed on throughout the ages of time, to allow the people – from peasants through to kings – to rise up and make the place better."

Sam gave that some serious thought, as he accelerated out of the corner.

A large grin formed. "I like that. Who's King Arthur for our generation?"

She met his smile. "I don't know. But sometimes I think our world needs one, and I like to believe the next embodiment of all that is good will rise like an Arthurian legend when our civilization needs it the most."

They drove in silence for another minute.

Up ahead, the road came alive with the red and blue flashes of an oncoming emergency vehicle. Sam pulled to the side of the road to make room, and watched as a Tillamook Sheriff's Ford F150 Interceptor raced by, with a single occupant at the driver's seat.

Sam turned the steering wheel to the left until it reached a full wheel lock, and accelerated in a sharp U-turn, before racing afterward.

Güinevere asked, "What the hell are you doing?"

"There was only one officer in the car."

"So?"

"You and I both know that there's true evil in that forest back there."

"I remember. We were both trying to escape it. So what are you doing taking us back there?"

Sam gritted his teeth. "I can't let a single officer drive alone into that sort of thing. Whoever they are, they're going to need help."

Guinevere shook her head. "When I said the world needed an Arthurian legend to rise up and help those in need, I didn't think you'd take it literally!"

Chapter Ten

British MI-6 Headquarters

Dexter Cunningham watched as the Director of MI-6 approached his office. The man was wearing casual clothing, which wasn't unusual. After all, if the head of a Secret Intelligence Agency can't work incognito, who can?

Dexter straightened himself up.

Plain clothes or not, the Director had an air about him that sent shivers down the spines of even the toughest operatives.

The Director entered his office, closed the door, and shut the blinds. Without preamble, he said, "I'm afraid we've lost Excalibur."

Dexter's blood turned to ice. "Are you certain? The project was shut down in 2008. Excalibur was to be put down."

The Director smiled at the euphemism for executed. "You know damned well what happened. The entire project was to be shut down long before that. But there was a complication..."

Dexter nodded. "I remember. The vessel he was being transported on sank."

The Director raised his eyebrows. "Yes. The report suggested a fire. But my guess is that Excalibur was behind it."

"You're kidding. He was sedated and restrained."

"What did you think he was going to do? He knew he was being sent to his execution. You didn't think he would let that happen so easily?"

Dexter nodded. "Sure, but the ship sank in the end. There were no survivors."

The Director's lips hardened into a flat line. "Dexter Cunningham, don't play games with me. I know damned well what happened after we tried to shut down the program. I also know that Excalibur went about systematically attempting to execute every man on the team. In 2011, either before or after killing Patrick, the *Hoshi Maru*, a Japanese fishing trawler, was destroyed by the devastating 2011 tsunami."

"I know. Dr. Jim Patterson and I were there. We were tracking Excalibur."

"You used Patrick as bait." It wasn't a question. Simply an acknowledgement that the Director knew everything that had happened, despite their secrecy at the time.

Dexter nodded. "We were trying to finish what we first set out to do. Excalibur had to be stopped. Although, we never predicted that a tsunami would be the thing to destroy him."

The Director's eyes narrowed. "Are you certain it did?"

Dexter nodded. "We watched the trawler get destroyed. Its captain had gambled, trying to take it back out to the safety of sea, but the die didn't roll quite as its skipper had planned. Instead, the *Hoshi Maru* took the brunt of the tsunami on its portside. A thirty-foot wall of water struck it causing the ship to broach and instantly reducing its steel hull to rubble."

"But where did that rubble end up?"

"As though that wasn't enough damage to destroy Excalibur, the *Hoshi Maru* was dragged back out to sea by the receding tide, where I'm guessing – or certainly hoping – the ship eventually sank, drowning Excalibur in the process."

"You're forgetting Excalibur was one hell of a swimmer."

"Sure, but out there in the middle of the ocean? How long could he have survived?"

"Long enough to reach the Oregon Coast."

Dexter coughed. "You mean, as in the US West Coast?"

The Director crossed his arms. "Afraid so."

"How?"

"The wreckage of the *Hoshi Maru* was indeed taken out to sea by the receding waters of the Japanese tsunami, where it was eventually picked up by a series of currents in the Pacific Ocean. Over the course of the past seven years, the ship has drifted, until a few days ago, when its hull washed up on Cannon Beach along the Oregon Coast."

"Good God!" Dexter said. "What are the chances?"

"Indeed."

"I don't suppose we had the good fortune of discovering that all occupants on board the *Hoshi Maru* were found dead?"

"They were. In fact, what remained of their bodies were all set up perfectly in the ship's dining compartment, as though Excalibur had gotten bored and decided to play with them."

Dexter pictured the gruesome scene. It was the sort of thing he could imagine Excalibur doing. "But no sign of Excalibur's body?"

"No. There was. In fact, the wreckage shows that someone had been alive on the *Hoshi Maru* when it finally came to rest along the Oregon Coast. Whoever that someone was, left on foot immediately. You and I can both guess where he was heading."

"You think after all this time his first thought was revenge?"

The Director raised his eyebrows. "Don't you?"

Dexter sat there in silence. He knew exactly where Excalibur would be heading, even though he didn't want to accept it.

The Director handed him a report. "Here, look at this. Live video feeds show him hitchhiking south along US Route 101 like he's on some goddamn vacation!"

Dexter picked up the report and fingered through the notes. An incredulous grin teased his lips at the sight of good Samaritans picking up the world's most dangerous man. "What's Excalibur doing there?"

The Director met his eye. "You know what he's doing there."

Dexter nodded. Breathing heavily. "Have you contacted Dr. Jim Patterson, to warn him?"

"Yes."

Dexter raised his eyebrows. "How did he take that?"

"He said he already knew about the wreck of the Hoshi Maru washing up on Cannon Beach. He already figured Excalibur had survived."

"How did he take that news?"

"How do you think he took that? What would you do if you discovered Excalibur had survived and was spotted on his way to find you?"

"I'd run."

"Exactly."

"Did he?" Dexter asked, his voice almost hopeful.

The Director remained silent for a moment. "No. Dr. Patterson said there was nowhere on Earth he would ever be safe while Excalibur was alive. Better that he bunkers down at his place, and rolls the dice. Live or die. There's a team of US Rangers – Delta Force I believe – on their way now to help."

"Did you tell them what they're up against?" There was an urgency in Dexter's voice.

"Of course I did."

"And?"

The Director placed the palms of his hands skyward. "They didn't believe me. How could they? If the roles were reversed, would you?"

Dexter thought about that for a second. His shoulders slumped forward. "No."

"That's right. And now they're flying into a trap."

"How many men?"

"Twenty. Two choppers. Two teams. It might be enough."

Dexter expelled a deep breath of air. "God help them. They have no idea what they're up against."

His assistant's cell phone rang. It made him jump with a start. He answered it on the second ring. "Yes?"

His assistant listened for a while, his face turning ashen gray. Finally he said, "Yes, I understand."

Dexter swallowed. "What is it?"

"That was the Commanding Officer of the US Ranger's Delta Force strike team. They just arrived at the doctor's house."

"And… what did they find?"

"Dr. Patterson's dead. His body was carved with surgical precision into small pieces and then set up to look like it was laughing at them all, like some sort of sick joke."

The muscles around Dexter's lips tightened into a grimace. He felt his gut churn. "Really?"

"That's what the Ranger said." His assistant sighed. "It's the sort of thing Excalibur would do."

Dexter sighed. "You're right, some weapons can't be destroyed."

"There's something else you should know."

"What?"

"They found a note written in the doctor's blood."

Dexter said, "Go on. What did it say?"

His assistant bit his lower lip, gritted his teeth. He expelled a deep breath of air. "It said, 'You're next, Dexter'".

Dexter was silent.

His assistant asked, "What are you going to do, sir?"

Dexter remained silent, his mind ticking over like clockwork, every answer returning to the same conclusion. If he stayed, he would be dead.

"Do we come clean about the project?" his assistant asked.

Dexter shook his head emphatically. "Oh God, no! We'll have civil rights groups from around the world breathing down our neck. No. We destroyed all records from that part of the program and shut it down for good."

"What about Excalibur?"

Dexter swallowed. "You mean, do we go after him again?"

"Yeah."

Dexter shook his head. "You saw what the project did to a god damned dog! What the hell do you think it would do to Jason Faulkner?"

"Ah… Christ!" The Director said. "I wasn't in charge when the program was running. The name of the man who became Excalibur was still a secret, even to me, as well as all the scientific and archaeological details. But I know Jason Faulkner. Whose stupid idea was it to test the program on an elite SAS soldier? It wasn't bad enough the man was already a trained killing machine, we had to imbue him with additional physiological powers!"

Dexter swallowed. "It was his own choice."

The Director considered that for a moment. "How long before you knew you had a problem?"

"Nearly six months."

"What went wrong?"

"Nothing. The ethics committee shut us down."

The Director lowered his eyes. "I know the whole program was kept in the dark, but I know damned well the ethics committee shut the program down on paper after it was revealed the test had been performed on a dog. So, don't give me this shit that everything was fine, and you only tried to destroy Excalibur because of an internal ethics committee."

Dexter nodded. "All right. All right. We knew early. But no one wanted to acknowledge it. By the time there could be no doubt, we were no longer in a position to eliminate him."

"Why? What had happened?"

"The experiment had the same effects on both of them – higher IQ, greater EQ, physiological changes including increased structural integrity at a cellular level…"

"Meaning?"

"They're tougher than you and I… and steel, for that matter."

"Go on. So, what was different? I was told the dog turned out perfect."

"There was something about the procedure. I don't know what caused it. Maybe it's just a side effect. Maybe it was there by design. I suppose this is the problem with tampering with someone else's research."

"For God's sake, Dexter, what happened?"

Dexter exhaled heavily. "Look. Where the procedure seemed to enhance Caliburn's natural good nature, the opposite could be said about Excalibur."

"You mean, the procedure enhanced Jason Faulkner's evil side?"

Dexter nodded. "I mean. He was an asshole before he became Excalibur. Maybe even before he became a secret operative for the SAS. Maybe killing people off the books had already turned him that way. I don't know. One thing I do know for certain is that after the procedure, he seemed to feed on evil. Growing darker by the day."

"That's when he went AWOL?"

"Yep."

The Director said, "Only he took seven men with him."

Dexter grimaced. He had been hoping he wouldn't have to go there. "Look. He was an asshole, but he was smart as hell and there was something about the procedure that gave him a way with people. Where it enhanced his evil, it also made his ability to command people supreme."

The Director nodded. "I'm sure all that money the seven of you were set to make made him all the more persuasive."

Dexter was past trying to deny it. Instead, he answered the next question that he knew the Director would be asking. "Excalibur became volatile. Dr. Patterson became concerned. When Excalibur refused to listen, we made a unanimous decision to execute him."

"Which clearly failed."

"Clearly..." Dexter turned his gaze away. "After the coup, Excalibur went around hunting down each and every man in that team."

"Patrick was on the *Hoshi Maru* when it was hit by the tsunami. The shipwreck's only been on the Oregon beach for a day and already he's managed to kill Dr. Patterson."

"And that leaves you as the only surviving member of the original team."

Dexter nodded. "The only one who knows the truth. He'll come after me for sure."

"What will you do?"

"What Jim Patterson never could."

"Which is?"

"I'm going to run like hell."

Chapter Eleven

Tillamook State Forest – Road House

Sheriff Emilee Gebhart was the first to arrive on the scene.

At the age of twenty-seven she was the youngest person to hold the position of Sheriff of Tillamook. Some said she had won the elected position because of her father, who had held the position for nearly twenty years. In some respects, Emilee believed that herself. Fact was, some people looked at the name of Gebhart and simply took it as the name they could trust. But truth be told, she earned the position as much because of who her father had been as because of his reputation. She had grown up as the daughter of Tillamook's sheriff, with all the expectations in terms of discipline, duty, and honor that her father instilled.

It was because of this, that she had lived her life, both professional and private, in such a way to set her up perfectly for the role. Whether or not she was voted in because of her father or not had soon become moot, as to anyone and everyone who now knew her in the position discovered she was the right person for that role.

She had already clocked off for the day, and was heading home, when the call came in.

It had taken her just twenty-two minutes to reach the old man's garage along the Wilson River. She pulled the Ford F150 Interceptor off the blacktop onto the dirt entrance to the garage.

In those twenty-two minutes, everything had changed.

While racing to the site, she'd been contacted by both Senators from Oregon, the head of the Oregon Department of Fish and Wildlife, and a senior official from the FBI. The general consensus was unanimous. No one had a fucking clue what was going on, but whatever it was, one thing was for damned certain. She needed to keep a lid on it, before journalists around the world had a field day.

She glanced overhead.

There were more Sikorsky Blackhawks overhead, most likely carrying another team of Delta Rangers, brought in to do God knows what in order to shut down whatever this was. The entire response was massive overkill for some coyote that had gotten into its head a desire to kill humans.

Which meant someone was lying to her.

And this whole thing had nothing to do with a rogue predator animal.

She considered waiting for her deputies to arrive. They might still be another twenty minutes behind her. It would be better practice in the event this thing turned out to have nothing to do with a wild animal, and everything to do with some homicidal psychopath. Hell, even one of those she could confront. What had her really spooked was the military's involvement. There had been Sikorsky military choppers in the sky all afternoon, as though they were searching for something.

Of course, if it turned out to be all a lot of fuss about nothing more than a starving mountain lion that had decided to attack a lone mechanic, and she hadn't even attempted to confront it on her own… well, that just wouldn't do for the brand-new Sheriff in town. Especially not one that was trying to prove she won her position out of merit, instead of nepotism.

That thought finished any concern about her own safety.

She switched the engine off, and retrieved her shotgun from its holster where it rested in the spacing between the two front seats. It was a Mossberg 590A1 Tactical, twelve-gauge, six shot 18.5-inch barrel, with a collapsible stock. She unfolded herself from the driver's seat. At her hip holster, she wore a Sig Sauer P220 semiautomatic.

At six feet exactly, she was tall and lithe, with long arms and legs more akin to a model than a sheriff. But there was strength behind those arms and legs. She was disciplined, and a lifetime of trying to live up to her father's expectations meant that she was tougher than any other law enforcement officer out there. Her face was set with the hard determination of someone who knew she had everything to prove.

She took in the scene at a glance. The garage was old and dilapidated. Its night time sensors had switched an overhead security light on, that lit up the entire driveway and parking area, like a photo shoot. The general store had glass windows and from what she could see was completely empty. The door to the log cabin – presumably where the mechanic had lived – was open, with a line of string beads in place to keep the flies out.

"Hello. This is the Sheriff. Is anyone in there?"

There was no response.

She felt the strange sensation of being watched. It was teasing at her, like a sixth sense, and she didn't like it.

Emilee turned around.

The place was well lit, and there was no one to be seen.

Yet still, she felt as though something was watching her. She still didn't like it.

It felt sinister somehow. Worse than that. It felt evil.

"If there's anyone in those bushes, I suggest you come out now before I fire off a couple rounds."

It was an idle threat. There was no way she was going to go off idly firing into the woods at something she hadn't even seen – although she sure as heck felt it watching her.

Emilee aimed her Mossberg shotgun toward the dense section of forest across the road. Although the sky had already turned dark, that area was in the darker shadow of the mountain range. It would have been the perfect place to hide. Definitely her choice if she was the predator.

She was even close to squeezing the trigger.

A moment later, she saw the headlights of a car. She lowered the barrel of her weapon and glanced at the vehicle as it slowed to a stop in the middle of the road house's parking lot. It was a yellow Ford Thunderbird. Looked old. Something her father's parents might have driven when they were growing up.

It was the same one she'd passed on the side of the road earlier.

There was a man and a woman with a dog – a golden retriever by the looks of it – in the middle of the two. It was the dog that put her at ease. If these were the people responsible for murdering the mechanic, there was no way a dog like that would have been sitting comfortably, without a care in the world.

She watched as the man climbed out.

He was in his mid-thirties. The man carried a Remington 12-gauge shotgun, with its barrel pointed toward the ground. The golden retriever followed him, and the woman stepped out and stared into the woods at the identical place where Emilee had been staring a moment earlier.

Sheriff Gebhart met the man's eyes. He must have been the one to call it in. "Sam Reilly?"

"Yes, ma'am." His gaze drifted from her back to the woman who he'd arrived with. "This is Guinevere Jenkins. She was hiking in the forest when it happened."

"My name's Emilee Gebhart, sheriff for Tillamook." She glanced at the dog. "Your dog?"

"No, ma'am. I found him in the woods. He protected me from something evil, and then followed me back here."

Her eyes narrowed, and her lips curled with incredulity. "Something evil?"

"I don't know what else to call it. It's just a feeling I got from whatever it was out there in the woods that's killing people."

"I was told it was most likely a coyote or a cougar. It's been a dry summer. Their natural food supplies have been down, so it's being forced to take risks by attacking humans. There's nothing evil about that. Just a predator animal, trying to survive."

The small lines in Sam Reilly's face hardened. He opened his mouth to speak, and then stopped himself, as though thinking better of his first decision.

"What?" she asked. "You don't think we're dealing with a coyote?"

"No, ma'am, I don't."

She glanced at him. He had an intelligent face, with dark blue eyes, and a strong jawline covered in two day's stubble. "Why?"

He filled her in about everything from the events of the past few hours, including the wild birds fleeing the forest, the golden retriever trying to protect him, and the strange evil creature in the woods. He spoke with confidence, and was able to articulate the events like someone used to being in a position of command, confidently reciting facts as opposed to fleeting thoughts and imaginings.

"You're in the military?" she asked.

"Was," he replied. "Past tense."

"What do you do now?" she asked.

"I work in ocean salvage, but mainly offer unique consultation on a variety of maritime and hydrology problems."

"Like what?" she asked, genuinely interested, and also trying to gauge his credibility.

"Right now, the state of Oregon has requested my services to locate the source of heavy metals entering the Columbia River. I'm heading there now to meet up with my team."

She glanced at his antique Ford Thunderbird. "You were heading there in that?"

Sam smiled. "Yeah. I was taking some leave. One of my directors is leading the project. I'm due up there in a few days."

Gebhart made a mental note to find out more about him. Then, returning to the task at hand, she said, "What about Mr. Potter?"

"Who?"

"The mechanic that lives here. You said he was murdered."

"Oh. I'm sorry. I never got his name." Sam pointed toward the log cabin. "He's in there."

"Okay, thanks. You can stay here, and keep an eye out for that evil creature roaming the woods."

Sam didn't take the bait. Instead, he just nodded and said, "Yes, ma'am."

Emilee entered the mechanic's residence. She found the man with his head sitting in his lap, the eyes ripped out of its sockets.

She took a deep sigh, picked up her cell phone and called the number from the FBI.

A man answered on the first ring. "Yes?"

"It's exactly the same as the others."

There was a moment of silence on the line, before the man said, "All right. We'll do the best we can. Delta Force are on site. Let's keep this contained. The official word is this is a coyote attack. Nothing more."

"I understand. I'll see what I can do."

There was a pause while the man on the other end of the line went quiet.

"What is it?" she asked.

"Have you heard about the ship?"

She closed her eyes for a moment and sighed. "Yeah, I know. I heard about the ship this morning. I've heard the legend too. I'll try my best to shut this thing down before any more rumors get out and the press have a field day."

Chapter Twelve

It was dark in the Tillamook State Forest by the time Sam Reilly finished up giving his statements to the sheriff. The once secluded garage in the forest was now riddled with the sheriff's deputies, FBI agents, and military personnel.

She finally said, "All right, thanks for your help. You're good to go."

Sam stood up, his focus drifting toward the Tillamook ridge. "Do you mind telling me what your team found at the log house up on that ridgeline?"

Sheriff Gebhart sighed. "Look. We've been up to that log house. There's nothing there. Nobody lives there. Hasn't for a number of years."

Sam raised his eyebrows. "No one's lived there for a number of years?"

"That's what my deputy says. I haven't been there for a while. But I know last summer the place was vacant, a dilapidating shack more than anything else, left in permanent disrepair."

"What about the military helicopters?"

Sheriff Gebhart made a wry smile. "What about the Blackhawks?"

"What did they find at the log cabin?"

"What is it with you and the log cabin?" she asked in return. "I mean, what do the military helicopters have to do with it?"

"I don't know. I saw two helicopters hovering directly above the clearing where, in the day time, you can see the small outline of a log cabin. When I was up there, I noticed soldiers, rappelling down from those helicopters. I just wondered what they found, that's all…"

Sheriff Gebhart's lips pressed into a thin line. "I'm afraid you must be mistaken Mr. Reilly, those helicopters are here conducting routine low-level formation flying, nothing more."

"Are you trying to tell me I didn't see two teams rappel into the forest?"

Her gray eyes narrowed and lips parted into a beautiful smile. "I don't know what to say. You're an intelligent man. Think this through, why would the military send two teams of Delta Rangers to investigate an 'evil thing' in the woods?"

"Why indeed?" Sam countered.

She laughed. "You're reading too much into it."

"What about the dog?" Sam asked, "I thought his owner might have lived there."

She gave the dog a cursory glance. "Maybe his owner once did. There's always a chance he's been living out here in the wild for some time now."

Sam looked at the dog. "Are you kidding? That mutt looks in better shape than I am. No, he's way too well-groomed to be a stray. Somebody owns him."

"The tag doesn't have an address. So I'd say, if someone did, they don't anymore."

Sam asked, "So what are you going to do with him?"

"I don't know. He will have to go to the pound if no one claims him."

Sam sighed. "That's a shame. He's an intelligent dog."

"You want him?"

Sam said, "I'll take him if no one else wants him. I'll make sure he finds a nice home."

"Go for it," Sheriff Gebhart said. "He's all yours."

Sam looked at the dog. "What do you say, Caliburn, you want to come with me?"

The dog barked, his tail suddenly wagging wildly.

Chapter Thirteen

Sam Reilly got back in the yellow Ford T-Bird.

Caliburn jumped into the box seat next to him, and Guinevere sat down in the passenger seat. Sam turned the ignition key and switched on the headlights.

"Sheriff Gebhart said that they've shut down the OR-6 East."

"Is there another way to Portland?" Guinevere asked.

"There's always another way. It just depends how far off course you want to go."

Guinevere made a weak smile. "No. I mean, is there another road that runs parallel or something? How much of a detour are we talking?"

"I don't know. Maybe another hour or two. We'll have to backtrack along the coast and then take the US-26. It will probably be close to midnight by the time we get into Portland."

Guinevere's face was set with indifference. "I'm in no rush. We'll get there when we get there."

"Okay, great."

Sam released the handbrake and headed back toward the coast.

They settled into the drive at a more leisurely pace.

The T-Bird was originally marketed as a sporty two-seat convertible, set to compete directly with the more powerful Chevrolet Corvette, but Ford changed its marketing strategy to focus more specifically on selling it in the newly developed personal luxury car market, which emphasized comfort and looks over performance and practicality. As a consequence, the T-Bird was a highway traveler, and once she got moving on the highway, the miles just kept rolling past.

Caliburn adjusted his position, turning his whole body round twice, before finally opting for a position with his head on Guinevere's lap. She patted the dog behind his ears, and Caliburn gave an appreciated mewl.

Sam said, "So what brings you out to this part of the world?"

"The US?"

"That too. But I was actually referring to Tillamook State Forest."

"Oh. I was out here to look at some locations for a healer's retreat."

Sam asked, "A what?"

"A healer's retreat. Somewhere far from the city, locked in the cleansing confines of nature. The sort of place where people can come for healing."

"What sort of things are you trying to heal?"

Her lip curled in a half-grin. "Are you talking about me, or the retreat?"

"Either."

"I don't know what I'm looking for," she said, and Sam felt there was something in her voice that suggested she was being surprisingly honest, while burying something dark in her past. "And I still don't know if this is the place I'm meant to find it."

Sam said, "And the retreat. What sort of things is it supposed to help heal?"

"I don't know that yet, either." She looked out toward the stars that rose from the horizon, her gaze distant, as though she were a thousand miles away. "People who need healing I suppose. People who are suffering physically, mentally, emotionally, or spiritually – I'd like to help."

"That's noble." His words came out more condescending than he meant. He quickly said, "What sort of healing do you practice."

"You probably haven't heard of it." She made a coy smile. "And if you have, you probably wouldn't believe in it. But hey, whatever, works, right? In the past few years I found it's helped heal me from wounds deeper than any you could ever see."

"So, it's in the pseudoscience category then?"

She laughed. "Some believe so. But you'd be surprised that not everything that helps can be explained by science."

Sam said, "I believe you."

Guinevere met his eye for a moment. "I believe you do. But I don't know why."

"Why not?"

"I don't know. I know people. It's a gift. I see what people are hiding as though it were in plain sight. Just one of those things that I have."

Sam grinned. "And what do you see in me?"

"I was there when you spoke to the Sheriff. You're military through and through. I know the type. You work with exact numbers, practical solutions, and hard facts to get the job done. Even as a civilian, you look like you're in command of everything and everyone around you, while juggling the near razor sharp edge of balancing that command by being both authoritative and leading by example in such a way that those around you genuinely want to follow you. Honor, dedication, and duty are the unreserved codes governing your every choice in life – and I see that you're a genuinely good person." She laughed. "Or did I get all of that wrong?"

"No. You're pretty good. So, what do you practice?"

"I'm a Reiki Master," she answered.

Sam looked at her. "Sorry. A what?"

"I practice the ancient Japanese art of Reiki. Basically, the idea is that an unseen life energy, known as a person's *Ch'i* flows through us all. If this life-force is low, then we are more likely to get sick or feel stressed, and if it is high, we are more capable of being happy and healthy."

"Interesting," Sam said. "Does it work?"

She made a genuine smile. "It did for me."

"Good for you," Sam said. He meant it, too. Deep down, many people are looking for something in life, and very few have the good fortune to find something that works. There were plenty of things he didn't understand, but if Reiki helped her, who was he to judge?

He said, "How long have you been out here?"

"Just a few days."

"A few days. Where's all your stuff?"

Guinevere looked bemused. "What stuff?"

Sam said, "I don't know. Change of clothes. Food. You know… that kind of thing? I noticed you're only carrying a day pack."

"I travel light. I find the universe generally delivers what I need. Not always what I want, though."

"What do you want?"

She made a coy, teasing smile. "Actually, right now, I'm kind of hungry."

"I don't know what's open at this time of night, but I've got some muesli bars in the glove box, if you'd like."

She went to answer, but Caliburn beat her to it. The dog sat up, his ears perked, and he made several quick barks.

Sam laughed. "You're hungry too, are you Caliburn?"

The dog barked again.

"Well… help yourself." Sam said, "They're in the glovebox if you want them."

Caliburn barked with delight and pressed his paw against the glovebox button. The lock unclicked, and the glovebox fell open, revealing a handful of muesli bars.

Sam grinned and turned to Guinevere. "Smart dog."

"Really smart dog," Guinevere replied.

"Do you think he knew what I was saying, or he could have just picked up the scent of something to eat inside?"

Guinevere shrugged. "Beats me. But these muesli bars are sealed in plastic wrappers. There's no way even a dog could pick up the scent through that. Besides, if he had just smelled them, why did he wait until right on cue to sit up and try to find them? No, I think it's safe to say Caliburn happened to be listening to what it was you had to say."

Sam said, "I mean, that can't be normal, can it?"

"I've never owned a dog. But don't think so."

"Are you just really smart, Caliburn?" Sam asked. "Can you understand what I'm saying?"

Caliburn mewled and nudged the plastic wrapper.

Guinevere said, "He's only interested in the food. At least that's more what a traditional dog would do."

She opened a bar and gave it to Caliburn, who gave an appreciative bark before hoeing into the meal with tremendous gusto.

Guinevere took a bite out of the second one and offered the third to Sam.

He took it, opening it and eating it with about as much delicacy and temerity as the retriever.

The dog stared at the fourth one still in the glovebox.

Guinevere said to Sam. "You want it?"

"No. I'm okay. You have it."

"Okay, Caliburn. I'll split it with you."

Caliburn barked and offered a paw to seal the deal. She gave it a perfunctory shake, and then handed the dog half of the remaining muesli bar.

Sam grinned at the sight.

The day had had its share of ups and downs. But at least it was finishing on a high. He, Guinevere, and Caliburn made a ridiculous union of traveling companions. She was intelligent and fun to be around and Caliburn vacillated between super intelligence and the silliness of a much younger dog.

A moment later, the smooth sound of the engine wavered to something resembling metal on metal. Sam took his foot off the gas, trying to ease the pressure on the 1956 engine. Instead, the sound became increasingly loud, before something made a great bang, and the car went silent as the engine stalled.

Sam tentatively tested the accelerator pedal, but nothing happened.

He went into damage control mode, and coasted the Thunderbird over into the break down lane.

He tried the ignition key.

Nothing happened.

Which meant all three of them were out of luck.

Chapter Fourteen

Sam glanced at the small set of engine gauges. Every one of them appeared to be within their normal range.

He tried the ignition again.

Nothing happened.

He opened the glovebox and retrieved a flashlight. He switched it on and then popped the hood. A cursory glance of the engine block showed that everything was where it belonged. The mechanic's repairs to the radiator appeared intact. The coolant reservoir was full. The sparkplugs were all connected.

A moment later he stopped and fixed the flashlight's beam on the rusted remains of a split timing chain. Sam sighed. That must have been what the mechanic had spotted when he removed the radiator to work on it. The timing chain was mostly concealed under normal circumstances.

It was obvious now.

But that was only because the timing chain had snapped.

Sam said, "Well, it looks like the T-Bird's not going anywhere tonight."

Guinevere took it with carefree equanimity and insouciance. "Like I said, I'm in no rush. We'll get to Portland when we do. I'm sorry about your car though."

"Don't worry about it. Cars can be repaired."

Guinevere glanced along the empty highway. "Don't suppose you know where we are?"

"At a guess, I'd say we're about three or four miles from Cannon Beach."

She grabbed her back pack. "Okay, so I guess we have some walking to do."

Sam grabbed a backpack which carried what little items of clothing he had for himself. He thought about locking the Remington shotgun in the safe in the trunk, but decided against the idea. Even though they had traveled nearly sixty miles from where the evil creature had attacked all three of them, he had an unusually strong misgiving about leaving his weapon behind. It wasn't like him to think that way. Especially not along the idyllic west coast of Oregon.

They walked north along US 101, the Oregon Coastal highway, with Caliburn happily leading the way. It turned out they had nearly twelve miles to cover.

At 1:22 a.m. they reached downtown Cannon Beach.

With the exception of a few street lights, and the flicker of motel *No Vacancy* signs, the place looked like it had gone to sleep for the night.

Sam said, "There won't be any mechanic on through the night. We'll find a garage and get the T-bird towed in the morning."

Guinevere glanced at the *No Vacancy* sign by the nearest two motels. "There doesn't seem to be a great deal of places left to stay."

"Yeah. I wonder what's going on. It seems unusual for the town to be booked out midweek. Come on, there's a few more to the north."

Ten minutes later, they reached another motel.

Caliburn gave a soft bark.

Sam asked, "What is it, boy?"

Guinevere made a wry grin. "I think he's suggesting the motel has some vacancies..."

Sam turned his eyes toward the motel. Its, *No Vacancy* sign wasn't lit up. But neither were the lights at the front desk. Most likely the manager had gone to bed.

He looked at Caliburn and laughed. "What... you can read signs now?"

The dog ignored him, but wagged his tail with joy.

Caliburn barked again happily. His eyes fixed on something next to the main entrance. It read, *Pets Welcome.*

Sam shook his head. "Did you see that, Guinevere. The dog can read."

She gave him a patronizing look. "I think he just likes the smell of the place. The place reeks of barbecued meat."

The scent wafted in through Sam's nostrils. Some vacationers had definitely used the BBQ earlier in the night, leaving cooked meat scraps in the nearby bin.

"All right, let's go see if they have a couple rooms available."

Sam rang the night bell. It was one of those electronic buttons, more like a door bell, that makes not sound, but lights up, giving the hint that it might wake up the night manager from wherever he or she was sleeping.

No one arrived after thirty seconds and Sam pressed the button again.

Nearly a full minute went by, and the lights turned on in a room at the back.

A dreary-eyed gentleman in his sixties greeted them. "Yes? What can I do for you?"

Sam said, "Sorry to wake you, sir. We're looking for two rooms, please."

The man shook his head. "I'm sorry. We only have one vacancy left."

Guinevere said, "We'll take it. Thank you."

Sam glanced at her. "You have it. Caliburn and I will keep walking and find another."

The motel manager said, "I'm afraid you won't find anywhere else to stay tonight. Everywhere is all booked up."

"Really?" Sam asked. "Why?"

"It has to do with that shipwreck that washed up onto the beach. People have come from all over the place to gawk at it. Lots of people are wondering where it came from. Of course, the fact the FBI are all over the place has done nothing to allay their curiosity."

Sam's interest was piqued. "Interesting. What are they saying?"

The manager said, "It was clearly a large fishing trawler, but it's been floating out at sea for many years. Some say it's Japanese, others say it's Chinese. Some think it's washed here all the way from Japan, after the tsunami all those years ago, while others argue that it's merely been drifting out in the North Pacific Gyre – you know that great garbage vortex they say is larger than England?"

Sam nodded.

He'd seen the place. Despite the common public image of islands of floating rubbish, its density was quite low, less than four particles per cubic foot, which prevents detection by satellite imagery, or even by casual boaters or divers in the area. It consists primarily of an increase in suspended, often microscopic, particles in the upper water column. The patch is not easily seen from the sky, because the plastic is dispersed over a large area.

Sam said, "But no one has been able to locate the ship's origins?"

"Not yet." The motel manager crossed his arms. "Now, did you want that room?"

Guinevere answered, "Yes please. For all three of us, thank you."

The manager ran his eyes across Caliburn. "Is she toilet trained?"

Guinevere smiled politely. "Yes, and it's a he."

The manager shrugged, as though he didn't really care either way. "All right, that will be ninety-eight dollars."

Guinevere paid in cash.

Sam said, "You sure you don't want Caliburn and I to keep looking?"

"No. Don't be ridiculous. It's all right. I trust you."

"Why? You only just met me."

"Hey, you saved my life. I think I can trust you."

"Really?"

"Yeah. Besides, you have that whole honor, courage, duty thing plastered all across your face."

"All right. But you can have the bed, and Caliburn and I will have the couch."

"Like I said, you have too much mensch to do anything inappropriate." She grinned. "And as for the couch, I wouldn't have it any other way."

The hotel manager gave them a key, pointed to their room, and then handed them a local newspaper. "Here's the article about the shipwreck, in case you wanna go check it out in the morning."

Sam took the paper, while Guinevere took the key. "Okay, I think we will. Thank you."

Guinevere glanced at the image of the shipwreck on the beach, with the Haystack and Needles rock formations in the background, in a dark sea beneath dense clouds. There was little of the original vessel's hull still visible. Years of drifting in the ocean had left it encrusted with barnacles nearly a foot thick. The newspaper had highlighted a second image of a brass nameplate, with the words *Hoshi Maru* clearly visible.

Her face turned white and she audibly gasped.

Sam placed his hand on her shoulder, almost expecting her to collapse. "What is it?"

Guinevere said, "It came from Japan, where it was wrecked while trying to leave Minamisōma Harbor at precisely 3:12 on March 11, 2011."

"Really?" Sam asked. "You sound pretty certain. Why?"

She swallowed. "Because my brother was on board when the tsunami hit. They never found his shipwreck."

"I'm sorry," Sam said, feeling like the weakness in the words for the moment.

She looked away. "What's worse is he told me two years earlier that he'd run away from civilization to avoid being murdered."

Chapter Fifteen

Upper Columbia River, Portland Oregon

The motor-yacht formed a dark silhouette along the river. At a length of 180 feet and a beam of 45 feet, it was shaped more like a bullet than a traditional yacht, with a long black hull and narrow beam tapering in to a razor-sharp prow.

She looked like a predator stalking the river.

The trailing whitewash, a stark contrast against the near black river against the night's sky, was the only demonstration of the vessel's unique combination of raw power. She was powered by twin Rolls Royce 28,000hp MTU diesel engines, and twin ZF gearboxes that projected the force of the combined 56,000 hp into four HT1000 HamiltonJet waterjets. This power was married to her unique hull, which used a series of hydraulic actuators to alter her shape in order to achieve the greatest speed and stability given any type of sea conditions. She was able to lift out of the water onto the aquaplane at speeds of 60 knots – making her the fastest motor yacht of her size in the world.

To the south the snowcapped crest of Mount Hood rose up against the backdrop of a velvet night sky. The vessel turned south, following the natural curvature of the river as it snaked through the gorge. Up ahead, a single propeller light aircraft disappeared as it lined up and came in to land at the nearby Columbia Gorge Regional Airport.

Moonlight shone across her dark hull and the vessel's name came into view…

Tahila

A name Sam Reilly, the ship's owner had given her, yet refused to tell anyone of its meaning or purpose. A small pool of guesses had circulated among the crew on board as to its hidden meaning. Some Googling and guessing came up with an interesting array of answers, which Reilly had thus far refused to acknowledge as either right or wrong – in an unusually stubborn display of mystery.

Some of the more popular suggestions were that it referred to the Hindu meaning of the name Tahila, which literally translates to, *Darkness*. A pertinent name for a dark vessel, capable of stealth. Although the image matched, it was hardly what the ship's acclaimed owner was going for as a means of offering assistance and scientific refuge to study the sea. Others considered the Hebrew meaning, which translated to, *A Song of Praise*. Again, few people on board believed that Sam Reilly would have named the yacht after a song they had never heard him sing.

Elise, a computer hacker with an Intelligence Quotient well and truly off the charts, argued that it was a derivative of the ancient Greek word, *Thalia*, which was the youngest sister of Algaea and Euphrosyne. Usually found dancing in a circle, they were the daughters of Zeus and the Oceanid Eurynome, a goddess of good order and lawful conduct. Sam Reilly, she argued, was using it as a play on words. The *Tahila* was a weapon of Goodness, while also representing the modern-day Greek word, which means, *rich, plentiful, luxuriant and abundant* – referring to the vessel's raw power and beauty.

At 3 a.m. Tom Bower stepped onto the sleek top deck. Despite his six foot-four-inch stature, and two hundred forty pounds of muscle, he was little more than a speck on board the dark bow. He stared at the giant gorge surrounding them.

His jaw was set firm and his dark brown eyes pensive as he stared at his ancient surroundings in awe. Only humans could be so destructive to threaten the very existence of such a wondrous place. The Columbia River was the largest in the Pacific Northwest region of North America, having started out in the Rocky Mountains Trench and the Columbia Lake – 2,690 feet above sea level – and the adjoining Columbia Wetlands form the river's headwaters. The trench is a broad, deep, and long glacial valley between the Canadian Rockies and the Columbia Mountains in BC. From there the Columbia flows northwest along the trench through Windermere Lake and the town of Invermere, a region known in British Columbia as the Columbia Valley, then northwest to Golden and into Kinbasket Lake. Rounding the northern end of the Selkirk Mountains, the river turns sharply south through a region known as the Big Bend Country, passing through Revelstoke Lake and the Arrow Lakes.

Out in the Rocky Mountains of British Columbia, Canada, it flowed northwest and then south into the US state of Washington, turning to the west to form the border between Washington and Oregon, before emptying into the Pacific Ocean.

The river is 1,243 miles long, and its largest tributary is the Snake River. Its drainage basin is roughly the size of France and extends into seven US states and a Canadian province. The fourth-largest river in the United States by volume, the Columbia has the greatest flow of any North American river entering the Pacific.

Matthew Sutherland, the ship's skipper, stepped onto the deck.

Tom asked, "What is it?"

"Sam Reilly wasn't on that flight."

Tom frowned. Sam was meant to be in Portland hours ago, and had booked a flight to meet them at the Columbia Gorge Regional Airport to come aboard the *Tahila* and take command of the project. Until then, Tom, as his deputy director, would be in charge.

Tom said, "Really? What does he think's more important than this project right now?"

Matthew shrugged. "Apparently his car broke down."

Tom suppressed a smile. "Of course his damned Thunderbird broke down! The thing's more than sixty years old. I don't know what his love affair is with old cars, when he can afford the best modern engineering has to offer."

Matthew turned to walk back down below.

Tom stopped him. "Did he have a revised ETA?"

"Heck. Right now, I don't even know if he has a place to sleep for the night. He'll probably call in the morning. Until then, he said that you're to take over the command of the project."

Tom nodded and stared out at the river, as Matthew disappeared below deck. As his eyes searched the dark gorge while the *Tahila* motored on through the Columbia, his mind wandered, imagining all that was at stake with the current leaked nuclear radiation.

The Columbia and its tributaries had been central to the region's culture and economy for thousands of years. They had been used for transportation since ancient times, linking the region's many cultural groups. The river system hosted many species of anadromous fish, which migrate between freshwater habitats and the saline waters of the Pacific Ocean. These fish – especially the salmon – have provided food for the region's First Peoples and European settlers, through to modern day fish producers.

All of that was at risk now, due to human folly and greed.

In the late 18th century, a private American ship became the first non-indigenous vessel to enter the river; it was followed by a British explorer, who navigated past the Oregon Coast Range into the Willamette Valley. In the following decades, fur trading companies used the Columbia as a key transportation route. Overland explorers entered the Willamette Valley through the scenic but treacherous Columbia River Gorge, and pioneers began to settle the valley in increasing numbers. Steamships along the river linked communities and facilitated trade; the arrival of railroads in the late 19th century, many running along the river, supplemented these links.

Since the late 19th century, public and private sectors have heavily developed the river. To aid ship and barge navigation, locks have been built along the lower Columbia and its tributaries, and dredging has opened, maintained, and enlarged shipping channels. Since the early 20th century, dams have been built across the river for power generation, navigation, irrigation, and flood control. The fourteen hydroelectric dams on the Columbia's main stem and many more on its tributaries produce more than 44 percent of the total US hydroelectric generation. Production of nuclear power has taken place at two sites along the river.

Then in 1943, the river was irrevocably changed.

Plutonium for nuclear weapons was produced for decades at the Hanford Site, which is now the most contaminated nuclear site in the US. These developments have greatly altered river environments in the watershed, mainly through industrial pollution and barriers to fish migration.

In southeastern Washington, a 50-mile stretch of the river passes through the Hanford Site, established in 1943 as part of the Manhattan Project. The site served as a plutonium production complex, with nine nuclear reactors and related facilities along the banks of the river. From 1944 to 1971, pump systems drew cooling water from the river and, after treating this water for use by the reactors, returned it to the river. Before being released back into the river, the used water was held in large tanks known as retention basins for up to six hours. Longer-lived isotopes were not affected by this retention, and several terabecquerels entered the river every day. By 1957, the eight plutonium production reactors at Hanford dumped a daily average of 50,000 curies of radioactive material into the Columbia. These releases were kept secret by the federal government until the release of declassified documents in the late 1980s. Radiation was measured downstream as far west as the Washington and Oregon coasts

The nuclear reactors were decommissioned at the end of the Cold War, and the Hanford site is the focus of one of the world's largest environmental cleanups, managed by the Department of Energy under the oversight of the Washington Department of Ecology and the Environmental Protection Agency. Nearby aquifers contain an estimated 270 billion US gallons of groundwater contaminated by high-level nuclear waste that has leaked out of Hanford's underground storage tanks. As of 2008, one million US gallons of highly radioactive waste is traveling through groundwater toward the Columbia River. This waste is expected to reach the river in 12 to 50 years if cleanup does not proceed on schedule.

But it hadn't been all bad news.

Large amounts of federal funding had been put into the Hanford Uranium Site in recent years to keep the uranium from leaching into the Columbia River at Hanford just north of Richland. For nearly a decade, the project had been expanded with tests showing very good results.

It was a good news story of humankind triumphing over prior mistakes.

Wells were being drilled now to inject a solution into the ground to bind the contaminating uranium to the soil and prevent it from migrating into the groundwater and then into the river. Much of the soil contaminated with uranium at the Hanford 300 Area has been dug up down to 15 feet, removing the majority of the contamination that could reach the groundwater.

But all that changed just three days ago, when dormant Geiger-Müller Counters, stationed throughout the Columbia River, suddenly came alive with reports of skyrocketing levels of deadly alpha particles, beta particles, and gamma rays.

Something had changed.

And their greatest fears had all been realized. The worst of the uranium rich, toxic groundwater, was now flowing directly into the Columbia River.

While politicians, EPA directors, and on-site cleanup project managers debated who was responsible, and what had gone wrong, the *Tahila* had been sent to locate the source of the catastrophic leak, and find a means of shutting it down.

Chapter Sixteen

At six a.m. Sam Reilly left the keys to the Thunderbird with a mechanic, thanked him, and headed south along *S, Hemlock Street* to find Guinevere and Caliburn, who had gone ahead in search of a local diner. The main street ran parallel to Cannon Beach, and reminded him of an old American town, with its log buildings, quintessential to every depiction of the wild west, clad with pine shingles that looked like they belonged to another century entirely. There were American flags raised high and a lone Sheriff making his early morning patrol on foot.

The entire town was still heavily bedded in fog.

Sam thought about the *Hoshi Maru* as he walked. Last night, Guinevere had revealed that her brother was on board the *Hoshi Maru* when it disappeared more than seven years ago during the Japanese Tsunami of 2011. What she hadn't revealed was why someone from the UK had chosen to move to a small fishing village in Japan.

When Sam asked her, Guinevere had simply told him that her twin brother had left out of the blue in 2008. For some time, she had wondered whether he'd had a problem with the law or something, but in 2010 Patrick had called her and told her that he was living on a fishing boat in Japan. Patrick had told her he missed her and loved her, and if anyone ever came around asking, that it was imperative she didn't tell them where he was living.

Sam walked with the determined stride of a soldier, his movements standing out from the rest of the pedestrians whose casual stroll and meandering spoke of tourists on vacation rather than people in active employ. Even the shopkeepers and café workers, who were still setting up their tables and chairs along the street, appeared to be doing so at a slower pace, as though vacation mode had seeped into their veins.

To the left, he spotted an open sign, that read, *The Driftwood. Pets Welcome.*

He stepped inside, where a small beer garden had been set up to serve early morning breakfasts to people and their pets. Seated in a corner booth, was Guinevere, with Caliburn next to a bowl of water near her feet.

"Good morning," Sam said.

"Hello," Guinevere replied.

Her head rested on her hand, her dark red curly hair falling forward, like a breaking wave. There was a faint scent of fresh shampoo. She looked great despite having only five hours of sleep. All the tension from the night before had vanished, and in its place was nothing but peace, interwoven with something else, too... some sort of teasing sense of adventure, barely concealed behind the sparkle of her gold speckled, green eyes.

The sight nearly took Sam's breath away.

Caliburn, as observant as ever, tilted his head and met Sam's eye with a tone close to reproach, and then returned to chasing a low buzzing fly with an apathetic snap of his teeth.

"Nearly got it," Sam said, patting the dog on its back.

"I took the liberty of ordering us both the Big Breakfast. I hope you don't mind, but Caliburn and I couldn't wait, and I figured that you, being a typical man, would be happy to eat anything placed in front of you."

Sam grinned. "And you would be right. Thanks."

"No problem." Guinevere said, "Did you find a mechanic?"

Sam nodded. "Yep."

"Any luck?"

"Yes and no. He says he can tow the T-Bird to the safety of his garage until it can be fixed…"

She pressed him. "But?"

Sam sighed. "The car's an antique. So, it might take him a couple days to track down a genuine timing chain."

"And you need that before we drive to Portland?"

"Yeah, kind of…" Sam replied. "There's probably a bus that will take you there if you're in a rush."

Guinevere smiled. "No. It's fortuitous. Just another time in my life where the universe simply delivered what I needed, rather than what I wanted."

"You wanted to go to Portland."

She nodded. "I have a flight back to London tomorrow. But I think I need to see where my brother died."

Sam said, "You know the *Hoshi Maru's* been floating in the Pacific Ocean for more than seven years since the Japanese Tsunami. Hell, that amount of time exposed to the corrosive seawater, and the ship no longer looks recognizable. You know we're not going to find your brother."

"I know. But still. I would like to see the place where he had once lived." Her eyes focused on the dark clouds in the distance. Her mind closed to the past. "Do you know he called me once? Just once when he was on board."

Sam let her speak. "How did he sound?"

"He seemed good. Better than I had heard him for a number of years."

"Why?"

"I don't know." She opened her mouth, closed it again, and expelled a breath. "Look. My brother spent most of his adult life in MI-6." She paused and met his eye. "You know what that is, right?"

He nodded. "The British Secret Intelligence Service."

"Right," she confirmed. "When Patrick got out, he was a different sort of man. He'd seen things, done things that no human should ever have to do or see."

"He was suffering from PTSD?"

"Almost certainly, not that he showed it. My brother was a hard man, capable of concealing his darkest thoughts to the deepest recess of the mental equivalent of a locked vault. But this was different."

"How so?"

"He sounded scared."

A waiter brought their food out.

Their conversation took a pause, as they devoured some breakfast. Sam glanced at the food. There were two large plates, filled to their edges with food. Grilled tomatoes, capsicum, fresh avocado slices, garnished with roughly torn fresh cress and rocket, a sweet potato hash brown and wholemeal bread.

The waiter placed a bowl of jellied salmon that looked good enough to eat down in front of Caliburn, who mewled with joy, and immediately began to eat it.

They thanked the waiter.

Sam turned to Guinevere and said, "I thought you got us the Big Breakfast?"

"I did." She smiled. "Didn't I mention I'm a vegetarian? Is that all right?"

"Why did Caliburn get meat?"

"What do you mean?" Guinevere asked. "Have you ever heard of a vegetarian dog? That's nuts!"

Sam bit down on his food, devouring it within minutes. "It's good."

She laughed. "See, I told you, men don't care what they eat – as long as it's in front of them."

"Hey, I don't deny it."

He waited until she finished her meal.

Guinevere asked, "Where was I up to?"

Sam said, "Your brother sounded scared."

"Not just scared. In the years earlier, he was becoming increasingly paranoid after coming back from some mission. He kept on talking about Excalibur."

"Excalibur?" Sam asked. "As in the legendary sword?"

She frowned. "Yeah, like I said, he was losing it. The way he rambled I figured he had PTSD. Sometimes I thought he was talking about a monster and other times he seemed to be just talking about an ancient mythical blade."

"A monster?"

"Yeah. Some sort of creature that was hunting him. An ancient predator, released from its Earthly confines."

Sam looked directly at her, and held her hand. "Do you think he was crazy?"

"I don't know. I had never known him to lose it before."

"Or do you think there was some truth to what he was saying?"

She breathed heavily. "That's just it. He'd been delusional in other conversations after he'd left MI-6, but this one seemed like it was firmly rooted in reality."

"And?"

"Patrick told me about an ancient monster – forged through fire and hardship every bit as strong as a traditional blacksmith might make – that was coming after him and every man in his team. It had killed most of them. Of the seven men in his team, he was one of only three left."

"Do you know who else was part of his team?"

"No."

Sam stood up. He paid the bill and left a generous tip. "Then, I guess we'd better go check out the wreck of the *Hoshi Maru*, and see if we can finally find some answers."

She put her hand on his shoulder. "But there's something else I haven't told you…"

"What?"

"The *Hoshi Maru*'s last radio transmission referred to its crew being attacked by a mythical Japanese beast, called a *Nue*."

Chapter Seventeen

Sam made his way down to Cannon Beach, Oregon.

Guinevere walked next to him with the determined stride of someone who knew with certainty that they were heading toward danger, but had to go there anyway. Caliburn, on the other hand, looked ten years younger, as he ran along the beach, sniffing new and wonderfully rotting scents, and chasing birds.

In the distance the thick mist rose eerily over Haystack Rock, the distinctive 235-foot high sea-stack, and its surrounding smaller intertidal rocks known as The Needles. In the shallow water between the sea-stacks and the beach, lay the remains of the *Hoshi Maru* – a jumbled barnacle laden mass barely resembling a once proud ship. Crepuscular rays shone on the shipwreck, turning it golden in the sea of gray.

"She's not much to look at," Guinevere said, stopping to stare at the shipwreck. "But my brother told me she was spectacular."

"I believe it," Sam said, thinking of the many once-majestic ships he'd seen languishing and dilapidating on the sea floor. "Come on. Let's see what they found inside."

They walked down toward the wreck.

Caliburn barked, and pounced on the fish in the shallow waves.

An Oregon Fish and Wildlife Officer stood guard next to the hull. His eyes were bloodshot, and Sam suspected the man had been there all night.

The Officer looked up to greet them, his jaw set firm, but not unfriendly. "Good morning. I'm sorry, I'm going to have to ask you folks to walk right around the shipwreck. It's currently been quarantined until we can work out where it's come from, and what sort of marine parasites it might be carrying."

Sam said, "I can't tell you what parasites she's carrying, but I can tell you her home port was Minamisōma Harbor, and she was lost during the tsunami that originated in Tōhoku, Japan, in 2011."

The Officer grinned. "Hey, with a name like Hoshi Maru, we could guess that she most likely originated from Japan. But there's no certainty she was lost during the tsunami. The seas surrounding Japan can be dangerous. No reason to think that she wasn't claimed by heavy seas. Nor any reason to think, just by looking at her, that she hasn't been in the water a lot longer than seven years. Heck, she might have been stuck in the North Pacific Gyre for decades."

"No. She was lost trying to get out to sea in the port of Minamisōma Harbor. The vessel reached the outer harbor and was swamped by the initial thirty-foot waves."

The Officer crossed his arms. "How could you possibly know that?"

Sam turned to Guinevere. "Because her brother was on board the *Hoshi Maru* at the time."

The Fish and Wildlife Officer took off his hat. Holding it to his chest, he met Guinevere's eye directly and said, "I'm very sorry to hear that, ma'am."

She said, "Thank you. After all these years, it's just nice to finally have some sort of closure."

Sam said, "That's why we would like to take a quick look on board."

"You know I can't let you do that, sir."

"Because of the quarantine?" Sam asked. "I'm a marine biologist by trade. I know how not to disturb the marine life and afterward, we'll bag our shoes. Please, it's very important to her."

The Officer shook his head and frowned. "I can understand why, but all the same, I have my orders to protect the security of the shipwreck until someone higher up than me takes possession and ownership of the scene."

Something about the way the man spoke gave Sam the odd impression that they weren't just dealing with a routine quarantine of a shipwreck from a foreign port. "Why? I thought this sort of thing fell in the direct jurisdiction of Oregon Fish and Wildlife Services."

"Normally it does," the Officer replied. The man opened his mouth to provide more of an answer to the question, but thought better of it, and closed it again.

"Who's taking over your scene?"

The Officer's eyes darted around, cautiously, as though someone might be eavesdropping on their conversation. Then, having determined the entire beach was empty, less a couple of people walking along the beach far in the distance and a Golden Retriever playing in the waves, he said, "Look. The FBI are taking over this one."

"The FBI?" Sam asked. "Does that seem strange to you?"

"No. Why? The FBI look to protect against foreign attacks against the United States. This ship certainly isn't from around here."

Sam made a coy grin. "It's hardly an attempted attack on American soil, either."

"You can say that, but if some of these parasites that have hitched a ride on its hull over the past several years end up in our water system, it can be every bit as dangerous and costly to the people of America to deal with."

"Sure, but that's why you're here," Sam said. "Isn't that your area of expertise?"

The Officer shrugged. "Yeah. Ordinarily. But this one's different…"

"Why?"

"Because the ship's come from Japan."

Sam made a conspiratorial sigh. "Sure, but this is the third vessel from Japan to wash up on Cannon Beach this year. I looked it up. And yet this is the first one the FBI have taken any notice of."

The Officer placed his palms skyward, the muscles of his face going taut into a slight grimace. "Look. I don't know what you think you're getting at, but right now, my only job is to keep tourists, and would be snoopers from dangerously climbing on board this shipwreck. So, unless you have something else to offer, I suggest you two keep walking."

Sam glanced at Guinevere, who was wild with frustration, and then back to the Fish and Wildlife Officer. "Okay."

"Thank you for your understanding, sir." The Officer looked hopeful to be done with the challenging questions. "You two have a lovely day. Once again, I'm very sorry for your loss, ma'am."

Sam said, "I have another theory why the FBI are involved in this."

The Officer met his eye defiantly. "Yeah, and what would that be?"

Sam took a wild leap. "I bet it would have something to do with the bodies."

The Officer swallowed down the bile that rose in his throat at the thought. He knew exactly what he was referring to, but didn't know how he'd heard about it so fast. He hadn't even had time to make his official report yet.

Instead, the Officer remained silent. "What about them?"

"It's a pretty bizarre scene. Those men were probably dead before the tsunami hit, weren't they?"

The Officer went pale. "How could you possibly know that?"

Sam persisted. "The skulls were all separated from their bodies. Each one intricately arranged, set in delicate poses, as though a child was playing with some sort of dolls. That's the case, isn't it?"

The Officer nodded. "Sure. I found the remains of four sailors set up with their skulls facing each other on a dining table as though they were having a conversation. Someone obviously put a lot of time and effort into the hoax."

"Or something evil, with the mindset of a child, was playing with the bodies of those it murdered," Sam countered.

The Fish and Wildlife Officer arched an eyebrow. "You think it was a monster that did that to the bodies?"

"Don't you?"

"No. I think someone found the boat before we had a chance to board it. Seeing the remains of the four sailors, with their flesh long since eaten away by fish, decided to piece the bones together to set up a bizarre scene on board. You care to have another explanation?"

"Yeah, sure…"

"What?"

"I think your monster murdered everyone on board the *Hoshi Maru*, before inevitably becoming stranded there until the wreckage, half afloat, half sunk, managed to drift all the way to the shores of Oregon."

"If this… monster, so you say, lived all those years on the disabled ship, where is it now?"

Sam said, "It got off the shipwreck as soon as it reached land… and like any other predator would do, it went immediately in search of new game."

"What makes you so certain?"

Sam Reilly crossed his arms. "Because I just came from Tillamook State Forest, where I witnessed a scene just like that…"

Chapter Eighteen

There was no doubt in Sam's mind that the Fish and Wildlife Officer had been shaken by his news. Even so, the man wasn't going to budge about letting them on board. It was strange. In his heart he knew it was unlikely that they would find any answers for Guinevere, but somehow, he still wanted to try, for her sake.

Sometimes, even finding nothing was closure enough.

He picked up his cell phone, scrolled through his contacts list, and pressed the call button over the one listed as Secretary of Defense.

She answered immediately. "Reilly, do you know what's happening at the Hanford site?"

"Not yet, Madam Secretary. I've been delayed…"

"You're not on the site, yet?"

"No, ma'am. The *Tahila* motored up the Columbia River late last night. It should be on scene shortly. I was to meet them in Portland, but my car broke down."

"Really?" The Secretary didn't try to hide her disapproval. "We're talking about what may end up being one of the worst environmental disasters involving nuclear waste in America, and you've been delayed by a faulty car? How incredibly careless of you."

"Yes, ma'am."

"I suppose you have Tom Bower running the show until you get there?"

"Yes, ma'am. He'll give me a report as soon as he has eyes in the water."

"He's going to dive the site?"

Sam answered immediately. "Most likely. He'll probably use an array of submersible ROVs to locate the primary source, but once he does that, he'll want to see it for himself. Trust me, nothing's been delayed while I'm stuck here."

"I don't need to remind you what's at play here, do I?"

"No, ma'am. I understand. Forgetting the obvious environmental disaster that awaits, this is a political crucible, a boiling pot, ready to explode. A nuclear processing plant leftover from the original Manhattan Project, its nuclear waste in the production of plutonium stored and slowly seeping into the underground water basin. A ticking time bomb, which a number of Administrations have ignored since its final reactor, N Reactor, was finally shut down in 1987. Ever since the general public became aware of its existence, the government has been telling people that they'll be safe. Now, all of a sudden, you've got a rogue leak into the second largest river system in North America, they're going to be pissed – and they have a right to be."

The Secretary of Defense remained silent for a few seconds. "Yes, that just about sums it up. We have teams of construction workers and engineers ready to create a physical barrier, but first we have to know where the leak is coming from – and as you know, there's a ground water basin beneath the entire site, which means that leak could be anywhere along the fifty miles of direct river frontage – or possibly even farther away."

"I understand, Madam Secretary. Tom's well aware of the stakes. The team will be on site soon, and they'll have answers for you."

"Good." Direct to the point, the Secretary said, "Now, if you didn't call to update me about the Hanford Site, what did you call about?"

"It's about a shipwreck along the Oregon Coast."

"What about it?"

"My car's being repaired, and as it is, I've come across a shipwreck on Cannon Beach. It's quite interesting actually… the ship's called the *Hoshi Maru* and has been drifting ever since its crew was killed by the 2011 tsunami…"

"Mr. Reilly, are you trying to tell me, while I'm dealing with the political fallout of the impending environmental disaster at the Hanford Site, you're exploring some shipwreck that washed up on the beach?"

"Not exactly, ma'am."

"Get to the point."

"I believe the vessel was carrying some sort of creature. The Japanese call it a Nue, a type of mythical chimera involving the face of a monkey, the legs of a tiger, and the body of a tanuki…"

"I know what a Nue is!"

"Really? I didn't. Someone had to explain it to me."

The Secretary said, "What are you trying to tell me, Mr. Reilly?"

"I don't know if I believe in a Japanese Nue, but whatever monster has escaped from its drifting barge across the Pacific, has now been released on the Oregon Coast, and it's wreaking havoc. I know personally that it killed a mechanic last night in the Tillamook State Forest."

The Secretary was silent, taking it in, waiting for him to reveal anything else that he might know.

When she didn't respond, Sam said, "I'm hoping a search of the shipwreck might reveal something that will give insight into what it is we're dealing with here, and possibly how we can defeat it. I have reason to believe that whatever it was, it was originally built as a military weapon."

"What makes you say that?"

"I met someone else. She told me her brother was on board the *Hoshi Maru*." Sam held his breath, wondering how the Secretary would take his absurd theory. "He was with the British Intelligence Service, MI-6. He was involved in a secret operation. Whatever that was, this monster has gone about killing every member of his elite team. And now it's in the Tillamook State Forest."

"Mr. Reilly, I need you to investigate the wreckage. See what you can find about this monster. We have teams searching for it in the Tillamook State Forest, but so far, it seems to be outwitting them."

A wry and incredulous grin formed on Sam's lips. "So you think my theory about a monster from Japan is right?"

"I hope for God's sake that it is, because the more likely alternative is much more dangerous."

"What's the alternative?"

"I'm afraid I can't say."

Sam took a deep breath. "Ma'am, did we make this creature?"

"No. But there's a chance, we might have funded its development." The Secretary said, "Look. I need you to concentrate on finding out as much as you can about this monster. Contact me alone. Needless to say, this could be PR disaster, let alone a deadly accident rampaging its way across the countryside."

"What about the Hanford Site?"

"Forget it. As you said, Tom Bower can deal with it. I need you to work out what's coming after us."

Sam squinted against the bright sunlight that now permeated the mist. "I don't understand, ma'am… if this is just some sort of animal, or beast, surely a team of Rangers could take it out easily enough?"

"If I'm right, this monster was a weapon forged from the finest minds in the defense industry, and I'm not so sure this weapon can be destroyed."

"All right. I'll do my best. One more thing, ma'am… the Hoshi Maru is currently under quarantine by the Oregon Department of Fish and Wildlife."

"No, it isn't," the Secretary replied. "I'll make some calls. But, as of this moment, you're taking the lead over its investigation. That ship's in your custody."

"Thank you, ma'am."

Chapter Nineteen

Sam looked at the Fish and Wildlife Services Officer. "I think you'll be getting a phone call any minute notifying you of a change of plans."

"What's the change of plans?"

"I'll be taking over the investigation of this ship."

"You?" The Officer asked, his face set with incredulity. "Who are you?"

"My name's Sam Reilly. I work in maritime salvage around the world, but sometimes I consult to the US government."

The Officer shook his head. "And who's supposed to be calling to tell me you're now in charge?"

"I don't know. She just said she'd make some phone calls."

"Who's she?"

Sam grinned. "Margaret Walsh, Secretary of Defense."

The Officer laughed. "You expect me to believe that the Secretary of Defense just told you on a whim that this is now your investigation?"

Sam made a half-shrug. "I don't expect anything. She told me she'd sort out the authority on her end, and I'm going to wait until she's done that."

A moment later, the Officer's cell phone started to buzz. His eyes darted between Sam and the cell phone. His face plastered with disbelief. He picked up the phone. "Yes?"

Sam watched, as the man listened.

After about a minute, the Officer said, "Are you for real, sir?"

Sam waited until the man ended his call.

The Officer made a big conciliatory sigh. "Mr. Reilly?"

"Yes, sir?"

"That was my boss. The director of the FBI just called him personally to inform him that you're taking over the lead responsibility in the investigation."

Sam grinned. "Is that so?"

"Yes, sir. There's a boarding ladder we've attached amidships."

"Thank you," Sam replied. "I'm sorry, I didn't catch your name…"

"Scott Meyers."

"Thank you, Scott. You look like you've been up all night. When does your counterpart take over?"

"In an hour."

"Okay, make sure you get some sleep. When you get back, I want your department to continue its investigation into any pest-like marine creatures, and also I'll need someone to organize the logistics of removing this ship off the beach before it becomes a permanent blemish on your otherwise pristine shoreline."

"Understood, sir."

Sam gave a sharp whistle. "Caliburn. It's time for you to get to work."

The dog barked at the shallow wave and ran toward the shipwreck.

Guinevere laughed. "You're inviting the dog into the investigation?"

"Sure, why not?" Sam asked. "Did you know dogs have three hundred million olfactory receptors in their noses, compared to about six million in humans, making their sense of smell about fifty times as good as ours. Even the part of a dog's brain that is devoted to analyzing smells is, proportionally speaking, forty times greater than ours."

"I get it. Dog's have a good sense of smell. And you want that, why?"

"Because only Caliburn here can tell us without a doubt whether or not whatever evil creature we found in the Tillamook State Forest originated on this ship."

Guinevere nodded. "That makes sense."

Leveling his eyes at her, Sam said, "Are you ready for this?"

Her face was set with determination. "I'm ready to find out what happened to my brother. I've known he was dead for the past seven years. This is all about finding closure, not hope."

"All right. You go up first and I'll help Caliburn on board."

"Agreed."

Sam watched as Guinevere climbed up the Fish and Wildlife Services' boarding ladder. Afterward, he lifted Caliburn up onto the deck. The dog was roughly seventy pounds. It wasn't just the weight, but the shape of lifting a dog that made it so awkward. On the deck, Guinevere grabbed Caliburn by his torso and helped pull him on board.

On the stable steel deck, Caliburn wagged his tail wildly and licked Guinevere.

She said, "You're welcome."

Officer Myers said to Sam, "Be careful up there. A thing like that can be hard to ever get out of your mind."

Sam nodded. "We will be. Thanks."

He then gripped the boarding ladder and climbed on board the wreckage of the *Hoshi Maru*.

Chapter Twenty

Benton County, Washington – Upper Columbia River
The Tahila motored along the Columbia River heading northeast.

Inside, Tom Bower took a seat at the Round Table at the heart of the Mission Room. With Matthew, the ship's skipper, Veyron, the ship's submersible engineer, Elise, a computer whiz, and Genevieve, a retired Russian assassin whose unique skill set had been appropriated for the team, only Sam Reilly was missing from the table. It wasn't the first, or the last time he'd miss an operation, but everyone knew the stakes.

The Round Table was Sam's idea. He liked the concept that each person brought their unique wealth of knowledge and experience to any mission. Given that they all had, in previous events, risked their lives for each other for the greater good, he felt that the concept of a Round Table, with the voice of each person seated there being given equal weight and consideration, was good strategy. Tom liked the symbolism of the Arthurian ideal, and he always tried to keep it in the back of his mind when he took over the director position at any time.

Symbolism was where the Round Table's similarities to its Arthurian predecessor ceased. The table itself was a three-dimensional touch-screen projector, which allowed them to bring up 3D images, expand those images, and search through in-depth 3D renditions of buildings, ships, locations, mine tunnels, and anything else the human mind could imagine and engineers have once built.

Tom opened the briefing by putting up a 2D digital image of the Hanford Site in 1942.

"I just want to go through a bit of background information about the site and the project, before we talk about how we're going to pinpoint the specific location of the nuclear waste leakage." Tom increased the size of the image until it covered the entire table. "This is the original Hanford Site dated June 1942."

Tom pinched the table, zooming in to the section around the river. "The land is predominantly desert environment, receiving less than ten inches of precipitation annually, and is covered with shrub-steppe vegetation. Visually, little of that would change, but in terms of livability, the events of World War II were about to dramatically alter the landscape."

He swiped the table to the left, revealing a new building. "This is the S-1 Section of the federal Office of Scientific Research and Development, known as OSRD, which sponsored an intensive research project on plutonium. The research contract was awarded to scientists at the University of Chicago Metallurgical Laboratory, known as Met-Lab. At the time, plutonium was a rare element that had only recently been isolated in a University of California laboratory. The Met Lab researchers worked on producing chain-reacting "piles" of uranium to convert it to plutonium and finding ways to separate plutonium from uranium. The program was accelerated in 1942, as the United States government became concerned that scientists in Nazi Germany were developing a nuclear weapons program, led by Werner Heisenberg."

Tom took a breath and rapped his knuckles on the table. "So, in December 1942, General Lesley Groves dispatched his assistant Colonel Franklin T. Matthias and DuPont engineers to scout potential sites to be dedicated to plutonium research. Matthias reported that Hanford was "ideal in virtually all respects", except for the farming towns of White Bluffs and Hanford. General Groves visited the site in January 1943 and established the Hanford Engineer Works, codenamed "Site W." The federal government quickly acquired the land under its war powers authority and relocated some 1,500 residents of Hanford, White Bluffs, and nearby settlements, as well as the Wanapum people, Confederated Tribes and Bands of the Yakama Nation, the Confederated Tribes of the Umatilla Indian Reservation, and the Nez Perce Tribe."

Elise said, "That wouldn't be the first time the local people got screwed in the name of military progress."

Veyron shrugged. "Hey, they built the bomb, didn't they?"

Tom didn't want to get into the moral or ethical debate about the development of a nuclear bomb. That wasn't his job. His job was to find out where the leak was, so that the engineers could fill it with millions of tons of concrete.

Tom swiped to the side, bringing in a more modern photo. This one showed the reactors up and running. He said, "The B Reactor at Hanford was the first large-scale plutonium production reactor in the world. It was designed and built by DuPont based on an experimental design by Enrico Fermi, and originally operated at 250 megawatts."

"Megawatts?" Matthew asked.

"That's thermal, not electrical," Tom clarified.

Matthew nodded. "Ah, thanks."

Tom continued. "The reactor was graphite moderated and water cooled. It consisted of a 28-by-36-foot, 1,200-short-ton graphite cylinder lying on its side, penetrated through its entire length horizontally by 2,004 aluminum tubes. Two hundred short tons of uranium slugs, 1.625 inches in diameter by 8 inches long, sealed in aluminum cans, went into the tubes."

Tom lifted two imaginary reactor diagrams from the table, forming a holographic 3-dimensional image of the structures. Reading from the information chart next to them, he said, "Plutonium was produced in the Hanford reactors when a uranium-238 atom in a fuel slug absorbed a neutron to form uranium-239. U-239 rapidly undergoes beta decay to form neptunium-239, which rapidly undergoes a second beta decay to form plutonium-239. The irradiated fuel slugs were transported by rail to three huge remotely operated chemical separation plants called "canyons" that were about 10 miles away. A series of chemical processing steps separated the small amount of plutonium that was produced from the remaining uranium and the fission waste products. This first batch of plutonium was refined in the 221-T plant from December 26, 1944, to February 2, 1945, and delivered to the Los Alamos laboratory in New Mexico on February 5, 1945. The material was used in Trinity, the first nuclear explosion, on July 16, 1945."

Elise said, "And then in Fat Man, the bomb detonated over Nagasaki, Japan."

"That's right." Tom paused. "So why do we care about the technical stuff?"

There was a general murmur that people around the table were getting lost in early nuclear physics.

"We care," Tom said, "because all of this required extensive cooling. Water was pumped through the aluminum tubes around the uranium slugs at the rate of 30,000 US gallons per minute – and all that water had to go somewhere. From 1944 to 1971, pump systems drew cooling water from the river and, after treating this water for use by the reactors, returned it to the river. Before its release into the river, the used water was held in large tanks known as retention basins for up to six hours. Longer-lived isotopes were not affected by this retention, and several terabecquerels of radioactive material entered the river every day. The federal government kept knowledge of these radioactive releases secret. Radiation was later measured 200 miles downstream and as far west as the Washington and Oregon coasts."

Tom glanced at the worried faces around the table. "The water supply wasn't the only problem in the nuclear pioneering days. In fact, at Hanford, the plutonium separation process resulted in the release of radioactive isotopes into the air, which were carried by the wind throughout southeastern Washington and into parts of Idaho, Montana, Oregon, and British Columbia."

Matthew said, "Hey, I'm from Idaho…"

It was the first Tom had heard about Matthew's childhood origins. "Downwinders were exposed to radionuclides, particularly iodine-131, with the heaviest releases during the period from 1945 to 1951. These radionuclides entered the food chain via dairy cows grazing on contaminated fields. Hazardous fallout was ingested by communities who consumed radioactive food and milk. Most of these airborne releases were a part of Hanford's routine operations, while a few of the larger releases occurred in isolated incidents. In 1949, an intentional release known as the "Green Run" released 8,000 curies of radioactive iodine-131 over two days. Another source of contaminated food came from Columbia River fish, an impact felt disproportionately by Native American communities who depended on the river for their customary diets."

Tom opened up a slide with a series of statistics. He read them out loud. "By the end of the Cold War, the project expanded to include nine nuclear reactors and five large plutonium processing complexes, which produced plutonium for most of the more than 60,000 weapons built for the U.S. nuclear arsenal."

"Which brings us to what we're dealing with." He took a deep breath. "This level of nuclear productivity has left behind 53 million gallons of high-level radioactive waste, stored within 177 storage tanks, and 25 million cubic feet of solid radioactive waste. Any one of these storage tanks could have leaked, sending deadly levels of nuclear waste into the ground water, and effectively poisoning the Columbia." Tom glanced around the table. "Any questions?"

Elise asked, "How long have the reactors been dormant?"

Tom said, "Most of the reactors were shut down between 1964 and 1971, with an average individual life span of 22 years. The last reactor, N Reactor, continued to operate as a dual-purpose reactor, being both a power reactor used to feed the civilian electrical grid via the Washington Public Power Supply System and a plutonium production reactor for nuclear weapons. N Reactor operated until 1987, before being entombed in concrete in the same process that was used on the other nuclear reactors."

Tom pinched the side layer of the digital table, and then pulled up a new 3D rendering of the area's geological layers. "Since the decommissioning of the Hanford Nuclear Site, geologists have discovered a second water basin, nearly eighty feet below the nuclear waste storage tanks. In 2011, the Department of Energy – the federal agency charged with overseeing the site – 'interim stabilized' 149 single-shell tanks by pumping nearly all of the liquid waste out into 28 newer double-shell tanks. Solids, known as salt cake and sludge, remained. DOE later found water intruding into at least 14 single-shell tanks and that one of them had been leaking about 640 US gallons per year into the ground since about 2010."

Tom slowly superimposed the movement of the nuclear waste-affected ground water documented between 2010 to present day. "At current rates of movement, the plutonium production waste products are expected to reach the Columbia River in 2031 – so the question is, what else went wrong?"

He glanced at the crew's serious faces. "Any questions?"

Genevieve pointed to a series of horizontal passages leading toward the Columbia River. "What are those?"

"Those are wet tunnels. Once used to pipe millions of gallons of semi-filtered water back out to the river. They were shut down in the early seventies after plutonium by-products were discovered in the water around Portland. We'll be placing a Geiger-Mueller Counter in each of those tunnels to determine if any are responsible." Tom glanced around the table. "What's next?"

Veyron said, "Assuming we find the leak, what do we do about it?"

"We do nothing. Our job is to locate and report. That's it."

Veyron smiled. "Okay, what I meant was, what's the plan – for those who are going to be working on it – to stop the leak?"

Tom said, "There's a company of military engineers working out a plan B, while the DOE's emergency response team is already on its way to the site to block the leak."

"With what?" Veyron persisted. "Concrete?"

"Yeah, basically... and a whole lot of it." Tom said, "Look, the Hanford Site occupies 586 square miles – roughly the equivalent of half the total area of Rhode Island. The original site was 670 square miles and included buffer areas across the river in Grant and Franklin counties. Some of this land has been returned to private use and is now covered with orchards and irrigated fields. The fact is, when the Manhattan Project was running, in an attempt to prevent spies from gathering any useful information, each arm of the Manhattan Project didn't talk to the next one. There were many workers who didn't know until decades later that they had been inadvertently working on the development of a nuclear weapon. This means there could be water pipes, underground tunnels, and even old nuclear waste storage facilities at any of these surrounding locations."

Tom set his jaw firm. There was tension in his voice. "I don't need to say what's at stake here. Let's go out and find this leak."

Chapter Twenty-One

On Board the *Hoshi Maru*, Oregon Coast

Sam switched on his flashlight.

He fixed the beam on the side of the deck. There was a clear line along the deck where the barnacles had reached and then stopped. It was a funny outline. Sam closed his eyes and tried to picture the ships position, floating in the water.

Guinevere asked, "What is it?"

Sam smiled, still trying to imagine it. He fixed the beam of the flashlight on the deck at the exact point the barnacles appeared to stop as if by magic. "See this mark here?"

"Yeah..."

"We can agree that's the highest point the seawater reached throughout the *Hoshi Maru's* long journey adrift across the Pacific Ocean."

"Right. So what?"

"Well. Just try and picture the positions. If that's the case, it means that for the last seven years, water has been over two thirds of the ship's decks, leaving just the bow and forward compartments above water."

"Why didn't it sink altogether?"

"Good question. That's what I wondered too. My guess is, being a fishing trawler with live fish holds all sealed in water-tight compartments, the *Hoshi Maru* has multiple recesses to trap air, producing built-in buoyancy chambers."

Guinevere ran her eyes across the deck, trying to picture it. "So you're saying the *Hoshi Maru* got hit by a tsunami, rolled over – potentially multiple times – without sinking. Then, as the tsunami withdrew into the ocean, it dragged the *Hoshi Maru* out to sea. Meanwhile, the fishing trawler's built-in live fish holds kept part of the ship afloat."

Sam nodded. "Which is how our monster managed to stay alive, like a rat scurrying for shelter."

"How did it survive the original impact of the tsunami? For that matter, how did it not drown in the process?"

"I don't know. But you want to see something else interesting?"

"Shoot."

Sam fixed the beam of the flashlight to a point nearly thirty feet back along the hull. The color of the barnacles changed from a light gray, to a dark green. "Those are living barnacles. These, here," Sam said, pointing to the first line of barnacles, "are dead."

Guinevere made a curious half-grin. "What does that mean?"

"It means that the ship was fixed in this position in the water, and then, after many months, it miraculously changed into this position." He used the angle of the flashlight to demonstrate what he meant.

"What are you getting at?"

"I'm saying that someone or something on board the *Hoshi Maru* must have pumped whatever water remained inside the hull out to sea, thus providing more room to live and survive inside."

"But if someone was able to drain the water, why not do so completely?" She raised her palms upward. "You know, so that they had the most amount of room available?"

"No. Whatever did this, made the conscious decision to keep the boat low in the water."

"Why?" she asked. "To help with stability?"

"Possibly, but I don't think so. A ship like this would have inbuilt ballast, meaning that it was sound floating in any position in the sea. She was never going to the bottom. She would simply float adrift until she eventually washed up on some beach somewhere."

"So why did it keep most of the deck submerged?"

"My guess…" Sam said, his deep blue eyes severe as they raked across the vessel. "I think it was trying to keep the profile of the *Hoshi Maru* low in the water, to prevent anyone spotting her and attempting to make a rescue."

"Why?"

"Beats me. My only guess is someone willing to risk their own life to prevent being spotted adrift at sea must know a lot of people are out to hunt them, and if that's the case, whatever the hell it is we're searching for, it's smart."

Up ahead, toward the pilot house, Caliburn gave a sharp bark.

Chapter Twenty-Two

Sam followed the dog to the entrance hatch.

"What is it boy?" he asked.

Caliburn lowered his nose to the deck and started sniffing. He reminded Sam of the old Looney Tunes cartoons of Porky Pig and Charlie Dog. In the cartoon, the dog would sniff out Daffy Duck, which Porky Pig would inevitably attempt, and fail, to shoot.

Caliburn followed the scent inside.

Sam and Guinevere followed close behind.

Sam glanced at Guinevere. "Are you sure you don't want to just wait out here?"

"No way," she replied. "After seven years of wondering, I want to know the truth."

"All right," Sam said.

He stepped inside the pilothouse.

The place looked surprisingly clean, given that it had been drifting on the Pacific Ocean for more than seven years. The wheel was still intact. The instruments and gauges were all there. Despite the outward appearance of the barnacle encrusted shipwreck, the pilothouse may as well have been that of a fully functioning, seagoing vessel.

Caliburn sniffed again and barked toward the internal stairwell, leading into the main compartments of the forward hull.

Sam said, "You want to lead the way?"

The dog backed away from the stairwell, leaving his tail tucked between his legs. He made a sort of mewling sound, and then turned to face the outer hatch to the pilothouse.

Sam nodded. "You don't want to go down there?"

Caliburn gave a short bark in acknowledgement.

"Is it because you don't like what we're going to find inside?"

Caliburn met his eye, holding it for a fraction longer than Sam had ever known a dog to do, before turning away.

Sam said, "Or is it because you don't like what used to live down there?"

Caliburn barked loudly.

"It was evil, wasn't it?"

Caliburn dipped his head.

Sam said, "All right. Go wait outside for us. We have to go see for ourselves."

The dog didn't need to be told twice. He immediately turned and walked outside.

Guinevere gave Caliburn a reassuring pat as he stepped outside.

Sam pointed the flashlight down into the main forward compartment. With barnacles thoroughly encrusted throughout the hull, blocking the portholes, it was completely dark inside. He carefully climbed down the iron steps. Each one made a resonant clang as he transferred his weight to the next one.

Inside, he found a recreational room. A cracked flat screen TV was mounted onto a wall. A bookshelf was stocked with various books. Their pages were dry but showed the brown discoloration of watermarks. The entire place had obviously been below the waterline at one stage, but someone, or something, had gone to the trouble to return it to its original state. The place was tidy, if not clean. Like someone had spent the effort required to keep it spotless. Two books were left open on the table. One was a Japanese book, its name Sam was unable to decipher, and the second one was a Japanese-English dictionary.

Sam turned to the remaining books fixed to the bookshelf. He assumed they had merely remained there after the ship had rolled over in the water because of the way the book shelves had been designed to keep the books trapped in their place. But now that he examined them closer, he realized the bookshelf had probably once been much fuller, and now, someone had specifically chosen which books to keep, and re-stacked them on the shelf.

He withdrew one at random.

It was in Japanese, but the pages had been well fingered with a series of dog-ears folded into the pages. They were all in Japanese. Hundreds of words had been underlined with a pencil.

Guinevere picked up the two books left on the table. Her face crunched up in a perplexed daze as she studied the Japanese book and the Japanese-English dictionary. Her red lips pursed as she tried to make sense of any of it.

Sam asked, "What's your first impression when you look around?"

"I don't know. It seems, tidy..."

"Maybe the monster or the person, or whatever the hell we're dealing with here, got bored and tried to keep himself occupied by tidying up and..."

"What?" She laughed. "Teaching itself to read in Japanese?"

"Hey, why not?" Sam asked. "It's no crazier than assuming a monster could already read in English."

That brought her out of whatever daze she might have wandered into. "What the hell are we dealing with here, Sam? I mean, whatever this is, it's not human. You've seen the footage of the 2011 tsunami. Those waves were thirty feet high, and carrying enough energy to devour five story buildings."

Sam's eyes narrowed. "What are you saying?"

"I'm saying, if this wasn't human, what the hell are we dealing with?"

Sam shrugged. "I have no idea."

A large, watertight door prevented passage to the aft section of the ship. Sam tracked the beam of his flashlight along the port side of the hull. The recreational room had two forward passageways open. Sam took the portside.

He glanced at Guinevere. "You want to take the starboard side?"

"Without you?" She grinned. "Hell no! I think I'll keep you company."

"That's fair enough."

Sam continued forward. He spotted a series of small sleeping quarters. One of the perks of a large fishing trawler was the increase in space over smaller vessels. This one was large enough to offer multiple sleeping quarters for its crew.

He shined the flashlight inside the first one.

It was clean, the bed was made, but looked like it hadn't been slept in for years. Sam stared at the bed a moment longer and stopped. He reached down and pulled on the sheets.

Guinevere's lips twisted into a wry smile. "What? You're checking on the quality of their bed making skills now?"

"No." Sam sighed and shook his head. "Look at this. Someone made this bed. But I bet you a hundred dollars whoever that person was, it sure as heck wasn't some fisherman living out at sea."

"Why not?"

"The people working on this ship were all fishermen. Judging by the size of the ship, they would have gone out to sea for a number of weeks, filled up their live fish holds to meet their quota, and then returned to their families. Those sorts of people are unlikely to want to have their beds perfect."

Guinevere shrugged. "So what? Who's to say there weren't any women on board? Besides, even if there were, who's to say that the men didn't just like to have clean sheets and a well-made bed?"

"First of all, you told me that your brother mentioned he felt like he was a bachelor again, living on a fishing trawler with a bunch of Japanese men away from their families." Sam pulled at the edge of the bed. "And secondly, those are hospital corners. They use them in the military and in hospitals all around the world. There's no way anyone casually did that."

"What are you saying?"

"I'm saying that sort of thing comes out of habit. You know, it's the kind of thing someone does without thinking if they've spent their life working in a hospital… or living on a military base."

"So our monster once lived on a military base?"

"It would seem so. The question is whose?"

They continued all the way through to the bow of the ship. Everything was dry and clean, with barely any brown watermarks. If he hadn't known better, Sam would have almost guessed that this part of the ship had never been submerged.

But he did know better.

Which meant that someone or something had gone to the effort of obsessively drying the entire compartment, and then cleaning it afterward. Again, that might be common enough for a person trapped on a giant raft for seven years – or someone who liked the comfort of a clean, almost sterile environment.

Sam turned around. "Come on, let's go check out the starboard passageway.

They moved quickly through the dark passageway, flicking the beam of the flashlight in a giant arc around the hull, trying to search for any clue as to the location of the original crew.

Sam stopped at the opening to the starboard passageway. There was no doubt in his mind what they would find in there. Scott Meyers, the Fish and Wildlife Officer had all but confirmed it to him earlier, when he asked about the strange set up of mutilated skeletal bodies.

He glanced at Guinevere, who took a deep breath and nodded reassuringly.

They walked inside.

It was the combined galley and mess area.

Four skeletal remains were set up at the table. Someone had used nylon fishing wire to tie the bones in various positions. Like the rest of the ship, even the bones had been well cleaned, making the sight less ghoulish and more like a morbid attraction at a museum. The bones might have been plastic toys the way they were set up.

One was reading a book. It's bony fingers still gripped the pages in an open position. Two were playing chess. It looked like the player with the black pieces was about to checkmate white and the other player was throwing his hands in the air as though he was angry about losing. The fourth one looked somber and almost pensive. Although how someone can make a skeleton look that way, Sam had no idea. The skeleton wore dog tags and in his hand was a single note.

Sam withdrew the note.

It was made from multiple cuttings of a book written in English glued individually onto a random piece of paper, the same way old ransom notes were written using newspaper cutouts.

Sam ran his eyes across the paper.

DR. JIM PATTERSON'S NEXT…

Guinevere glanced at the name on the dog tags and then removed the dog tag over the skull. She squeezed the tags close to her chest. "This was my brother."

Sam lowered his eyes. "I'm sorry."

"It's all right. I never expected to find him alive. At least I now know what happened to him. Even if I don't know why."

"You might have gained more questions than answers."

"Why?"

Sam handed her the note. "Any idea who Dr. Jim Patterson is?"

"No. Why?"

"I don't know. But apparently, he's next."

Guinevere glanced at the note and shook her head. "No. I've never heard that name mentioned before. Not that that means much. The fact is, my brother worked with the Secret Intelligence Service, so most of what he did and who he did it with were closely guarded secrets."

"I understand."

Guinevere looked at the four skeletons. They were set up with the same sort of imaginative demonstration as that of a child playing with dolls.

She met Sam's eye and asked, "How did you know?"

"About what?"

"The bodies. You practically told the Fish and Wildlife Officer what we'd find in here. So how did you know?"

"I didn't," Sam confided. "I just guessed. I figured Scott Meyers would have told me the truth with his eyes either way. Besides, I wasn't lying when I said the body that I found at Tillamook was set up like a child had been playing with its toys."

"You know what I don't understand?" she asked.

"What?"

"If someone's been living here all this time, where did they live?"

"What do you mean? Wouldn't they have lived all throughout the ship?"

She frowned. "No. I mean, where's the evidence of food, of fresh water, of living… I mean, this place looks like a museum. The entire thing appears artificial. Like the set ups of an historical diorama. There's no smell of recent human habitation. Those beds clearly haven't been slept in for years. The entire place looks… like something's missing…"

Sam nodded. "I get it. The place is like a vacuum. A shallow cardboard cutout of one's existence."

"That's right. So where's the doll maker?"

Sam flicked the beam of his flashlight around the room, and wondered who or what had been living there for the past seven years. What sort of creature would make up such games to pass the time while drifting aimlessly on a raft across the Pacific? What sort of creature could be capable of such ruthless killings, yet positively neurotic when it came to cleanliness and tidiness?

His thoughts were interrupted by the sound of Caliburn barking ferociously on the top deck.

Sam turned to Guinevere, and he shouted, "Quick!"

Chapter Twenty-Three

Sam ran up the flight of steel stairs into the pilot house and out onto the deck. There, along the heavily encrusted section of the aft deck, was a raised platform about twelve feet high. It might have once served as an aft living quarters, or storage section to house various fishing equipment, but years of the bottom half being predominantly underwater had left the lower section of the doors permanently rusted shut and fused with barnacle encrustations.

The fur on Caliburn's back spiked. He continued to bark nonstop at the structure.

Sam patted him on his back. "It's all right, Caliburn. What do you see?"

Caliburn stopped barking, his eyes fixed against what was once the opening to the structure. The muscles of his lips pulled taut, as the dog bared its teeth.

Sam squinted trying to imagine the internal make-up of the *Hoshi Maru*. If the internal structure had a large hatchway to the back, was it possible that there might be an internal stairwell that reached it, also? And if so, how could it be reached?

He patted Caliburn until he settled. Speaking in a soothing tone, he said, "It's all right Caliburn. Whatever it was, it's no longer here now."

Guinevere's eyes traced the outline of the raised structure, stopping at a hatchway two thirds of the way along the deck that appeared to open to the lower decks. "It looks like there might be a connecting passageway. What do you think, Sam?"

Sam nodded. "I had the same thought."

He leaned over the non-existent railing and shouted, "Hey Scott, you there?"

Scott stepped up to the third rung of the boarding ladder. "I'm here."

Sam pointed to the raised structure that had Caliburn in a frenzy. "Has anyone checked inside there yet?"

Scott shook his head. "No. We had a look at prying that hatchway open. But it won't be an easy job. Probably simpler to cut a hole in the wall with an angle grinder."

"Or reach it internally," Sam suggested.

"You can try, but the whole thing's been flooded."

"My dog's picked up the scent of something inside. I'm really keen to find out what it is."

Scott looked at him with skepticism painted across his face. "You want to go see what's got your dog in a terrified frenzy?"

Sam said, "I do."

Scott grinned as though the idea amused him. "Trapped inside the sealed, flooded, hull."

"Yeah…"

"Are you a decent swimmer?"

"I can swim," Sam said.

"I've got a snorkel and face mask in my truck on the beach, if you want to try swimming through. It's probably only about twenty feet. You wouldn't catch me doing it, but I don't see why you shouldn't try."

Sam said, "Thanks. That will save me going off to find one."

A few minutes later Scott returned with the snorkel and mask.

"Thanks," Sam said.

"You're welcome. Better you than me." Scott gave him a good hard look. "Have you ever been inside a flooded shipwreck before? It can be pretty dark and dangerous."

Sam nodded. "Once or twice. I'll be okay," he said with a grin.

"All right. Good luck and stay safe, because I sure as heck won't be coming in after you if you get into trouble."

"I'll be all right." Sam squatted down and patted Caliburn. "Good boy. I need you to tell me something."

The dog went quiet and sat down on its hind legs. The dog looked straight up at him, patiently waiting to find out what Sam wanted to ask.

Sam grinned. "I swear you understand every word I say, don't you, Caliburn?"

The dog tilted its head and mewled.

Sam's voice became hard and serious. "I need to know is there anything or anyone alive in there?"

Caliburn made a slight whimper at the reference to inside the aft deck, and turned his eyes away.

"Does that mean something is alive in there?"

The dog didn't make a sound. For a moment, Sam wondered if he'd been imagining all along that Caliburn was more intelligent than he really was. Maybe Caliburn didn't comprehend anything that he was saying. Perhaps most of it was just a natural response to his tone. Like a learned behavior of a typical animal, expecting to be rewarded with food.

But Sam didn't think so.

"Caliburn," Sam persisted, meeting his gaze directly. "I'm going to go in there, you know that?"

The dog whimpered.

"Am I going to find something alive in there?"

The dog didn't make a sound.

Sam sighed. They weren't getting very far. Some sort of failure in translation more than lack of intelligence. "All right. Tell me this. The thing that was chasing us back in the Tillamook forest, that's where I met you by the way, it was evil, wasn't it?"

Caliburn gave an immediate, crisp, bark.

"Okay. That thing in the forest. Whatever evil thing it was. It was on this ship, wasn't it?"

Caliburn barked again. There was no mistaking the response. It was an immediate, and emphatic response.

Yes. The evil thing was here.

"Right..." Sam grinned. "You do understand me, don't you?"

The dog's mouth opened and it started to pant. Its tail wagged briskly.

Sam expelled a deep breath.

Guinevere's lips parted into a smile. It was nice to look at. Open, full of teeth, and suggestive of some sort of hidden wonder, a playful mischievousness unable to be bridled. Whether she believed Sam and Caliburn had a connection or not was not in debate. Instead, she was just enjoying watching the two try to communicate.

"All right," Sam said, "One last thing. Is it still here?"

Caliburn turned his head.

The answer was much less resounding. It might be. Then again, it might not be.

Sam stood up. To Scott Meyers he said, "Has someone secured and watched this ship the entire time since it became beached?"

"Ever since we were notified of its discovery."

"When was that?"

"Four days ago."

"Okay, and in that time, no one or nothing could have boarded the ship without you or one of the Officers noticing?"

Scott said, "No way."

"Thanks." Sam turned to Guinevere. "That's good enough for me. We know whatever evil once lived here has since been to the Tillamook State Forest. It might, conceivably have gotten back in since last night, but given that the place has been under the watchful eyes of Fish and Wildlife Services, I think it's safe to say that the living quarters inside the ship are no longer inhabited by that evil thing..."

Guinevere thought about it for a moment. "The logic's sound. I'm still glad it's you and not me trying to reach it. I'll wait here with Caliburn."

"Thanks."

Sam opened the hatchway amidships.

It looked like someone had scraped off any barnacles as they had formed and the hinges had been maintained with regular oiling. Meaning, there was no doubt in Sam's mind that something was using the hatchway regularly throughout the Hoshi Maru's trans-Pacific voyage.

He slid the facemask into position and took several deep breaths. A moment later, he placed the snorkel in his mouth, and with his flashlight in his right hand, he dipped beneath the deck, into pitch dark waters below.

Chapter Twenty-Four

Sam dived downward, using his feet to slowly propel himself through the flooded compartment. It was relatively narrow which was good. It was a passageway running fore and aft, as a means of checking on the various live fish holding compartments, fresh water storage compartments, and whatever other type holds the *Hoshi Maru* used. It meant it was wide enough to swim, but narrow enough to avoid any likelihood of becoming lost and entrapped.

The beam flashed through the still waters of the flooded shipwreck. The light struck the tiny stilled particles, turning them to gold.

Sam could hear the sound of his heart pounding in his ears. The beats slowed as he dived and the natural mammalian dive reflex kicked in. The ancient evolutionary response allowed physiological changes after immersion in water that override basic homeostatic reflexes. This optimizes respiration by distributing oxygen stores to the heart and brain, enabling extended submersion times.

Above, he passed the first hatchway.

He fixed his flashlight beam up at it, but kept moving. Based on his estimate, he needed to travel another ten or more feet before reaching the raised chamber. It wasn't a long swim. But he took it slowly, and cautiously. The passageway was filled with fishing lines. If he got caught up in any one of them, he would be hard pressed to cut them away before he ran out of air. His other concern was the fact that he might have to double his submersion time if the hatch on the opposite side ended up being locked or rusted in place.

Up ahead he spotted what he was looking for.

A single ladder rising from an even lower deck, all the way up to what he hoped would be the upper deck house. There was some light rising in the vertical shaft, good confirmation that he was on the right track.

Better still was the distinct lack of silt and marine life on the upper rungs of the ladder, while there were plenty in the lower section.

There was only one explanation – someone had used the ladder regularly to guide themselves through the murky waters.

Sam gripped the rung closest to him, and pulled himself through the water. He kicked hard in the water, picked up speed as he made his ascent, and emerged into a dry area.

He climbed the rest of the ladder until he was completely out of the water, standing on the dry deck spacing of the mysterious aft living quarters.

Sam swept the room with his flashlight. The beam flickered on the various walls and floors, and ceilings. There were three bunkbeds. All were made up, but one had the distinct appearance of having been regularly slept in over the past seven years.

If the *Hoshi Maru* was a residential house, then the aft quarters were its granny flat or poorer sibling. All the necessities of the forward hull of the ship were there, including a galley, beds, eating space, and some books. But instead of being surrounded by creature comforts, the place looked barren, and constructed out of necessity. At a guess, Sam figured the place was a shelter for fishermen during nightshift or in bad weather, to have a break.

The galley had large bottles of water and hundreds of cans of tinned food. As the flashlight beam skittered around the cupboards and living space, it became obvious that someone had been eating, drinking, and existing in the region for some time – but that person had also been careful to keep the place clean so that he could continue to live in it despite the harsh conditions.

In the ceiling above, Sam noticed several holes had been chiseled to increase the ventilation of the otherwise stale air, and also to provide a meager light source.

Sam searched the space for a few more minutes, before nearly concluding that there was nothing more to be learned for having discovered the monster's inner sanctum.

He turned to leave, and the beam of his flashlight caught the reflection of writings on the wall beside the hatch. It reminded Sam of a daily set of goals or objectives that one might post on their bedroom door to remind themselves of their simple purpose each day.

Sam stared at the writing.

It was a list of seven names.

The top four had been crossed out. The last one in that was Patrick Jenkins – Guinevere's brother. There were three names below it.

DR. JIM PATTERSON
DEXTER CUNNINGHAM
JASON FAULKNER

Chapter Twenty-Five

Sheriff Gebhart was in a bad mood.

It might have had something to do with getting very little sleep the night before, but it didn't. Instead it had everything to do with what had happened to her investigation. She glanced at the roadblock she was protecting like some rookie deputy. It was positioned on the Wilson River Highway – the main road running through the Tillamook State Forest.

Despite her years of training, all the fighting she had endured to achieve her position and prove that she was the right person for the job, at the end of the day she had been placed on watch duty, to oversee the shutdown of the forest to all civilians until the Defense Department could determine what the hell was really going on.

What made it worse, the FBI and the two teams of Rangers who were operating in the area, were treating her as an outsider, shutting her out from everything to do with the investigation. She watched a blue Porsche Cayenne approach. Its driver was in a business suit and looked unimpressed at the diversion. She almost took pleasure in turning him around, and redirecting him north to I-26.

When the car had left, she felt better.

Somehow the thought arose that no one ever truly controls their fate. Even the rich sometimes have their plans shut down – or in this case, at least diverted a couple hundred miles. Strangely, it put her at peace, and made her realize that being removed from the case might actually be a bit of a blessing in disguise. After all, there had been multiple deaths now and still no one had any real answers. The longer this went on the more of a political nightmare it would become. Heads would roll if things went badly – and by the looks of things, things had already gone badly.

No. They can keep it. She was there to serve the good people of Tillamook. Whatever was going on here, was clearly a federal issue. Someone had screwed up big if the Secretary of Defense had become involved in the investigation.

Her cell phone rang.

She grinned. It was likely to be another update. She answered it. "Sheriff Gebhart speaking."

It was a friend of hers, Scott Meyers. "Emilee, I think I have a lead on the case that you're working on."

"I'm not working on any specific case."

"I thought there was a murder in the Tillamook State Forest. When we spoke yesterday, you said the body was set up the same way the skeletons were set up in the wreck of the *Hoshi Maru*... you even said something big was happening, the FBI and two teams of Rangers were squabbling over jurisdiction."

"Something big is happening. I'm just not a part of it."

"They cut you off?"

Emilee made a half smile to herself. "Yeah. My whole department has been placed on babysitting duties, making sure no civilian inadvertently enters the area."

"I'm sorry. That's pretty lousy."

"Forget about it. It's all right. When things go bad with this one, someone's going to be crucified over it, so it's probably better that that someone's not me."

"All right… all right. I just have a strange question about your case… I mean, the case you were working on."

"Scott! I said I'm out of the loop."

"It's okay. Just hear me out."

"What?"

"The man in the forest. The first one you said was an older man in a log house. The recluse scientist…"

Her eyes narrowed on a squirrel playing on the branch of an oak tree. "What about him?"

"What was his name?"

"Scott. You know I can't release that kind of information. His next of kin haven't even been notified yet."

"Was his name Dr. Jim Patterson?"

That made her quiet. "All right. I understand. I'll pass it on to the FBI, but they're not interested in talking to me. I'm just here to make sure no one wanders into the place…"

"I was right, wasn't I?"

"You know I can't say that!"

Scott was persistent. "I'll take that as a yes."

"It might have been a no."

"I don't think so."

Emilee sighed heavily. "Scott, how did you know that name?"

Scott said, "Because that name was next in a list of seven names found on board the *Hoshi Maru*. The four names before it were all scratched out, leaving just three. We don't know who the first three were, but the fourth one was a man named Patrick Jenkins, who died on the ship."

"What are you saying… whatever got off the *Hoshi Maru* had made a list of people to murder?"

"It looks like it," Scott said. "Patrick Jenkins was on that list. He was a British expat living in Japan. Jim Patterson was the next on that list, and now he's dead. That leaves just two more names. Two people who could live anywhere in the world."

"Scott," Emilee's voice became firm. "Listen to me. You need to contact the FBI over this. That's an execution list. Someone needs to get those seven names and find out what they all have in common. This is no longer a local issue. Someone in the FBI needs to locate the two remaining survivors and get to them first."

"It's okay. Calm down. There's a maritime consultant who's taken over the investigation of the *Hoshi Maru* under the direct orders of the Secretary of Defense."

"Margaret Walsh, our Secretary of Defense?"

"Yes."

"I thought it was just an idle threat that she was interested in this case. Now you're telling me she has already assigned someone to investigate the *Hoshi Maru*?"

"Yeah, that's what I was trying to get at. It was her man, Reilly, who discovered the seven names on the execution list."

Gebhart arched an eyebrow. "Do you mean Sam Reilly? The maritime and hydrology consultant?"

"That's the one. Why? Do you know him?"

"Kind of. He happened to be in the forest when the killing first started. In fact, he was the one to call 911."

"Interesting," Scott said, in a manner that suggested he had other things more important to focus on right now than that sort of coincidence. "Look. I just wanted to let you know to be careful. Sam Reilly's contacted the Secretary of Defense and the Director of the FBI regarding the names on the list. There's a team at the Pentagon working round the clock to put it all together. But whatever's really going on out there, it's a heck of a lot bigger than we've been led to believe, so please, be careful."

"Cute, Scott. I'm glad to know you care about me."

"I'm serious. Promise me you'll take care of yourself."

"All right. I'll take care."

Sheriff Gebhart ended the call and put her cell phone back in her pocket.

What the hell's going on?

A moment later, she felt the prickly tendrils of fear tease her spine, as she heard footsteps come out of the forest behind her.

Chapter Twenty-Six

Sheriff Gebhart swore as she spotted the man.

He was tall. Roughly six foot two inches. A solid two hundred twenty pounds of muscles. His face was set hard, but good looking. He wore the military uniform of the 75th Ranger Regiment.

"Wow!" the soldier shouted, raising his hands defensively. "Don't shoot!"

Emilee expelled a breath. Her hip holster had been unclipped. It was an involuntary response. She didn't even recall doing it. She clipped the weapon back into the holster.

Meeting the soldier's eye, she said, "I'm sorry. You spooked me. I could have shot you!"

The man smiled apologetically at her. "My fault. I shouldn't have snuck up on you like that."

"You're damned right you shouldn't have." A slight grin formed on her lips. "Especially not since we're all out here trying to locate some deadly animal that's taken it into its head to start killing people."

"I'm sorry. You're right." The soldier offered his hand. "My name's Jason Faulkner. I'm with the 75th Rangers Regiment."

She took it. "Pleased to meet you, sir," she replied. Meeting his intense dark eyes, she asked, "Is there something I can do for you?"

"Yes. I'm hoping you might help me with our investigation."

Gebhart shrugged. "I'll try, but to be honest, your boss recently took me off the case. Declared the entire region of Tillamook a military crime scene, with the entire thing being run by the Department of Defense."

He nodded. "And your services, I presume are being squandered by managing roadblocks."

She gave a half-grin. "Hey, I serve at the whim of the people."

"And I'm sure you do." His eyes drifted toward the roadblock.

Gebhart said, "What can I do for you, sir?"

He smiled at her. He had a nice smile. It was warm, welcoming, and appreciative. It looked candid, but then again, given whatever clandestine shit-fight the military had got itself involved in, the smile and the genuineness might be all practiced.

Faulkner said, "It's about a dog ma'am."

She frowned. "A dog?"

"Yes, ma'am. A golden retriever. We believe it was with the owner yesterday and might provide some vital clues to what's going on in these woods. I don't suppose you saw a dog yesterday."

Gebhart thought about the two visitors in the yellow Ford Thunderbird with the lost dog and sighed. "As a matter of fact, I did. A man said he found the dog in the woods. It had a collar but no phone number or ID. The man was insistent that the dog belonged to someone who had cared for it, but without anything to go off, all I could suggest was that he take the dog to the pound."

"Did he?"

"No. He said it would break his heart to see a dog like that be put down. Instead, he said he'd look after it until he could find the dog a suitable new owner."

"Did he say where he was headed?"

She closed her eyes for a moment, trying to access her near perfect memory banks of the previous evening. "Yeah, the man said he was heading to Portland, Oregon."

"Did you get a name?"

She nodded. "Sam Reilly."

Chapter Twenty-Seven

Jason Faulkner cut through the forest of junior spruce-fir trees, turning from a fast walk to a run as soon as he was out of Sheriff Gebhart's sight. The pathway dipped along the ridge and came out at the US-101 junction at Tillamook.

A near-new Santorini Black Range Rover was parked on the side of the road.

He stepped up to the door, and the car's proximity monitor recognized the keys in his pocket and unlocked the doors. He opened the door and climbed in. The car still had that new car smell. And the scent of money. The cream Napa leather seats were piped with black. The previous driver was shorter than him. He took the time to make the array of adjustments to the electric seats.

He pressed the start button.

The 5L V8 engine started with a gravelly roar that bespoke of a time long before global emission standards within the motor industry.

Jason threw the Range Rover into gear. He turned the wheel all the way to the right, released the electric handbrake and planted his foot down hard, making a U-turn and heading north along US 101. The supercharged engine had great acceleration. Better than turbocharged. No lag. The high-end, sports SUV took off with a lurch.

His lips twisted into a smile.

There had always been something about driving that had made him feel good. A sense of speed and control over one's destiny, offered by the gift of a private motor vehicle. That gift only got better when it was an expensive SUV.

Of course, he'd stolen the car.

It hadn't been reported yet and given the state he left the previous owner in, he doubted very much it ever would be. More likely, someone would one day find the car abandoned and then put it together with the death of its owner – maybe.

Jason hadn't given it another thought. He would be long gone before anyone found the body or the car. He hadn't even bothered to bury the body of its owner. In fact, he'd barely played with the corpse. There hadn't been time. That thought had made him think of the sheriff. *What was her name? Gebhart? Emilee Gebhart.* She had given him her card and he'd kept it. She was a beautiful woman. Strong. Powerful. Intelligent.

Once he'd gotten through with what had to be done, he still might give her a call. That thought brightened his already fine day.

He glanced at the speedo. He was lazily doing 90 miles in a 45 zone. He took his foot off the gas and let the big SUV coast until it slowed to the speed limit. He'd already made much more of a show of Patterson's death than he had meant to, and judging by the military and FBI response, someone in government had already been alerted to the fact that he'd returned. That meant Dexter Cunningham probably knew it too.

So be it.

Still, it was a mistake to steal the Range Rover. If he was being honest with himself, which he certainly always aimed to do – because if you can't tell the truth to yourself, who else could ever believe you? – Jason knew it had been the wrong choice. It was a little bit of luxury after the hardship of the past seven years. That luxury might still get him killed, or at least, permanently incarcerated until someone found a good means of taking him apart, or experimenting on him.

That frightened him.

Despite the others' belief that he was near immortal, he knew that, given enough time, all weapons could be broken. And that is what he was. A weapon.

The thought of being trapped in a small cell and having all his power greedily taken from him frightened him more than dying.

He shook his head.

I shouldn't have taken the damned car.

It stood out as being British aristocracy. If he had been thinking he would have picked a more common American car. Something like a Ford, or a Dodge... which would have blended in with the rest of the local cars. It would have been a good precaution to take. Then again, he hadn't expected such a show of force at Patterson's place, and he hadn't taken into account that Excalibur would simply run...

He input a cell phone number into the Range Rover's touchscreen and pressed call.

A man answered on the fourth ring.

Jason said, "It's me."

Silence.

"Did you hear me, Arthur?"

The man audibly expelled a deep breath.

"I heard you, Excalibur."

"Good." Jason glanced to his left as the Pacific Ocean came into view. "Did your men manage to get the key from the old factory's vault?"

"Yes. My men have it." Arthur rediscovered his control. "What about you, Excalibur? Did you do your part?"

Jason fixed his eyes on the road ahead. "Patterson's dead. But the dog got away from me..."

"Really?" Arthur's voice was incredulous. "How the hell did that happen? You were supposed to be the sharpest weapon nearly a billion dollars of military research and development could produce. So what went wrong?"

"How the fuck do you think it happened?" Jason said, his voice curt and pugnacious. "They did the same damned treatment on the dog, so I'm going to take a wild guess, and say, the dog's a hell of a lot smarter than you are."

"All right. All right." Arthur's voice softened. "You know what that means, don't you?"

Jason nodded to himself. "Yeah. I had better find that damned dog or the deal's off."

"Good to see we have an understanding." Arthur's voice was emphatic, but he didn't belabor the point. They were both men of action. Mistakes had been made, but the project needed to be finished. "Do you have any idea where the dog would have gone?"

Jason grinned. "As a matter of fact, I do."

"Where?"

"A good Samaritan picked up the dog. He's heading to Portland Oregon in a yellow 1956 Ford Thunderbird. It's hard to miss. Let the rest of the team know to keep a look out for it."

"Okay, my men will deal with it."

"I'm on my way there now. And Arthur…"

"Yes?"

"Don't fuck this up. You know what's riding on it."

Chapter Twenty-Eight

Sam Reilly climbed down from the wreck of the *Hoshi Maru*, leaving the Department of Fish and Wildlife to take over responsibility for removing the vessel from the beach – most likely by towing it back out to sea on the next king tide. He also asked their team of marine biologists, who were in the process of determining if the ship housed an invasive species, to take samples and analyze the DNA located on the only recently used bed on board.

By six p.m. Sam, Guinevere, and Caliburn all returned to the motel. They washed and got changed. Earlier in the day, Guinevere bought a new pair of jeans and an opaline tank top that matched her eyes, and accentuated her figure. They ate dinner from a nearby diner and were back to the motel by seven-thirty.

Guinevere had been mostly silent about their findings on board the *Hoshi Maru*. Sam wondered if she was taking the loss of her brother hard, but from what he saw, she maintained her generally positive and mischievous persona. She looked good, better than he would be in her circumstance, but maybe she was just better than him at hiding her emotions. He didn't know and she didn't want to tell him, so he let her be.

Without anything else to do to kill the time, they headed to the motel's common room. It had table tennis, a pool table, and an old jukebox. At the back of the room was an old wardrobe with a sign noted, BOARD GAMES.

Guinevere said, "What do you want to play?"

"Sleep. I like sleep."

"You're no fun."

Sam's lips formed a half-grin. "But I'm happy to play whatever you like."

"Board games? Or pool?" she asked.

"Either... you choose."

"Okay, board games it is." She opened the cupboard. There was only one game inside. She removed the box and handed it to Sam. "It looks like we're going to be playing SCRABBLE."

Sam laughed, a coy grin plastered across his face. "Then I'm afraid I'll have to beat you."

She arched a delicate eyebrow. "Is that so?"

"I work with a computer whiz who's a genius. For nearly two years I've regularly played SCRABBLE against her. By now I'd say I can beat just about anyone."

"So you beat your friend then?"

"Elise?" Sam laughed. "No. Two years on and I've never come close, but I'm pretty good. Certainly, good enough to kick your butt."

"What do you want to bet?"

Sam asked, "What's on offer?"

"How about the motel's bed?" Before Sam could respond, Guinevere said, "Without me in it by the way."

Sam suppressed a smile. "Of course. I wouldn't imply otherwise."

She met his eye. "Deal?"

"Sure."

Caliburn sat down and placed his jaw on his paws, taking a rest on the motel's old wooden floor, his brown eyes watching them as they set up the classic old word game. His eyes, lazily tracked their movements with mild amusement, as though interested in their progress.

Guinevere took the first move.

She licked her lips and played MUZJIKS.

Sam's eyes narrowed. "You're kidding me, right?"

"Hey, MUZJIKS is a word. It means Russian peasant." She grinned. "As in, the MUZJIKS were starving in the field, while the Tzar was eating a feast in the palace."

"Who knows that sort of thing?"

Guinevere made a coy smile and added up the score. "Hey, the Z is over the double letter score, that's a total of 39 points, doubled for being the first word played. That's seventy-eight…"

Sam steepled his fingers. "Well played."

She glanced at the dog. "What do you think of that? Seventy-eight points straight off the bat!"

Caliburn gave a short, baritone, bark.

"You're right, Caliburn. I do get a bonus fifty points for using all my letters! Let's see, that takes me to one hundred and twenty-eight points!" Guinevere laughed and gave him a firm pat. She took a new set of seven letters, and then looked at Sam. "Your turn. See if you can beat that."

Sam couldn't.

He played well and caught up to within fifteen points of her by the end of the game, but never beat her.

Afterward, he asked for a rematch.

She agreed.

This time he won.

Guinevere frowned. "Best out of three?"

"Sure," Sam replied, happy to keep playing with her.

They drew letters to decide who played first. The rule was that whoever picked the letter closest to A went first. Sam drew an M and Guinevere picked an S, meaning that Sam went first.

He said, "I guess I go first."

Guinevere replied, "You need all the help you can get."

Sam glanced at his seven letters.

XOGLDYI

Caliburn barked once. His wail started wagging eagerly.

Sam smiled. "What is it, boy?"

Caliburn nudged the SCRABBLE board and leaned forward on both paws.

Sam said, "Hey, careful with that."

The dog barked again.

"What is it, boy?" Sam asked, giving him a good pat on his thick mane.

Caliburn nuzzled into him and then locked his eyes on the board game, giving another crisp bark.

Guinevere laughed. "I think he wants to play."

Sam's lips curled into a smile of incredulity. "Is that it Caliburn, you want to play SCRABBLE?"

The dog tilted its head to the left, as though considering what he had to say, and then looked directly at Sam and barked in affirmation.

Sam shrugged and pushed the gameboard and letter pieces toward the dog. "Okay. I don't have much I can make with this anyway. See if you can do better."

The dog stared at the seven letters. His brown eyes seemingly fixated on the strange writings, like an archeologist studying ancient petroglyphs with no apparent meaning.

Sam opened his mouth, a slight dimple forming at the corner of his lips. His gaze drifted toward Guinevere. "What do you think of this?"

"I don't know." She artificially set her voice deeper, mocking Sam, and said, "He certainly appears to be taking the game seriously."

The dog stared at the letters, but after nearly a minute he did nothing.

Sam said, "Are you going to take your move, Caliburn?"

The dog barked, and nudged the small placard holding the seven letters over.

"Hey…" Sam said, his voice set in a tone of mock chiding. "I thought you wanted to play? You're just making a mess. Besides, now Guinevere knows what letters I have. Don't you know it's meant to be a secret?"

Caliburn ignored him. Instead, he barked wildly, and nudged the letter pieces around.

Sam watched him. At first it looked like the dog was simply jumbling up the letters into random patterns.

After a few seconds, Sam leaned in to pack up the game, but Guinevere stopped him with a single hand gesture – *let's wait and see what the dog does...*

Sam grinned.

Okay, I'll wait...

Nearly a full minute later, the dog had arranged three letters side by side.

Sam's eyes narrowed as he read the letters out loud. "DOG."

Caliburn tilted his head again and barked. There was nothing difficult about interpreting the dog's meaning.

It said, *well, what do you think of that?*

"Cute, Caliburn." Sam grinned as he added up the score for each letter. "D's are two points. O's are just one, and G's are two points. That's just five points. You get double for playing first. That's ten in total. Pretty lousy way to start the game."

The dog placed its jaw on the wooden floor, and stretched both its paws forward, as though covering its eyes in shame. The dog mewled sheepishly, and tucked its tail between its legs.

Sam said, "Hey, don't worry. I couldn't do any better."

Guinevere said, "Did Caliburn really just write DOG?"

Sam nodded. "I think he did. I told you he wasn't just any old lost dog. Caliburn's the smartest dog I've ever met."

"Even so," Guinevere replied, "I don't think it's possible for a dog to read, let alone spell."

"What are you saying?" Sam turned the board so that the word DOG faced her. "This was a coincidence?"

"It might have been..."

"Sure, with odds of about a million to one that he'd pick that word in particular," Sam countered.

"All right. If Caliburn can read and spell, let's simply try him with another word."

"Okay. That makes sense." Sam emptied the rest of the letters on the floor beside the game board. He riffled through them, searching for some specific letters. "Hey Caliburn... do you want to play again?"

The dog's tail started wagging again. Slowly at first, then fast and uncontrollably.

Sam nodded and placed seven new letters in front of the dog. "See if you can make the word cat."

Caliburn stared at the letters.

AXOGDCT

The dog barked and repositioned the letters using his snout.

Sam grinned as he watched him form another three-letter word. "DOG. Well, there you have it. Someone trained this dog to recognize the name of his species. That's impressive, but not impossible. Nowhere near as amazing as being able to spell any random word."

Caliburn barked, as though still waiting for praise.

"Good try, Caliburn," Sam said, giving him a pat behind the ears. "But I'm afraid the word we were looking for was CAT."

The dog glanced at the board, and the letters, as though examining them better might provide another outcome. When it didn't come naturally, he merely mewled uninterestedly, and returned to his predominant position of sleep as if bored by the whole thing.

Guinevere said, "Well, what do you make of that?"

"His owner has clearly taught him to recognize the word DOG. Neat party trick, but nothing more."

She arched an eyebrow. "You really believe that?"

Sam sighed. "Not even a little."

Chapter Twenty-Nine

The next morning Sam and Guinevere took Caliburn to a local vet.

The doctor was a forty-something year old Texan who'd recently moved into the area to escape the dry heat. Sam filled the man in about how he'd found Caliburn in the Tillamook State Forest, about the dog knowing where the glovebox was, and about the bizarre trick of spelling the word, DOG. The vet was mostly unimpressed, arguing that dogs are smart animals and can be trained to perform any number of tasks.

Sam doubted there were many dogs that had been trained to read or spell simple words, but he bit his lip and let the doctor assess Caliburn.

The vet did a quick assessment and looked at Sam. "I can tell you one thing."

"Yes?" Sam and Guinevere asked, simultaneously.

"The dog's not a stray. Or if he was, he's only just become so. The fact is, he's very healthy despite being an older dog of say, ten or eleven years. His fur is clean and well groomed. His paws are clean and his claws trimmed. His teeth are superb. I don't know if his owner was a dentist or something, but I've never seen a dog of any age with such good oral hygiene."

Sam patted Caliburn. "That-a-dog. Well done."

The vet continued, checking Caliburn's temperature, and taking a small sample of blood for testing. He rotated the medical vial so that the blood mixed with the chemicals designed to prevent it from clotting. "The DNA blood tests might take a few weeks to come back."

Sam frowned. "That long?"

"That long. Unless you know a geneticist who can do it for you quicker?"

Sam held his hand out for the blood sample container. "As a matter of fact, I do. I'll send it to her today."

"All right, I'll leave that for you." The vet ran a series of behavior tests to judge Caliburn's logic and reasoning abilities. When he was finished, the vet said, "Caliburn's a healthy dog in good shape and as you said, he's very intelligent. He's well behaved and his behavior tests, designed to assess his intelligence, are off the chart."

"Thank you. That's reassuring to hear." Sam said, "Can you tell us anything about his background from his collar?"

The vet looked at the collar. It was made of a thick piece of metal and had the words, *Caliburn* neatly engraved on one side. "Anything in particular, you're looking for?"

Guinevere said, "I thought dogs were meant to be microchipped or something? We were hoping maybe the collar might have the dog's details."

The vet nodded. "Yeah, most dogs are required to be microchipped when they're sold, but that's not always the case. Sometimes you have people who buy illegally from non-breeders, dogs who accidentally have litters, you know? But for the most part, dogs are microchipped."

"But Caliburn isn't?" Sam asked.

"No. Caliburn isn't," the vet confirmed. "A dog like this wasn't an accident, and by the looks of things, the owners sure as heck didn't try and take shortcuts."

"So, what are you saying?"

The vet twisted the palms of his hand toward the sky. "I don't know. I'm sorry I don't really have anything more to tell you. I'm saying it's more likely whoever owned Caliburn had another reason for keeping him without a microchip. A dog of his class might have come from overseas – possibly even somewhere we don't accept dogs from, through the regular emigration channels."

Guinevere asked, "What about the weight of the collar tag. It seems awfully heavy for a nametag, don't you think?"

The vet picked it up again, and twisted it in his hand.

His lips, previously set in a firm line, turned upward. He unclipped the dog collar, slid something out of the nametag, and handed it to her. "Would you look at that, the thing's a hidden USB flash drive."

Guinevere asked, "Do you have a computer we could use?"

The vet crossed his arms. "I don't know. There might be something bad on it."

"Aren't you curious?" Guinevere persisted.

The vet relented. "Yeah, I won't say that I'm not at least a little bit curious." He pulled a chair back behind his work computer and said, "All right. Help yourself."

Guinevere inserted the USB flash drive into the side of the computer.

It asked for a password.

She sighed. "Anyone have any ideas."

Sam said, "Elise, a computer whiz who works for me would probably make pretty short work of it. But I'd love to know what's on here."

The vet reached around and said, "It looks like you're going to have to wait. No one's getting through there in a hurry."

"We might get lucky," Sam replied. "I'll give my friend a call and see if she has any suggestions."

"There's no way that will help." The vet's voice was emphatic. "That's a 256-bit military grade encryption right there."

"Really? How do you know? I mean, that might just be a paranoid owner with a long password, right?"

"No. I'm afraid not." The vet leveled his eyes at Sam and Guinevere. "See that emblem there in the top right hand corner?"

Sam glanced at the security seal. "Yeah?"

"That's a code. It means the password is 256-bit encrypted to military standards. I know, I have a brother in Special Forces, and it's the same as he uses…"

"What are you saying, Caliburn belongs to the military?"

The vet frowned. "Not necessarily. But I wouldn't be surprised if Caliburn was purposely genetically designed to be some sort of ultra-intelligent dog."

"For what purpose?" Sam asked.

The vet sighed. "Beats the hell out of me."

Chapter Thirty

Sam walked out of the veterinarian clinic. It overlooked Cannon Beach. Sam's gaze traced the line of the beach, the Hay Stack and Needles rising out of the water, before settling on the *Hoshi Maru* wrecked in between the two.

The faint lines across his face hardened.

He pursed his lips.

What the hell is going on here?

Guinevere glanced at him, almost reading his thoughts. "What do you make of all of this?"

Sam shook his head. "I don't know, but I intend to find out."

He picked up his cell phone and called Elise.

She picked up immediately. Without preamble, she said, "I heard you had some car trouble?"

Sam stepped to the edge of the beach, staring out at the gentle swell of the Pacific Ocean. "That, among other things. Look. It's a long story, but I need you to break a 256-bit encrypted USB flash drive. Can you do that?"

"Do you really have to ask me?"

Sam grinned. "That's what I thought. How long would it take you to break it?"

"That depends. When can you get it to me?"

"My T-Bird should be repaired by this afternoon. I'll drive up the 84 by tonight."

"All right." Elise paused. "Sam…"

"Yeah?"

"What's on the flash drive?"

Sam said, "I have no idea, but I'm dying to find out!"

"Don't worry. I'll have the answer for you soon after you get here tonight."

"Thanks." Sam asked, "Do you know how the Hanford Project cleanup is going?"

"Bad so far. Emergency crews haven't started to plug the leak yet."

"Really? Why not?"

"They can't find it."

Sam's eyes narrowed. "What are you talking about? I heard that the alpha particles, beta particles, and gamma rays flowing into the Columbia were off the chart!"

Elise said, "They are, but we haven't reached the accident site, yet."

In the background, Sam heard Tom ask, "Is that Sam?"

Tom took the phone. "Sam, is that you?"

"Hi Tom. Elise tells me you're having some problems?"

"Well, it's not good."

"That bad?"

"Something nearby is leaking large amounts of uranium and plutonium into the upper Columbia River, so I'd say no matter what the outcome, it's bad."

"So, it is the old Hanford Nuclear Site that's leaking?"

"I'm not so sure."

"Really?" Sam asked. "Where else could that amount of uranium be coming from?"

"I don't know," Tom agreed. "But one thing's for certain… we've been all along the stretch of river that meets the Hanford Nuclear Site – and that's definitely not the source."

"There's nothing there?"

"No. The radiation is coming from farther upstream."

"How much farther?"

"We don't know yet. A long way by the looks of things. We're still working our way upward. We have clean-up teams in place, but no one knows where it's coming from. I have a theory, but we won't know until we get there, and I'm guessing no one's going to like hearing it when I do."

"What's your theory?"

Tom said, "Two theories to be exact, and both are bad."

Sam said, "Go on."

"One is that there's an unaccounted-for subterranean river system that's flowing beneath the known water basin at the Hanford Site. Something's changed recently, and thus, the toxic water is now flowing into the Columbia."

Sam considered that, mentally picturing the topography of the river and nearby landscape, trying to piece together some sort of logical explanation. Having found nothing, he tried to jam in some illogical ones. But it was all the same. Like trying to squeeze a square peg into a round hole. Subterranean rivers took years to alter course. It seemed highly unlikely that it would suddenly shift now. There were no known seismic activities within the area. But it might be possible.

"What's option two?" Sam asked.

"They lied to us about the size of the Hanford Site all these years!"

Sam thought about that. It would be an enormous betrayal against the people, but in a location that was set up to produce the first nuclear bomb in secret, there really was no telling what truths had been allowed to fully surface. "Have you asked the Secretary of Defense?"

"Yeah."

"What did she say?"

Tom said, "That she hadn't been briefed on any nuclear storage facilities near the Hanford Site that hadn't yet been acknowledged publicly."

"She hasn't been briefed on it?"

Tom expelled a breath. "Yeah, her words. She was quite specific about the wording."

"It might be a habit of hers," Sam mused. "After years of juggling politics and reporters she withholds things like that just in case she doesn't like what you find when you locate the leak. But..."

Tom finished what he was thinking. As Tom spoke, Sam could hear the incredulity in Tom's voice over the phone.

"If I'm right, it's one hell of an admission."

Sam nodded to himself. "All right, keep me posted on the progress. I know the Secretary of Defense and the President have a lot riding on this – not to mention the good people of Portland and the outlying townships – all the way through the coast, down into California and up into Vancouver."

"No worries. We'll find it."

"Good luck."

Sam checked his cell phone.

There was a message from the mechanic – *The T-Bird is fixed and ready to go.*

Chapter Thirty-One

Sam settled into the drive along highway 26.

It was long and straight, with a predominant speed of 55 miles an hour – exactly what the old T-Bird was designed to do. Caliburn nestled into Guinevere's lap, positioning his head half inside and half outside the window.

Guinevere stroked the back of his ears and the dog mewled contentedly. To Sam, she said, "What is it with dogs and car windows?"

Sam shrugged. "What's not to get? It's the same reason middle aged men buy cars without roofs… there's something rejuvenating about the wind blowing across your face."

"You're saying dogs and men are the same?"

"No. Probably not…" he turned to face her. "Dogs are better than men in every respect."

Her lips parted in a smile. "Really?"

"Dogs are infinitely loyal, when you come home they race to greet you, not because they want anything at all from you, but simply because they missed you and have been looking forward to your company…" Sam took a dramatic breath of air and continued. "A dog's love is permanent, irrespective of any changes you might make along the way. They don't ask for anything in return. Dogs acknowledge your faults, but are quick to forgive. Dogs are infinitely more capable of love than most humans."

"Wow…" she laughed. "You really like dogs."

"Not really. I just think we have a lot to learn from them, that's all."

She fixed her jade eyes on him, seriously. "You don't own a dog?"

Sam took his right hand off the wheel, holding it palm upward. "No. I don't have time."

"Time for what, exactly?"

Sam looked at her. His ocean blue eyes, honest, and sincere. "To give the love that all dogs deserve."

Caliburn tilted his head to look at him. The dog gave an almost inaudible bark.

Guinevere said, "Hey, it looks like you've upset Caliburn!"

Sam glanced at the dog. "Not you Caliburn. You're different."

Caliburn tilted his head, trying to make sense of what he meant, and then finding little meaning in it, he turned his head and went back to sleep on Guinevere's lap.

Sam pushed the accelerator down hard and the T-Bird overtook a slow-moving logging truck. In front of it, he took his foot off the gas and settled into a few miles over the speed limit again.

Guinevere said, "What are you going to do with Caliburn?"

Caliburn glanced at him; his big brown eyes regarded him beseechingly, but he remained mute.

Sam said, "I don't know. We'll work something out."

"Will you keep him?"

The dog continued the imploring look.

Guinevere persisted. "Will you?"

Sam sighed. "I don't know. Like I said before, I don't have a lot of time to give a dog, even a very human one like Caliburn, enough attention."

Caliburn mewled.

Sam said, "Sorry, Caliburn. I promise we'll find you the perfect home."

Caliburn turned his head away.

Sam looked at Guinevere. "What about you? What are you going to do when you get back to England?"

"I'm not sure. I'd like to follow up on a few things from my past. Also, what we've discovered since searching the wreck of the *Hoshi Maru* has made me more determined to find out what my brother was really involved in."

Sam said, "Tell me about your brother."

Guinevere's gaze drifted toward the Broadleaf Lupines that lined the rolling roadside. The drought-tolerant perennials produced long silvery leaves and spires of blue-violet flowers, which announced the arrival of spring and early summer. Her smile twisted into indecision.

He concentrated on the road, letting her decide in her own time whether or not she wanted to confide in him.

After a few minutes Guinevere said, "Patrick was different than most people. He wasn't always a good person. He had a dark side, we all do, but for the most part, he chose not to let it control him. But sometimes, the darkness crept in. Do you know what I mean?"

Sam nodded. "I think so. We all have it in us. Good and bad, even the best of people. For the most part, good is in control, but sometimes… when our guard is down, or under the right set of deadly circumstances, the bad can come out."

"That's right. Even murderers have some good in them. And some very good people are capable of evil given the… what did you call it?"

"The right set of deadly circumstances?"

"That's it," Guinevere said. "The most obvious is in the form of vigilante killings. But often those are mistakes. People being too lazy to control their primal urge for revenge. Sometimes, it's simply a case of built up pressure. One thing, then another, until the person just snaps and does something evil."

Sam heard the tension in her solemn voice. "Was that your brother?" Sam asked. "Did he do something evil because of something terrible that happened in your life?"

Guinevere held her breath, still unsure that she could let go and finally confide the truth. "No. My brother was pure evil."

Sam waited for her to explain. When she didn't, he said, "But you said he kept the darkness at bay?"

"No. I tried to keep him from embracing the darkness, but it was a battle too great for me."

"What happened?"

She pursed her lips and sighed. "He joined the army. I convinced him that, if he had to kill people, it might as well be for his country."

"Where did he serve?"

"Everywhere and nowhere. From what I understand, my brother killed a lot of people all over the world. Bad guys I guess… people that our country told him were bad. But somewhere along the line he got involved in something worse. The killing wasn't enough."

Sam's eyes narrowed. "You think killing bad guys wasn't enough?"

She nodded. "It's a definite possibility. I know he got involved in something new and whatever that was, it eventually cost him his life."

"And you have no idea what he was involved in?"

Guinevere shook her head. "No. He never talked about it. You see, he worked with MI-6 – the British Secret Intelligence Service – they were working on some project."

"Do you know what that was?"

"No."

"After he died, did you ever look into it?"

"Yeah. But all I ever found was parts of the name of the project."

"Do you remember them?"

"Sure, but they didn't make any sense."

"Shoot."

"King Arthur's Blade."

"What the hell did MI-6 want with an old Arthurian tale?"

"Beats me."

Sam's eyes narrowed. "Did your brother leave you anything when he died?"

"You mean in a will?" Guinevere replied.

"Yeah."

She pursed her lips, unsure how far to go. "Yeah, he left me the name of a book, and said to look into it if anything ever happened to him."

"Really. What was the book?"

"*Historia Regum Britanniae.*"

Sam grinned. "The History of Kings in Britain?"

Guinevere smiled. "That's right."

"So did you read the book?"

She shook her head. "No."

"You're kidding me!" Sam made a wry smile, filled with incredulity. "Your brother says he's left a clue about his death, and you don't bother to read the book?"

Her smile turned hard. "He didn't say that! He gave me the name of a book and said to look into it if he died."

Sam persisted. "Which you never bothered to get around to doing?"

"Did I mention the book was released in 1136?"

"What? You haven't heard of Amazon and Kindle?" Sam asked. "All the better about the age, it means the book's well and truly out of publication, and is probably free on Kindle!"

"It is," she said, "I checked."

"Then why didn't you read it?"

"It wouldn't help," her voice was soft, but the words emphatic.

"Why?"

"Because the cipher Patrick left me was designed to be used against the original edition of the book, not an e-book, or a modern-day appropriation or print."

"That might make it a little harder. Are you sure it's the right book?"

"Yeah… I mean, how many books can there be that reference King Arthur and were written that long ago."

Sam thought about that for a moment, and said, "So let's go find the book."

"That sounds great, but do you know where we're going to find a book written in 1136?"

Sam grinned. "As a matter of fact, I know a bookstore in Portland that might just have a copy."

Chapter Thirty-Two

Powell's Book Store, Portland Oregon

It was raining by the time Sam Reilly drove the yellow T-Bird into the Pearl District of Portland, Oregon. It was an area formerly occupied by warehouses, light industry and railroad classification yards but since the 1980s had transitioned into a trendy area noted for its art galleries, upscale businesses, and residences.

He pulled onto Union Avenue, once the location of the old viaduct. The traffic light changed and he accelerated past the Portland Streetcar and along 11th Avenue, finding a parking spot right at the front of Powell's.

The bookstore was reputed to be one of the largest privately-owned brick and mortar stores in the world. It encompassed a full city block between NW 10th and 11th Avenues and between W. Burnside and NW Couch Streets and contained over 68,000 square feet of retail space, spanning five levels and nine color-coded rooms displaying 3,500 sections of books. More importantly, it was said to have one of the largest stocks of rare, collectible, and antique first edition books – and according to its website, it currently was in possession of one of the few remaining original copies of Welsh bishop Geoffrey of Monmouth, *Historia Regum Britanniae.*

Sam left Caliburn in the car. "You'd better wait here old boy. We'll find some food to bring back afterward, okay?"

The retriever watched him and Guinevere leave, licking his lips.

Sam and Guinevere entered via 11th and Couch.

They descended a few steps into the Orange Room and were greeted by thousands upon thousands of journals and stationery.

Guinevere glanced around the massive room as they followed it through to the Rose Room. She turned to Sam. "Do you have any idea where to start?"

Sam frowned. "There's meant to be a Rare Book Room somewhere here, but I have no idea where to find it."

A young woman with brown hair, dark eyes, and a small nose ring stopped to help. "You look lost."

Sam said, "We are… a little. We're looking for a very old book on the Kings of Britain. Any idea where we might find that?"

She smiled. "How old?"

"Twelfth century."

"I don't know. That's going back some. If the store has such a book, it would be in the Rare Book Room."

Sam asked, "Where's that?"

"Top floor. At the end of the Pearl Room." There was something about her that was incredibly cute and trendy, making her fit in perfectly at the store. "I'm heading that way myself, I'll take you there."

"Thank you," Sam and Guinevere replied in unison.

They took the first set of stairs up into the Red Room, before looping back with another set of stairs going up into the Pearl Room. They passed the Basil Hallward Gallery and entered the Rare Book Room.

Sam ran his eyes across the room. It was filled floor to ceiling with dark wood shelving, ambient lighting, antique furniture, and carefully selected works of art. Most importantly though, the Rare Book Room was home to several thousand of Powell's most valuable books, including an extensive library of reference works about antiquarian books.

He glanced at the woman's nametag. It read, Carly Nelson. Sam said, "Thanks for your help."

"You're welcome," she replied. "I'll leave you with Lindsay here, who will help you find what you're after."

"Thanks."

Lindsay looked up. She had blonde hair, and striking blue eyes, but aside from those differences, Sam figured the two women might have been sisters. "What are you looking for?"

Guinevere said, "We're looking for an original copy of *Historia Regum Britanniae*."

Lindsay's eyes lit up with pleasure as she proudly said, "That's one of our oldest books."

Chapter Thirty-Three

Guinevere sat down at an antique mahogany desk.

At the nearby sales counter, a salesperson took a copy of Sam's driver's license and an imprint of his credit card for security in case any of the books being examined were damaged in the process. Sam Reilly had donated various antique research books to Powell's over the years, giving him a little more credit than most people.

A few minutes later, Lindsay brought out the original edition of the 1136, *Historia Regum Britanniae*. The book was made of discolored paper, bound by leather hide.

"Is there anything you particularly want to know about the book?" Lindsay inquired.

"My brother left me with this," Guinevere said, showing a sheet of plastic the exact size of one of the book pages, with dozens of single letter-sized cutouts. "It's a cipher key designed to match an original edition of *Historia Regum Britanniae*. He died unexpectedly a few years ago, and left me with this, with a note saying that this will give me the answers to what happened to him."

"That's weird," Lindsay said, a wry smile forming in her parted lips. "Your brother really didn't want to make it easy for you, did he?"

Guinevere nodded. "No. Apparently he had never heard of leaving me a letter. Instead, he's making me jump through some pretty difficult hoops to work out what he was involved in and what happened to him."

"All right, I'll leave you to it. I'll be right over there if you need anything. This looks like it might be kind of personal."

"Thanks," Guinevere said, and she watched Lindsay leave.

She placed the plastic cipher delicately on the first page of the book and made a note of each of the legible letters that were still visible. Guinevere finished the page and stared at the letters on the notepad.

They were all gibberish.

She turned the cipher around and tried doing it the opposite way.

Again, it all came out as gibberish.

Sam put away his wallet and took a seat next to her. "Any luck?"

Guinevere frowned. "Not yet."

"What are you getting?"

"Nothing. Random letters. Nothing more."

Sam pursed his lips. "Are you sure you have the right page?"

"Patrick never gave me a page. Just that I was to read *Historia Regum Britanniae* using the cipher."

"All right, keep going. Try the next page."

She tried the next three, but none of them revealed anything meaningful or even legible for that matter.

Sam said, "There must be something we're missing."

Guinevere nodded. "I know, but that still doesn't alleviate the simple fact that I have no idea what clue my brother was trying to give me."

"All right, let's start at the beginning and read the book."

Guinevere frowned. "We might be here all day. It's a long book."

"I have the time."

"No, you don't. I thought you had an urgent project up at the Hanford Nuclear Site, and besides, have you forgotten we've left poor Caliburn waiting in the car?"

Sam said, "Okay, you're right. Let me see the beginning of the book, and maybe I'll flick through the book and see if anything stands out."

Lindsay's ears pricked up, and she moved over to greet them. "No one will be *flicking* through the book. That's survived since the twelfth century and the pages are very delicate!"

Sam made a sheepish half-grin, forming a dimple on his cheek. "I'm sorry. Wrong use of words. I just want to scan through the book, looking for something in particular."

Lindsay met his eye, "You'd better not wreck that book."

Sam lifted his hands in a placating gesture. "I won't, I promise."

Guinevere turned the pages until she reached the start of the book.

On the first page, Welsh bishop Geoffrey of Monmouth, noted his purpose in writing the history.

Sam read the statement out loud, "I have not been able to discover anything at all on the kings who lived here before the Incarnation of Christ, or indeed about Arthur and all the others who followed on after the Incarnation. Yet the deeds of these men were such that they deserve to be praised for all time."

Guinevere said, "And that's why we have Monmouth to thank for introducing the world to King Arthur and his honorable kingdom."

"Pity most of it was made up though…" Sam said, as he scanned the next page. "But maybe not all of it."

Guinevere said, "I don't care if it is all made up or not. I just want my cipher to work so that I can find out what my brother was trying to tell me."

She turned the next page.

It was written in old English, making it difficult to understand. The book itself contained nearly three hundred pages. It might take them days to make sense of any of it, and assuming her brother had used the book for the cipher based solely on its rarity, they would have wasted all that time.

She turned to Lindsay. "I don't suppose you have a condensed version of this book?"

Lindsay smiled. "I thought you specifically needed an original copy of the book?"

"We do. But I want to get a better understanding of the whole book. I was hoping you might have a study guide or an abbreviation of the text in a format where I'm not going to damage this copy?"

Lindsay nodded. "I'll see what I can find."

She returned a couple minutes later with another book. This one was thicker and contained a reprint of the original *Historia Regum Britanniae,* as well as a study guide, and a highly abridged version, condensed into just a few pages.

Lindsay handed Guinevere the book, and said, "Try this."

Guinevere took it and thanked her.

She and Sam then ran their eyes across the pages.

The *Historia Regum Britanniae* was made up of twelve books.

They scrolled through the description of each of the twelve books, but when Guinevere and Sam had finished reading the outline of the book it hadn't revealed any clues about her brother.

She looked at Sam and said, "Well, that clears it up, doesn't it?"

Sam sighed. "Yeah. It all sounds pretty fanciful."

Lindsay approached them again. "Any luck?"

Guinevere shook her head. "No. It's an interesting story about the development of early England, but I can't for the life of me think what my brother's trying to tell me by getting me to read it."

"The cipher didn't work?"

"No. Not even close. I don't suppose there's anything else that might be close to the original *Historia Regum Britanniae?* Something that maybe my brother got confused about? Like, maybe yet another version?"

Lindsay thought about that for a moment. "Actually, I've been giving this some thought. Did your brother specifically tell you that the answers you were looking for were in *Historia Regum Britanniae?*"

"Yes," Guinevere said. Then, thinking about it, replied, "No. He said I needed to look for the earliest edition of the King Arthur Legend. I assumed that was the same thing. Monmouth's book has been widely accepted as the first reference to King Arthur and the Sword in the Stone."

"Actually, that's not true."

Chapter Thirty-Four

Guinevere looked up at the helpful antique book specialist. "There's an older version?"

Lindsay said, "No. You have the first edition of *Historia Regum Britanniae*. But that book was most likely based on the 830AD book, *Historia Brittonum*."

Sam asked, "What's it about?"

"It's written by a Welsh monk named Nennius."

"Did he have a first name?" Sam asked.

Lindsay shrugged. "If he did, no one knows it."

Guinevere said, "So what did this Nennius write?"

Lindsay said, "It was basically an earlier version of the history of Briton. Some scholars believe that, if an historical Arthur ever existed, he was a sixth-century chieftain who helped Britons hold back the tide of Saxon invaders. Nennius describes Arthur by name, only he was never a king. Instead, Arthur was referred to as a chieftain who was larger than life, credited with winning many battles against the barbarians, single-handedly slaughtering nearly a thousand foes in a day."

Sam said, "I don't suppose you have a copy of that book?"

"Yeah, we do," Lindsay said. "It's worth close to a million dollars, but if you're very careful you can look at it."

"Thank you," Sam and Guinevere said.

They waited while Lindsay brought the ninth century book out onto the mahogany table. It was written on vellum – made from fine quality lamb skin – and written in old English.

Guinevere found herself holding her breath.

Lindsay carefully turned to the first page.

Guinevere set the cipher over the top of the words. She started to copy the visible letters down. Her heart thumped as she quickly realized the cipher was producing real words.

GUINEVERE YOU MUST FIND BOTH PARTS OF KING ARTHUR'S FIRST SWORD!

USE IT TO KILL EXCALIBUR!

Sam grinned. "After so much discombobulation, that seems very specific."

Guinevere sighed. "Sure, but do you have any clue where to find the damaged pieces of King Arthur's sword, let alone how to forge it together again?"

"I don't know about finding it, but when we do, maybe we just need to find a good blacksmith, I suppose."

"You can't be serious."

"No. It doesn't matter; I couldn't tell you what happened to Arthur's sword, much less why it's in two pieces."

Lindsay said, "I can answer that!"

"Really?" Guinevere and Sam asked.

"Sure. According to legend, Arthur was thought to have been mortally wounded fighting in the Battle of Camlann during the 6th century. As it turns out, Arthur survived, after he was taken to the Isle of Avalon and healed by the Seer Merlin, who went on to construct an even better sword for the famed king named Excalibur."

Sam asked, "Who was Arthur fighting?"

Lindsay said, "Some believe that he was fighting his sworn enemy, Mordred, who ruled the invaders of Britain."

Guinevere said, "And others believe?"

"That Arthur fought alongside Mordred, his protector. No one knows the truth and how to differentiate between fact or fiction, history or mythology. But one thing most people agree on was that the sword was split into two, with one shard being taken back to the Isle of Avalon to help heal Arthur, while the second half was taken as a token of victory by Mordred."

Sam said, "Great. So, assuming Arthur and Mordred were real, we need to find out where Arthur's part of Excalibur ended up and where Mordred took his part. Then, we need to work out a way to magically forge the two parts together – and use it to kill Excalibur. Is that how you read all this, Guinevere?"

Guinevere made a coy smile. "Yeah, that's about it."

Lindsay said, "I don't suppose your brother simply left more clues in the book about where to find these things?"

"Good point," Guinevere said, as she turned the vellum, and placed the cipher over it.

All three of them gasped.

It was a list of three locations.

GLASTONBURY ABBEY ENGLAND

JERUSALEM ISRAEL

DRAGON BREATH CAVE - MAJORCA

There was no doubt in any of their minds about the meaning. King Arthur was buried in Glastonbury Abbey, Mordred and his sword were buried in Jerusalem, and the Dragon Breath Cave held the fire to forge the sword whole again.

Guinevere tried the next page.

Nothing.

She turned the vellum, but the book was short, and there were no more writings.

Sam asked, "Can you think of anything else Patrick might have left you?"

"No, nothing at all," Guinevere lied.

"All right. It's not a lot to go on, but I'll have some of my researchers see what we can find at those locations."

"What are you saying?" Guinevere asked.

Sam grinned. "I'm saying we're going on a Quest to restore King Arthur's famous sword."

Sam turned to Lindsay and said, "Do you have a digital copy of these books I can buy?"

Lindsay said, "Yes, of course. Come this way."

Guinevere watched as Sam left to buy the digital version.

As soon as his back was turned, she flipped the cipher over and placed it on the last page of the book. It immediately revealed more writings.

She felt the rush of adrenaline as she read the words the cipher had revealed to her.

ONLY YOU GUINEVERE CAN DRAW THE SWORD FROM THE STONE

Chapter Thirty-Five

Sam thanked Lindsay for her help. A moment later, he heard a distant scream. He stepped outside the Rare Books Room looking for its source. His eyes glanced across the Pearl Room, along the Basil Hallward Gallery.

Nothing.

He turned around, and came face to face with a man in a black balaclava. The man leveled the barrel of a handgun at him, and said, "Get your hands out where I can see them!"

Sam slowly moved his hands upward. "Okay. What are you after?"

Two more men in balaclavas entered the Pearl Room.

The man holding the gun against Sam said to them, "Secure the Rare Books Room! And hurry, the police will be here any minute!"

Sam heard Lindsay scream at them not to damage her books.

"I found her!" One of the attackers said. "Patrick's sister. Guinevere!"

"Good," the first attacker shouted. "Turn around Mr. Reilly."

Sam did as he was told.

An instant later, he felt the cold, hard barrel of a handgun being pressed against the base of his spine.

"Let's go. Walk and don't do anything stupid."

Sam watched as another two men covered in black balaclavas moved with military precision, securing the escape routes of the Pearl Room. All this time he thought he'd been dealing with Excalibur the monster, or Excalibur the man, but this was the first he'd realized a well-funded organization might be behind it.

These men, he realized, were most likely mercenaries. Hired elite soldiers. Guns for hire. It was going to be difficult to find a way out. Best case scenario, it was still likely to have significant collateral loss of lives.

Swallowing hard, he said, "Okay. You're the one with the gun. I'll do what you say."

"Good decision."

They stepped into the Rare Books Room.

A man inside had his arm around Guinevere's neck, so that his elbow applied pressure to her throat. The man had a gun pressed at her head. Lindsay was standing next to the checkout section, with her hands behind her head.

The third mercenary was throwing expensive, rare, books around, ripping pages, and cursing.

"Where is it?" The soldier shouted at Guinevere. "I know you came here for the last copy of *Historia Brittonum!*"

"I don't know what you're talking about," Guinevere replied.

The mercenary punched her in the gut once. It was hard, and Guinevere winced in pain.

Sam tried to step forward, but the man behind him said, "Don't…"

He stopped.

Across the room, Guinevere stood up. Her jade eyes widened, and became piercing like fire.

The soldier asked, "Now do you have something to tell me?"

Her mouth twisted in disgust. "Yeah. Didn't your mother ever tell you not to lay a hand on a woman?"

The mercenary laughed. "All right, I was happy to do this the easy way. Single bullet to the head and all. For Patrick's sake. But, if you want to make it painful, be my guest."

Guinevere tried to hold her hands up placatingly. She tried to say something... but the man holding her throat made it come out in barely a whisper.

The man who appeared in charge cupped his hand to his ear and said, "Sorry, what was that darling? I couldn't hear you?"

The man holding her looked up at the man as if to say, *what do you want me to do, boss?* The leader gestured to give her space.

The man stepped backward, letting Guinevere go free.

She took a deep breath in and out before adjusting her position, trying to get a comfortable stance.

The leader met her eye. "Now, what do you want to tell me?"

Guinevere said, "I just wanted to say..."

"Yes?"

"If you walk out that door now, there's a good chance you might get away with this..."

"And if I don't?"

She shrugged. "I don't know. I think I heard your friend say something about the police being here any minute..."

"You'd better tell us where the book is then."

"I'm afraid I can't do that." Guinevere's lips twisted into a wry smile. "But if you touch me again, none of you are getting out of here alive."

The man laughed.

He then punched her hard in the gut.

Only this time, she stepped forward to meet him.

With a retractable razor blade she'd picked up from the stationery desk a minute earlier, she turned and lunged, so that the blade sliced straight through her attacker's throat.

In an instant, it cut through the tough tendons, ligaments, and cartilage that were designed to protect the vital pieces of a person's windpipe and large carotid blood vessels.

The leader's eyes widened in terror.

His hands reached to his throat to stem the bleeding.

Before they had gotten there, Guinevere had already taken his handgun. It was a Walther P99. A first-generation 9mm version, with a green polymer frame. Developed by the German company Carl Walther Sportswaffen of Ulm, the semi-automatic was popular in law enforcement, military, and by the looks of things, mercenaries.

The next few seconds happened lightning fast.

The soldier holding Sam asked, "Are you all right?"

Instead of answering, the leader fell to the ground, dead.

Sam pushed hard against his captor.

And Guinevere raised the Walther P99, and fired a single round into the man's head.

She didn't wait to see if the round had connected.

Instead, she swung around and shot the man who'd been holding her twice in the chest.

The man gasped for air as his lungs quickly filled with blood.

Guinevere moved like a demon. She gripped his head with her hands and whispered, "I warned your friend, no one was getting out of here alive if he touched me again."

The man tried to say something, but it came out as a bloody gurgle.

Sam said, "We've got to go."

Guinevere said, "You're lucky… I'm not so big on the revenge thing."

An instant later, she pushed hard, and snapped the man's neck.

Chapter Thirty-Six

Sam took his dead captor's handgun.

It carried 20 rounds of 9×19mm Parabellum in a detachable box magazine. None of the rounds had been fired.

Outside, he heard the two mercenaries guarding the Pearl Room debate their next move. Sam didn't wait for them to come up with a plan.

He glanced at Guinevere, who had already taken the second soldier's handgun, and carried one in each hand. Sam mimed the positions of each assailant, indicating that he'd take the one on the left, and she would take the one on the right.

She nodded.

And they both stepped into the Pearl Room.

Their attackers got as far as aiming, before both had been shot dead.

Sam's eyes raked the room. There were a few civilians lying on the ground with their hands over their heads.

Guinevere stepped back into the Rare Books Room.

She grabbed the *Historia Brittonum.*

Lindsay looked at her as though she was going to stop her.

Guinevere said, "I'm going to need this. I'm sorry, but you heard them. They were willing to come in here during broad daylight to steal it by force. That means they know something I don't. I'll make it up to you when we return it, I promise."

Lindsay looked like she was going to complain, and then, having thought better of it, she said, "Okay, that will be fine. I'll just mark an I-Owe-You… or You-Owe-Me, shall I?"

"Sure."

Police sirens rang out.

Sam said, "Guinevere! We've got to go!"

They ran down the stairs the way they had come, through the Red Room, down into the Rose Room, and out the Orange Room.

Sam climbed into the T-Bird.

He swore. "Caliburn's missing!"

Guinevere looked around. The dog was gone. "Drive!"

"We're missing Caliburn!"

"It doesn't matter! We need to go!"

Sam gritted his teeth. She was right. He planted his foot on the accelerator, and the T-Bird set off with a jolt.

He turned right into SW Riverside Drive, following the Willamette River, passed Lewis and Clarke College before turning off into a residential area.

"What are you doing?" Guinevere asked.

"I'm getting off the main roads. Someone knew about the T-Bird. They know what we're driving and they're actively hunting us. We need to find somewhere to lay low until we can get help."

Guinevere cocked an eyebrow. "You got a plan?"

"Yeah. There's a house nearby, surrounded by giant pine trees that will block anyone with satellite access from locating the car. The place has been vacant for years."

Next to him, he heard a dog bark.

Sam swore.

And Caliburn sat upright on the bench seat. His tongue was out, and panting hard.

Sam glanced at the dog.

There was nowhere for it to hide in the T-bird. It was a two-seater.

His brow furrowed. "Where the hell did you come from, Caliburn?"

The dog tilted its head and barked happily.

Guinevere said, "I saw what happened!"

"Really?" Sam said. "That's great, because to me it looked like he just appeared out of nowhere."

"That's because he did."

"Oh great. So now we have a dog that reads and spells, and what… goes invisible?"

"He was camouflaged."

"You're kidding me."

Guinevere sighed. "Hey, I'm just telling you what I saw. The dog's fur matched the color and material of your T-Bird precisely."

Sam leveled his eyes at the dog. "Is that right, Caliburn?"

The retriever barked.

"How is that even possible?" Sam asked.

"I don't know. Other animals in the wild are capable of it. Think of a chameleon or some of those marine creatures that change their colors to hide from predators…"

Sam said, "You mean octopus, cuttlefish, and some squid?"

Guinevere shrugged. "Sure, those things too."

"All right, but Caliburn's a dog. No amount of breeding can cause a dog to develop such an efficient natural camouflage technique, can it?"

"I don't know. Beats me. It's just one of those bizarre things I have no explanation for."

Sam grinned. "On that subject…"

"What?" Her liquid eyes met his, her jaw set with defiance, as though daring him to ask.

Sam said, "I thought you said you were a healer?"

"I am." She smiled. "I do Reiki energy work."

Sam took a right and turned into Military Road, Dunthorpe. "Do you care to tell me how you learned to kill with such efficiency?"

Guinevere swallowed hard; she bit her lower lip, and said, "Before I was a healer, I was an assassin with British Military Intelligence."

Chapter Thirty-Seven

Sam slowed the T-Bird to a crawl.

He took his eyes off the road and looked at Guinevere, genuinely studying her face all anew. She was strikingly beautiful. Her liquid jade eyes were full of intelligence. Her fiery red hair framed her strong jawline. She met his gaze straight on. Sam knew he was good at reading people. But somehow, all he could see was kindness.

He frowned. "You weren't always like this, were you?"

"No." Her voice was soft. Her eyes glassy.

Sam turned his attention to the fork in the road up ahead. "When you spoke about your brother having this natural evil inside him, and the fact that the two of you were identical twins, you were speaking about yourself as much as him... that's it, isn't it?"

She took his hand and squeezed it. "I can't explain it. Our parents were fine. Our upbringing was normal. No one hurt us; no one abused us as children. Our desire to hurt others was inbuilt in our DNA. That's the best I can do to explain it."

"You joined the Army together?"

"Yes."

"And both of you were selected for special – off the record – operations with MI-6?"

She nodded. "They said we shared a certain set of moral parameters and flexibilities that made us uniquely valuable to them."

"Did you work together?"

"No. We completed basic training and then field training together, but after that, we went our separate ways. Truth is, most assassins like to work on their own. It becomes more dangerous, to the government and to us, if we work as part of a team. My brother and I needed to kill people. We killed the people that our government told us were bad – we were legal killers – but if we were really honest with ourselves, we would have just as happily killed the same people if our government told us they were good."

"What happened?" Sam squeezed her hand back. "I mean what made you change?"

"You're certain I've changed?"

Sam's response was emphatic. "Yes."

Her eyes turned somber, but her voice was filled with defiance. "When my brother died, my desire to hurt people left with him. It wasn't a conscious decision. Just something that happened. As the time went on, I knew I needed to make amends with the world. I needed to serve people, and make the place better. For seven years, that's all I have done – until today."

"You had to kill those men. They would have killed us otherwise."

She grimaced. "I know. But I didn't have to enjoy it."

Chapter Thirty-Eight

Sam stopped the car outside 11607 Military Road, Dunthorpe.

He let the car idle.

Guinevere looked at him. "What is it?"

He stared at the three big new houses. "Change of plans."

"Why?"

Sam realized he was still holding her hand. He squeezed it gently and let go. "Nothing. My grandparents lived in this house. It was a big old classic American house. It was sold when they died, but has remained vacant for years ever since while the developers decided what to do with it."

Guinevere glanced at the big brand-new houses. "It looks like the developers worked it out."

"It would appear so. By the looks of things, the old family house has been knocked down to make way for three even bigger houses." He shook his head as he looked at the last tree remaining on the property. It was an old redwood. A really good example of the ancient monsters, too. Big enough that if you cut a hole through the middle of the base of it, you could just about drive a car through it. It was the last one left. "When we were kids, I remember playing at this place. There was a whole forest of trees here. My brother and I used to get lost for hours out there. Now look at it. Paradise has been replaced by a few McMansions."

Guinevere looked at the houses. "They look nice."

Sam shrugged. "They probably are. It's just a reminder that time waits for no one."

She said, "I'm sorry about your grandparents."

"It's all right. They led good lives. Full of adversity, mixed in with luck and success."

Caliburn mewled and placed a sympathetic paw on Sam's lap.

Sam grinned. "It's okay, Caliburn. Really it is."

Guinevere asked, "Do you have a plan B?"

Sam shoved the Thunderbird into gear. "Yeah."

He turned out onto the main road again and started driving south. To their right, the rich green forest of Tyron Creek raced by them.

Sam drove hard, but not dangerously fast. The last thing he wanted was to be picked up for speeding. Especially since he wasn't yet certain who else was involved in this. It was possible that their attackers were entirely made up of mercenaries, but the thought crossed Sam's mind, if the British used assassins off the books, who's to say the American government didn't use a similar program?

No. They were better off getting off the grid for a few days until he could rendezvous with his crew and the safety of the *Tahila*.

They drove past Lake Oswego.

Sunlight filtered down through the clouds, scattering reflections of light across the picturesque lake.

Guinevere stared at the stunning vista. "I'd love to live somewhere like this!"

Sam said, "You know I own a house overlooking the lake?"

"Really?" She smiled. "So why aren't we driving there?"

"Because if they knew we were headed to Powell's they definitely have gone to the trouble of looking up the address where the T-Bird is generally garaged."

"You think they're waiting for us at your place?"

"I'd bet my life on it."

Guinevere gripped the handgun she'd tucked into her pants. "You know, I could be convinced to kill a few people just to stay at your place out here for a few days."

Sam said, "No. I think we had better not. I think you might end up having to kill a lot more people than you bargained for."

"Okay, okay. Your house must be beautiful. Do you ever use it?"

"No," Sam said, honestly. "My family and friends sometimes meet there for Christmas. But truth be told, I don't get there much. I really should sell it, but it's nice to have roots somewhere. I spend more time on my ship than I ever have lived on land. Maybe one day."

"Why do you keep it?"

"The house?"

"Yeah."

"I don't know. It reminds me that family matters. Your roots, where your parents and where you grew up matters. Of course, all that could be nothing more than garbage. My team is my family and my ship is my home."

"If we're not going to your house, where are we headed?"

"I have an old friend in Tualatin. His name's Mike. I haven't seen him for a few years. Never been to his house before. Whoever those people back there were, they knew we were headed to Powell's. That means they probably know I have a house in Lake Oswego. I have an Aunt, named Janice, who lives there too, but I don't want to risk dragging her into this."

"But you're happy to drag your friend into it?"

Sam shrugged. "Hey what are friends for? Besides, no one will know about the connection."

"Does your friend know we're coming?"

"No. He's out of town."

Ten minutes later, Sam pulled up in front of his friend's house in Tualatin.

He switched off the ignition and got out. Caliburn jumped out of the car, happy and eager to be free from his confinement for the day.

Sam pulled out a lockpick.

Guinevere stared at him, accusingly. "Is this really your friend's place?"

Sam laughed. "I swear it is."

"And he's not going to mind you breaking into it?"

"Under the circumstances, I'd hope not."

"What about the back to base security alarm?"

Sam looked at the warning sticker, and the alarm on the roof. "Okay, that I didn't know about."

Guinevere said, "Well, I guess that's it for that plan."

"No. I can fix this." He picked up his cell phone, found the person he was after, and pressed call.

Guinevere asked, "Are you calling your friend?"

"Yeah."

"The one who owns this house?"

"No. Someone who's going to help me break into it."

Elise picked up the cell phone. "Where are you Sam?"

"It's a long story, Elise. I need some help."

Something about his voice told Elise it was urgent. "What can I do for you?"

"If I give you the phone number for a back to base security firm and an address, can you find me the alarm code to disengage the alarm?"

Elise chided him. "You're not breaking and entering again, are you, Sam?"

"Just get me the code, Elise. I need a place to lie low for a little while."

Sam heard typing in the background. It was so quick, it sounded more like a machinegun than the staccato of an old-fashioned typist.

A moment later, Elise said, "Okay, the alarm's been disconnected. You're free to enter… or break and then enter?"

"Thanks, Elise."

Sam inserted the lockpick into the keyhole, adjusted the internal latches of the lock, and then turned the handle.

The door swung open.

Guinevere smiled. "You've done that before."

Sam said, "You'd be surprised how such a skill comes in handy."

She frowned. "It's disturbing how easy that was for you."

"Hey, I'm not the healer who also happens to be a highly capable, yet reformed, assassin."

Guinevere shrugged. "Touché."

"You'll get no complaints from me."

Chapter Thirty-Nine

Mike owned a big German Shepherd.

He and his family were away for a summer vacation, but Sam was certain he'd find some canned food for Caliburn, who by now must have been starving.

Sam rifled through five different cupboards until he found what he was after. He opened the can of dog food and placed it in a bowl for Caliburn.

The dog watched him, and licked his lips.

Sam poured some water in a bowl and placed it next to the food.

Caliburn sat upright and barked.

Sam said, "You don't have to ask permission. Go on, eat!"

The retriever didn't need to be told twice.

Guinevere found some frozen food in the fridge and unceremoniously dumped it in the microwave. It was a type of lasagna. More than they could eat together. Sam parked the T-Bird in the garage and shut the roller door so that it wouldn't be spotted by any passersby. When he returned to the kitchen, the sight of the melted cheese made Sam salivate. He hadn't realized how hungry he was until then. They ate it out of the packaging. His mother would have killed him for being lazy, but he justified it on the grounds that it was bad enough that he was eating his friend's food, no reason to use his plates.

Sam watched Caliburn curl up on the couch, getting ready for sleep. He came and sat next to the dog, running his fingers through the dog's thick golden mane. Caliburn nestled in as though to request more of a pat.

Sam stopped. "Now Caliburn, we need to talk."

The dog sat upright and mewled.

Sam said, "It's about your magic trick. You changed the color of your fur."

The tension seemed to instantly evaporate from the dog, as he adjusted his position on the couch ready to go back to sleep.

Sam said, "I'm serious. I need to know about it!"

Caliburn tilted his head, as if to ask, *what do you want to know?*

"Do you have control over it?"

Caliburn barked.

Sam said, "I don't know if that was a yes or a no? I sure wish we had the SCRABBLE board to ask him."

Guinevere went and grabbed her bag. She unzipped it and said, "In that case you're in luck."

Sam looked at the SCRABBLE board. "You stole the motel's SCRABBLE board! Who are you?"

"Hey, I figure our needs are a bit more important right now than some vacationers trying to have family time."

Sam wasn't so sure, but he was glad to have the SCRABBLE board even so. He emptied the game letters out onto the floor. Finding the letters, NO, and YES, he laid them out so that Caliburn could easily recognize the two of them.

Sam said, "Okay, let's try this again. Caliburn, can you control it?"

The dog nudged two letters from the board together to form the word, "NO."

"Did someone experiment on you?"

"YES."

"Your old master?"

"YES."

Sam met the dog's eye. "Were you the only one?"

"NO."

"Who?"

Caliburn nudged some of the other game pieces together to form the word, ANOTHER.

"Do you know his or her name?"

Caliburn tried to maneuver some of the letters on the floor, but struggled to form a word.

Guinevere said, "Was his name, King Arthur?"

The dog nudged the word, NO.

"Crusader?"

Caliburn looked blank.

Sam squinted and said, "What about Excalibur?"

Caliburn's ears pricked up.

Sam's eyes narrowed. He said, "Excalibur. The other experiment's name is Excalibur?"

The dog gave a single affirmative bark.

"Look. I want to take some blood directly under your fur. It won't be a big sample."

Caliburn jingled the game pieces to spell, "WHY?"

"I need to find out what makes you so special?"

The dog simply used its nose to point toward the same set of letters. "WHY?"

"Because whatever experiments they used to achieve your extraordinary abilities, I'm afraid they've used them on something else, too, haven't they?"

"YES."

"Only the program failed with the second test, where it worked perfectly for you?"

"YES."

"What went wrong with the second test?"

It took some time, but Caliburn eventually spelled something resembling, "NOTHING."

"Nothing?" Sam raised an incredulous eyebrow. "Then, why was the program shut down?"

"EVIL."

Sam's eyes narrowed. "What was evil? The people experimenting on you?"

"NO."

Sam swallowed. "The second test subject. That's it isn't it? The experiment emphasized your intrinsic state of being. Where you were naturally good natured, a dog filled with duty, honor, kindness, and unconditional love, the second creature was filled with hatred, vengeance, and pure evil... is that it?"

"YES."

Sam said, "Don't worry. Whatever it was out there that you were afraid of, he can't find you here."

The dog tilted its head.

Almost as if to say, *you don't know what's coming for me.*

Chapter Forty

Sam called Aliana Wolfgang.

The two had very nearly gotten married a few years back, but their distinctly different lifestyles and all-encompassing work schedules never seemed to gel together. In the end their relationship became more or less platonic, based on mutual friendship and respect for one another. But they had always remained close and for Sam at least, the sound of her voice never ceased to stir some pretty strong emotions.

Aliana was a geneticist and a leading expert on microbiology. She owned a pharmacological research and development company in North Dakota. Early that morning, Sam had sent her samples of Caliburn's blood as well as some possible DNA samples of whatever creature had lived and survived inside the drifting wreck of the *Hoshi Maru*. If anyone could tell him what they were dealing with, and what they were up against, it was Aliana.

She picked up on the seventh ring, right before it went to voice mail.

Sam asked, without preamble, "Did you get the data I sent you?"

"Hi Sam, how are you?" Aliana teased. "It's nice to hear from you too. I'm well. Thanks for asking…"

Sam grinned. "How are you Aliana?"

"I'm well. Life's good. What are you doing?"

"I'm in Tualatin, Oregon. It's a very long story, starting with getting stuck in Cannon Beach yesterday after my granddad's old T-Bird broke down, and I needed to wait for parts to make the repairs."

"How perfectly mundane of you." There was a tone of laughter in her voice. "That's an incredibly normal problem for you to have. I'm almost disappointed for you."

Sam laughed. "If it makes you happy… there was a Japanese fishing trawler that washed up on the beach. The ship was called the *Hoshi Maru*. It was last seen trying to leave the harbor at Minamisōma, Japan just before the 2011 tsunami hit."

"So I heard. It's the third one this month."

"You heard about it?"

"Okay, I read it in a newspaper. Apparently, it has taken the majority of the lost ships about this long for the natural winds and currents to bring them here. All the same, that sounds more like a typical ecological disaster waiting for the right marine biologist to solve. I expected more from you."

Sam said, "Did I mention the ship was carrying a biological monster. Some sort of Japanese chimera called a Nue – a mythical combination of a tiger…"

Aliana didn't let him finish… "I know what a Japanese chimera is!"

"Yeah, well this one is pure evil. It's gone on a killing spree, which very nearly involved me last night and this afternoon, too."

Aliana said, "And there's the typical punchline. Everything ends up with someone, or in this case, something, trying to kill you. Things never change with you." She spoke with a tease, but there was a harsh undertone of disappointment in her voice.

"Hey!" Sam said, "I don't like very nearly getting killed on a regular basis, either! It's not like I go out of my way to find these problems!"

"Sometimes it sure seems like you do…"

Sam said, "I'm all right you know. But thanks for your concern."

"I knew you were all right. Takes more than an evil mythical creature from Japan to kill you. Besides, you're here to talk to me about the dog, aren't you?"

Sam's eyes widened. "You got the results!"

Aliana ignored him. It wasn't every day that she had him desperate for something she had. "Let me guess, you picked up the dog while being chased by the evil monster?"

Sam said, "You know, you'd be surprised by how right you are."

"No, I wouldn't."

Sam felt a lump in his throat. "You knew?"

"Not at first. But I did as soon as you mentioned being chased by some evil monster."

Sam grinned. "Hey, you don't think I'm crazy?"

"Sure I do, Sam. But in this case, you might be right."

"What did you find?"

Aliana said, "Tell me about the dog. It's really smart, isn't it?"

"Aliana, just tell me what you know about the dog."

"It's a chimera."

"From Japan?"

"No. A chimera was traditionally any sort of mythical beast that shares the spliced DNA of two or more species. Of course, with modern medicine, as well as strange chance occurrences, these two different genetic strands can naturally bind together."

"You're saying it's no longer mythical?"

Aliana said, "Hell, it's not even science fiction anymore."

"How does it work?"

"Basically, an animal chimera occurs when a single organism becomes composed of two or more different populations of genetically distinct cells that originated from different zygotes involved in sexual reproduction. If the different cells have emerged from the same zygote, the organism is called a mosaic."

"Zygotes?" Sam asked. "In English, please!"

"A zygote is the union of the sperm cell and the egg cell to achieve fertilization. As the egg is fertilized, the zygote begins as a single cell but divides rapidly in the days following fertilization. After this two-week period of cell division, the zygote eventually becomes an embryo."

"I still don't get it," Sam said. "How does the single egg split into two distinctly different species?"

"Not all chimeras include different species. The most common human chimeras shared cells with distinct DNA from two or more people."

"How does that happen?"

"Naturally, or through artificial assistance?"

Sam said, "Both."

Aliana said, "The primary cause of chimerism in humans is during a bone marrow transplant. If a person required a bone marrow transplant, the donor's erythropoietin – the cells that are responsible for producing new red blood cells – have a distinctly different DNA than the receiving person. As a consequence, the recipient becomes a chimera, having his or her normal DNA and someone else's DNA in their bloodstream."

Sam's eyes narrowed. "But some people can be chimeras from birth?"

"Yes. When a mother is carrying fraternal twins, there is a high likelihood that one of the embryos might die very early in the pregnancy. It's been estimated that this might happen as much as 20-30 percent of the time in the case of fraternal twins. Of course, it happens so early that the mother never realizes her loss. Instead, the other embryo can absorb some cells from the deceased one. The resulting baby ends up with two sets of DNA."

"And artificially?" Sam asked.

"In research, chimeras are artificially produced by selectively transplanting embryonic cells from one organism onto the embryo of another, and allowing the resultant blastocyst – that's one of the earliest cells to develop in the embryo – to develop as two or more distinctive DNA sets."

Sam swallowed. "And scientists are actually doing this sort of stuff?"

"Yes," Aliana replied. "And they have been since the early eighties!"

"You're kidding me."

"No. In fact, one of the earliest primate chimeras artificially produced were the rhesus monkey twins, Roku and Hex, with each having six genomes. They were created by mixing cells from four totipotent blastocysts, totipotent meaning an immature stem cell capable of developing into any cell in the body. The experiment kind of failed, because the cells never fused, but they formed individual organs with unique DNA."

"Did anyone successfully develop an artificial chimera with more than one species?"

"They sure did. In 1984, the Institute of Animal Physiology in Cambridge, England successfully developed a Geep, by combining sheep embryos with goat embryos. But that's not where the research ended." There was something exciting, yet simultaneously disturbing about her enthusiasm.

Sam said, "Go on."

"In August 2003, researchers at the Shanghai Second Medical University in China reported that they had successfully fused human skin cells and rabbit ova to create the first human chimeric embryos. The embryos were allowed to develop for several days in a laboratory setting, and then destroyed to harvest the resulting stem cells. In 2007, scientists at the University of Nevada School of Medicine created a sheep whose blood contained 15% human cells and 85% sheep cells." She started to explain where current research was going, but Sam stopped her.

"Aliana… what other animals does the dog share its DNA with?"

Sam could imagine Aliana smiling as she answered him. "Not just the dog."

Sam took a deep breath. "The dog shares DNA with the monster!"

"Exactly."

"And what is the monster?"

"The deadliest of all creatures on Earth – homo sapiens."

Sam stared at Caliburn trying to picture it as a chimera with shared human DNA. "There's a man with dog DNA out there?"

"Not just dog DNA. Both creatures have a third DNA type."

Sam couldn't believe what he was hearing. "What's the third type?"

"Octopus."

"An octopus?" Sam closed his eyes for a moment, trying to picture the near mythical creature. "So I'm being hunted by man with octopus's arms, and the whipping tail of a golden retriever?"

"Something like that…"

Sam stared a Caliburn. "But the dog looks normal. I mean, I'm looking at him right now, and even after being told that he's part human, part octopus, he still looks just like any other dog."

Caliburn shifted his gaze to meet Sam's, recognizing the conversation had turned toward him.

Sam patted the dog, and said, "It's okay, we're just talking about how unique you are."

Caliburn seemed to accept that, and rolled onto his back, with his tail somehow wagging side to side in the typically dangerous whipping fashion of a golden retriever.

Aliana said, "What are you trying to ask, Sam?"

Sam said, "I want to know why it doesn't have a face of a man, and eight arms and legs like an octopus."

Aliana laughed. "Chimerism is almost always undetectable without DNA tests. The exception to this is if they exhibit abnormalities such as male and female or hermaphrodite characteristics or uneven skin pigmentation."

The skin pigmentation comment jogged Sam's memory about Caliburn's chameleon like camouflage in the T-Bird. "We got attacked by a group of highly trained mercenaries today."

"A typical day in the Sam Reilly office." Despite the humor in her statement, her voice had a steely cold edge to it.

Sam said, "The dog was in the car at the time. When we tried to escape, we couldn't find him. It wasn't until a good ten minutes after we had left the scene of the attack that Caliburn seemingly appeared out of thin air."

"That would be the octopus DNA that accounts for the chameleon type ability to adjust its skin coloration."

Sam said, "It was perfect. It was as close to a magic invisibility cloak as I've ever seen and I've seen just how far DARPA was able to take that process with its cloaking technology."

Aliana said, "It looks like magic, but most animals use a very simple technique to alter their colors. They use special cells called chromatophores that respond to chemicals in the nervous system and bloodstream. Inside these cells are tiny sacs containing color and when the signal comes, this color is released and spreads throughout the chromatophores. They only have four shades to work with –yellow, red, blue and brown."

"Just four colors. That can't be right. Caliburn matched the blue stripes on the seating of the T-Bird perfectly."

"Just four colors," she confirmed. "But like artists, this type of camouflage requires the animal to mix colors to produce the perfect camouflage, even against extremely complex patterns. What's even more bizarre is that chameleons, the greatest artists in this field, are completely color blind."

"They're color blind?"

"Afraid so."

"That's the most ridiculous thing I've ever heard. And I've spent this week trying to makes sense of an old Arthurian Legend, as King Arthur's battle for the Sword in the Stone and the battle of good and evil plays out all around me!" Talking about King Arthur brought Sam back to his problem in hand. "All right. So I'm hunted by some sort of human chimera that's part dog, part octopus… he would presumably be very strong, capable of chameleon like camouflage, and smart as all hell, is that right?"

"Maybe… maybe not."

"Why?"

"A dog doesn't generally want to kill everyone."

"So what tried to come after me?"

"Hey, dangerous monsters attacking people in the dark woods and world ending scenarios are your problem, not mine." Aliana made a slow, dramatic sigh. "One thing I do know is that that dog wasn't the product of some mad scientist, or a kid on a farm trying to experiment with a unique breeding program. That dog is a work of scientific excellence. Someone has paid big dollars, and a team of leading geneticists to make this work. There's only one group I can think of who would have that sort of budget who would do that..."

"Who?"

"The military."

Sam thought about what the vet had told him regarding the USB-flash drive they had found hidden inside Excalibur's dog tag. "I think you're right, Aliana."

"Of course I'm right."

Sam said, "Thanks Aliana. I really appreciate it. I'll let you know how it goes."

"You're welcome." He could hear her breathy voice. "Sam..."

"Yeah?"

"Be careful. Whoever illegally built this thing, they're going to want it back. And they're not going to want to leave any witnesses to what they have done when they try to take it back. You know that, don't you?"

Chapter Forty-One

Sam ended the call and quickly briefed Guinevere on the developments.

All three of them headed upstairs, searching for a guest room or somewhere they could sleep for the night. Truth was, Sam doubted that sleeping in his friend's bed was any worse than breaking and entering his house. But it was funny where friends drew the line. They found a king bed. It looked big enough for all three of them, not that Sam was going to let Caliburn share his bed, no matter how smart or adorable he was.

When Sam had brought Guinevere up to speed, she asked, "How long have you been in love with Aliana?"

Sam laughed. "It's not like that."

Guinevere leaned up against the side of the bedroom's doorframe. Her face plastered with skepticism. "Really?"

"No. Look. Aliana and I have been an item for years."

Guinevere frowned. "And you've never gotten around to marrying her?"

"No."

"Shame on you!"

Sam shook his head. A slight grin forming on his lips. "Hey, it's not what you think."

"Then tell me. Why didn't you marry her?"

"She was already taken."

"I didn't figure that one. Who was the lucky guy?"

"Not a guy. Her work. Aliana Wolfgang will always be first married to her work." Sam dipped his head, avoiding the scrutiny of her gaze. "And, if I'm completely honest, I'm just as married to my work on board the *Tahila.*"

Guinevere crossed her arms. "That's it? Unrequited love because you're both too busy with work?"

Sam laughed. "That and Aliana doesn't like the fact that my job can be dangerous at times."

"That, I can appreciate. Hell, we can both appreciate that after the events at Powell's earlier today. I know your problem very well. The entire time I worked at MI-6 I never really let anyone get to know me. I dated for fun and pleasure, but never let anyone get really close. It was too difficult. So, I suppose, I can see how such a thing would happen for you. I'm sorry. I hope you find whatever it is you're looking for one day."

"Thank you," Sam said. "But right now, all I'm looking for is a mythical sword once owned by King Arthur."

Guinevere was persistent. "Does this sort of life make you happy?"

Sam grinned. "You bet it does."

"And you're not still seeing Aliana?"

Sam shook his head. "No."

"Are you really over her?"

"Yes," Sam said, and he meant it too.

"Good," Guinevere said, and she removed her top, revealing an athletic figure covered in cotton underwear. She was every bit as stunning naked as he had imagined. She grinned, lasciviously. "I was hoping you'd say that."

Sam glanced at Caliburn, whose somber eyes locked with his in some form of gentlemanly understanding, before he mewled and headed downstairs to take a defensive position before the front door.

"Good night, Caliburn," Guinevere said, and softly closed the door.

Guinevere stepped closer to Sam.

He looked at her admiringly.

She wrapped her arms around his neck, stopping with her lips close to his. He could feel the warmth of her breath.

She paused for a moment. Teasing. Testing his restraint.

In that instant, Sam knew he could fall in love with her in five minutes, but he doubted very much that the two of them could ever be just friends.

A moment later, her lips parted in a smile.

Sam closed the gap.

It was the easiest thing in the world to kiss her. She kissed him back, hesitantly at first. Then she put her hands behind his head and pulled him toward her, kissing him hard.

And Sam gave in to his every desire.

Chapter Forty-Two

Columbia River, Trinidad – Washington

Trinidad was originally a railroad stop and was named Trinidad by workers for the Great Northern Railway due to its geological and physical similarity to Trinidad, Colorado. Trinidad is located on the border with Douglas County directly above the Crescent Bar on the Columbia River. Once little more than a ghost town, Trinidad's population was growing as houses were being built to take in its sweeping views of the Columbia River.

In the early hours of the morning, as the night sky turned to the gray of predawn, the *Tahila* motored to a stop near the bank of Crescent Bar. The dark, sharp-angled and low-lying hull gave the ship a predator like image, as though it was stalking prey along the Columbia River. The east intermodal goods train snaked its way nearly a mile back, along the rising elevation of Crescent Bar, forming the only sign of movement and life across the bleak landscape of the gorge.

Inside the Tahila *Tom Bower* was preparing to dive.

They had located the source of nuclear radiation leaking into the Columbia River. It was entering from some sort of subterranean river that fed into the Columbia through a large opening. The question was, given that Trinidad was more than forty miles from the Hanford Site, where was the nuclear waste coming from, and more importantly, why had it only just started to leak into the river now.

Genevieve stared at Tom. Her face set hard. "Tell me again, why do you need to dive into a nuclear waste filled river?"

Tom said, "Because the tunnel's too long for an ROV to do the job."

"Right. Aren't you worried about the radiation levels?"

"No." Tom paused. "Yes. But it should be all right. I mean, nuclear divers do this sort of stuff for years. It should be fine. Besides, there's still only relatively low levels of spent nuclear material inside the subterranean river."

"As opposed to?"

Tom said, "Nuclear divers, who work in nuclear power plants, water cooling towers, and spent nuclear fuel pools. They're often compared to the SCUBA equivalent of HAZMAT workers, with the difference being their exposure to radiation instead of air borne contaminant."

"How do they make it safe?" Guinevere asked.

"Their dive suits are specifically built for it."

"And the *Tahila* carries these?"

"Yeah. Two of them to be exact."

Genevieve said, "Great. Where's the second suit. I'll go get set up now."

Tom frowned. "No way. You're not diving with me."

"Why not?"

"Didn't you hear me? I'm about to dive into a subterranean tunnel leaking spent nuclear waste."

The muscles of Genevieve's face hardened. Her piercing blue eyes met his. "I thought you said it's safe!"

"I lied! There's nothing safe about diving in nuclear radiation… I don't care how often nuclear divers do it."

That sealed it for Genevieve. She called out to Veyron. "Hey Veyron, can you find me the second nuclear dive suit. I'm going with Tom to make sure he doesn't do anything especially stupid."

Veyron walked into the dive room. He exchanged a glance with Tom, trying to determine who he was more frightened of in this situation, but said nothing.

Tom broke first. "It's okay, Veyron. You'd better get the second nuclear dive suit. I've seen Genevieve like this. I'm not going to be able to talk her out of it."

Chapter Forty-Three

Tom zipped up the outer section of his nuclear dive suit. It was made of vulcanized rubber, which was designed to limit the exposure to nuclear contamination, was easily cleaned, and mostly waterproof. The suit was composed of three separate compartments. The first was basically a dry suit. The second a water-cooling suit, designed to maintain a survivable temperature inside – more useful in the hot waters of a nuclear power plant – and the third layer is the heavy protection layer.

At this point, Veyron and Elise helped Tom and Genevieve don their two layers of rubber gloves, which attached to the hard cuffs on the dry suit. This allowed the diver to have dexterity while limiting the amount of contamination to their hands, especially if the outer layer happens to rip. Next, their external antenna was attached to their diving harness. The antenna was designed to automatically transmit to the dive room on board the *Tahila*, where Veyron and Elise could verify all dosimetry and make sure that neither of them was inadvertently becoming radioactive in the process.

Last was their heavy Desco air hat. It was the diving helmet of choice for nuclear divers, because its positive pressure free flow, and smooth cleanable surface, worked safely in the radioactive environment.

Tom and Genevieve waited while Veyron checked each of them individually.

Veyron said, "All right. You're both good to go. I've set up the sea scooters. You have ninety minutes of propulsion and four hours of air supply. I don't need to tell either of you that you don't want to surpass either of those times while you're down there. It's one thing to go cave diving, but it's a whole other world of crazy to add in nuclear radiation while you're at it."

Tom said, "I know the risks."

Veyron turned to Genevieve. "What about you?"

Genevieve made a defiant smile. "I know the risks. That's why I'm here. To make sure Tom doesn't get himself killed in the process."

Veyron nodded. "All right. I'll monitor your radiation levels from up here, and let you know if you're getting into trouble. Good luck."

Chapter Forty-Four

Tom and Genevieve sank to a depth of forty feet.

Their powerful headlights sent parallel beams of almost blue light through the clear waters of the Columbia River, like some sort of futuristic spacecraft.

He stared at the entrance of the subterranean river. It was roughly ten feet high, but twenty wide, and started at a depth of forty feet. According to early assessments taken by the Tahila, it drained into the Columbia River at a rate of just half a knot per hour. Slow, but not insignificant, given that they now had to swim against that current.

Tom asked, "How are you doing, Genevieve?"

"Never better," she replied. "You never cease to take me to some lovely places, you know that?"

He squeezed her hand through the thick rubber gloves. "Genevieve..."

"Yeah?"

"Thanks for coming."

"You're welcome." She smiled. Even through the hard-coated faceplate of the Desco air hat, Genevieve was visually stunning. Her intensely blue eyes radiated like stars. Her face set with determination, confidence, and unwavering strength. "Let's go do this thing."

"Agreed."

Tom set the buoyancy to neutral on his RS1 military grade sea scooter. It was basically an underwater motorcycle, only instead of being driven by a turning rear wheel, it used a forward positioned electric propulsion blade.

Attached to the sea scooter was an AMP 100.

The AMP-100 provides real-time, remote radiation monitoring for gamma and X-ray. Local readout of the hand-held meter functions as a portable survey instrument. It was also very useful for acquiring dose rates on items that might be found on the bottom. Due to the possibility of irradiated items, this will tell the diver if that item can be picked up or just pushed off to the side.

He checked the reading. The device measured radiation in Rads.

The reading was 200.

It was a low radiation level, high enough to cause symptoms on exposure to humans but far from being immediately lethal.

Tom switched on the main power to the sea scooter. Its dashboard lit up. Positioned at the front of the sea scooter was a sonar array, which projected a detailed bathymetric map of the seafloor and surrounding submerged tunnels ahead. It also self-projected a reciprocal course, in the event that they become lost underground and underwater.

He used his right thumb to depress the speed rate button, and the little propeller began to spin with a whine.

Genevieve gave him a ten second head start and then followed from behind.

Tom's headlight, positioned at the front of the sea scooter next to the sonar transducer, flicked light off the walls of the tunnel. It was as dark as any cave Tom had ever explored, but the water was clear, its visibility perfect.

The cave system turned left, before rising upward, where the subterranean river had once punched a hole through the softer limestone.

Inside the new section, the passage became narrow. No longer ten feet by twenty feet, the subterranean river took on the specific image of a narrow tunnel. It was big enough to drive the sea scooter, but they would have trouble turning it around if they needed to. It would be doable, but difficult in the narrow confines.

He knew he was taking a risk, but he continued to follow the tunnel.

The AMP-100 pinged, noting that the Rads were rising.

Tom glanced at the reading – 300.

It would have been considered quite high if they were outside of their nuclear dive suits, but still low enough not to kill a person on exposure.

Still, he was glad he was inside a dive suit and breathing self-contained air.

The river system continued in an unnaturally straight line for nearly a mile.

Tom said, "Something's not right here."

"What do you mean?" Genevieve replied. "We're diving through an underground river, filled with nuclear waste, what could be wrong?"

Tom said, "Subterranean rivers, like their sisters above ground, tend to snake and meander, as the flowing water tries to find a path of least resistance…"

Genevieve shined her headlamp along the walls of the tunnel. "This one's perfectly straight."

"Yep."

"Which means?"

Tom said, "It didn't develop naturally. Someone built it."

"Why?"

"I have no idea. If I had to guess, I'd say someone was using it to bring water into something. Or illegally drain water into the river."

Genevieve shook her head. "It seems like a lot of work to achieve that."

"Yeah. I don't know why."

At around the mile mark the tunnel came to an abrupt end.

Tom looked around. "Where the hell is the water flowing from?"

Genevieve said, "Look up!"

Tom turned his headlamp upward. The tunnel suddenly widened into a large opening, like looking up from the bottom of a bath plug.

The AMP-100 went berserk. Rad levels skyrocketed well into the thousands.

It was safe to say they had found the source of the nuclear radiation.

Tom slowly maneuvered his way through to the opening.

As soon as he was in the new cavern, he realized they had entered a large subterranean lake. The bathymetric readings, displayed at the front of the sea scooter's monitor, showed them to be in what appeared to be nothing less than an underground sea.

"Where are we?" Genevieve asked.

Tom shined his flashlight across the bottom of the lake. Large cylindrical nuclear fuel rods littered the floor, surrounded by thousands upon thousands of 144-gallon drums, marked with the black and yellow trefoil – the international symbol for nuclear radiation.

Tom angled the sea scooter upward and gave its throttle a short burst. It was enough to set him in ascending motion.

And after a few seconds, the sea scooter broke the surface of a subterranean lake.

Chapter Forty-Five

Tom used his hand-held flashlight to search the grotto, its beam running along the ceiling and distant horizon in giant swathes.

Genevieve said, "This is clearly a nuclear waste holding site."

"Agreed. Judging by its size, I'd say it's the largest one to serve the Hanford Nuclear Site. It's also undisclosed, which means the politicians and the military have been lying to the American people for many years."

Genevieve shrugged. Growing up in Russia as the daughter of a leading mafia boss, she often saw things in simple, clear cut ways. "It was supposed to be a secret nuclear development site. It wouldn't have been very secret if they notified the people of the purpose of the Manhattan Project."

Tom sighed. "You're right. This might have been the original disposal site during the initial testing and development phase of the Manhattan Project. Those records would have been kept secret until the nineties, after the Cold War had ended. If so, there's a good chance that everyone and anyone who knew about it is now dead."

"You think it's all a case of forgotten locations?" Genevieve didn't bother to hide her skepticism. "No, I bet you any amount of money, someone still knows about this location, and they'd go to extreme lengths to keep the secret buried."

"I hope you're wrong. But you're probably right." Tom fixed his flashlight on an iron platform built on the side of the subterranean lake. There was a sign over a doorway cut into the rockface. "Let's see what that is."

He opened the throttle and the sea scooter whirred as it raced through the water. Tom climbed a set of stairs built into the iron platform, careful not to let any sharp edges cut through his dive suit.

Genevieve climbed up after him.

Tom shined his flashlight on a brass nameplate next to the door.

It read, *Camelot Weapons Industries – Holding Site, 3.*

Chapter Forty-Six

It was nearly eight a.m. by the time Sam woke up. In the dark fog of an Oregon morning, and without anywhere to be, his internal body clock had allowed him a sleep-in. It didn't happen often. He rolled over and placed his hand on the bed next to him.

Guinevere was missing.

He sat up with a jolt, a sudden rush of fear teasing at his senses. He switched on the bedside lamp and pulled on a pair of blue denim jeans and a white polo top.

Sam listened, but didn't hear anything unusual.

He slipped his shoes on and reached for the Walther P99 handgun he'd taken from one of the mercenaries who'd attacked them at Powell's. It was most likely overkill, but something in his gut told him to be cautious.

Sam quietly stepped out of the bedroom and listened.

He was greeted by silence.

At the bottom of the stairs he waited, listened, and stepped out into the living room ready to shoot.

Guinevere lifted her hands up and said, "Don't shoot!"

Sam lowered his weapon. "Sorry. I thought something had happened."

She met his eye, a mischievous smile creeping up on her lips. "I hope you don't treat every woman you go to bed with like this the next day."

His brow furrowed. "Sorry. I'm normally a light sleeper. I woke up with a fright when I noticed you weren't in bed anymore. How are you?"

"I'm good. Caliburn and I are just playing a game."

She was already dressed in a pair of cargo shorts, and a dark green tank top. The green accentuated her eyes. She looked good. Better than good. Sexy and wholesome. He noticed the distinctive bulge of a handgun tucked into her shorts, and a second one in her left cargo pocket. One to fire quickly, and a spare to follow up with.

Sam's eyes drifted downward.

On the floor a new game of SCRABBLE had been set up. There were a number of words already played. Most of them were pretty basic. The sort of thing a primary school kid would have been proud of, rather than an adult. Even so, at a glance it was obvious that Caliburn had been making some pretty good words.

Sam said, "You're playing SCRABBLE with Caliburn?"

"Yep." She made a coy grin. "I think he's beating me."

"Whose turn is it?"

"Caliburn's."

"Your go then, Caliburn. I want to see you make your move."

Sam watched as the dog nosed around some letters to form another word. It was a slow process, but the dog eventually spelled, RUN.

Sam shook his head. "Sorry. It's too early for a run."

The dog nudged the word again, this time more emphatically, RUN.

The dog got agitated and started barking wildly.

Sam asked, "What's wrong?"

Caliburn focused all his concentration on the board and wrote the word, SCARED.

Sam frowned. "Of whatever we found at Cannon Beach?"

The dog dropped his nose onto his lap in affirmation.

"Don't worry about it. Whatever that was, it can't get here."

Then Caliburn spelled, IT FOLLOWED ME.

"No. It can't have." Sam's voice was emphatic, but already, his resolve was weakening. "Whatever it was, there's no way it followed us here. We're more than a hundred miles away by car. There's no way it could have followed us."

The dog's fur spiked upward. He sniffed and shuffled around, finally settling with his tail between his legs, nearby the fire. Sam patted Caliburn behind his ears, reassuringly.

"It's okay, Caliburn. No one followed us. No one knows where we are."

Caliburn barked once. The dog was scared. That much was certain.

Sam said, "How does it know you're here?"

Caliburn slowly maneuvered the SCRABBLE pieces to spell, CONNECTED.

Sam frowned. "You and he are connected? Like the swords. You're both forged by the same blacksmith leaving an indelible connection like a scar?"

The retriever tilted its head as though still trying to contemplate what was being said and what it meant. He then returned to some leftover food Guinevere had put out for him in the morning.

Sam shrugged. "I don't get it. First he's scared half to death and now he's bored?"

"Beats me." Guinevere stood up on her toes, wrapped her arms around his neck and kissed him.

Sam kissed her back. "Good morning."

Guinevere said, "I had fun last night."

"Me too."

A moment later, Caliburn's fur spiked, his brown eyes wide with terror, he released a soft growl.

Sam gave him the SCRABBLE board. "What is it?"

The dog carefully spelled, IT HERE.

Sam said, "What's here? Excalibur?"

Caliburn nudged the pre-made word, YES.

Sam glanced out the window. The fog was so thick he couldn't see where the driveway reached the road. There was no sign of anyone or anything at the front door.

He looked at Guinevere. "He's kidding, right? There's no way whatever that was followed us here."

Guinevere shrugged and made an uncomfortable laugh. "I don't know. He seems to understand a lot more than we've given him credit for. He might actually have a connection."

Caliburn kept moving the letters until it spelled, TO KILL ME.

Sam and Guinevere drew their handguns. Sam kneeled down next to Caliburn and patted him with his spare hand. "It's all right. You're safe with us. We're not going to let anything happen to you."

Caliburn nudged three more letters together.

Sam glanced at them, and then read it out loud, "RUN!"

Chapter Forty-Seven

Sam looked at Guinevere, their eyes making a quick exchange. They needed to get going. He reached for his keys. His heart raced. There was a tension in the air mixed with disbelief. No one could possibly know where they were. It was impossible to believe that Caliburn and Excalibur were really connected in some way.

Even so, there was something about Caliburn's reaction that turned his blood to ice. He raced upstairs to grab his backpack. Sam moved quickly. Guinevere had both her handguns out and Caliburn started barking at the front door.

Behind them, something started tapping on the window. Sam turned around.

There was nothing there. A small branch from a Red Alder tree was brushing up against the glass in the wind.

His eyes fixed on it, holding his gaze for a few seconds.

He withdrew the handgun and leveled it at the window.

Guinevere whispered, "What the hell are you planning on shooting?"

Sam shook his head. "I don't know, but there's something out there."

"It looks like a Red Alder tree to me."

Caliburn's fur shot straight up, and he bared his teeth, giving a deep, gravelly bark.

Sam kept his eyes fixed on the window. He swallowed hard. "Whatever it is, I can feel it. It feels exactly the same as the Evil we felt when we were attacked in the Tillamook State Forest…"

Guinevere stared at the window. "Oh shit! I feel it too."

The tip of the Red Alder branch twisted and bent all the way over until it was touching the glass. It was too obvious and purposeful a movement to have been caused by the wind.

Sam held his breath.

Caliburn's growl turned deadly silent.

The tip of the shifted branch started to sway. Tap, tap, tap. It was prying at the edge of the window, the slight gap in the window pane.

Guinevere whispered. "It can't get in there... the window's locked."

Sam aimed the Walther P99 directly behind the window.

The branch stopped moving.

Sam's eyes narrowed.

Was IT scared?

He considered that possibility. It might be more likely that there was nothing more than wind outside, and all three of them had become spooked by nothing more than a tree being casually shifted by the breeze.

Sam took a step backward, turning his back on the window. He took another one.

On the third step, the tapping started once more.

Sam turned to face it, and drew the Walther P99, aimed, and squeezed the trigger. He fired four shots in rapid succession.

The glass shattered. Fragments and shards splintered in every direction.

Sam, Guinevere, and Caliburn all stared at the broken window. If there had been something evil outside it wouldn't be alive anymore. Not with four shots of 9mm Parabellum somewhere in its torso. And even if Sam hadn't struck a vital organ, no one can take a bullet, let alone four without making a sound.

A few seconds later, the branch bent around with a gust of wind and started tapping on what remained of the shattered window.

Sam took a deep breath in and exhaled.

Guinevere said, "It was just the wind! Just the goddamned wind!"

And then the internal lock on the window frame began to turn on its own.

Chapter Forty-Eight

Sam and Guinevere opened fire simultaneously.

Together, more than a dozen rounds were sent down the barrels, each one landing somewhere near the window's lock, the broken window, and below the window. If anyone had been alive there, it would have been shot.

Something moved quickly, reaching inside to fully unlock the window. It moved so quickly that he couldn't really tell what it was. Instead, it looked more like a jumbled mess of colors. Like a camouflaged animal stalking its prey in the forest.

Only in this case, they were the prey.

Sam emptied the rounds in his chamber. He didn't wait to see if they had any affect. He shouted. "Run!"

All three of them ran through the internal door to the garage.

Sam pressed the garage opener, but the power to the house had been cut. The door didn't budge. He climbed into the car, took out his keys, inserted it into the ignition and turned it. The T-Bird started first try.

Caliburn barked.

Inside the kitchen, a person's feet could be heard crunching against the glass on the floor. Those feet weren't moving slowly. They were running – straight for them!

Sam revved the T-Bird's engine.

Guinevere reached into the spacing beneath the dashboard and retrieved Sam's Remington 12-gauge shotgun.

Sam shifted the three-speed shift-o-matic into reverse, released the handbrake, and planted his foot on the accelerator.

Something came through the internal garage door.

Guinevere fired the shotgun at the shapeless form running toward them.

The Thunderbird smashed through the pine garage door.

Sam held his foot hard on the accelerator.

In front of him, he watched the shapeless figure run straight for them. Guinevere fired again and again, until she'd emptied all four rounds into whatever creature seemed to be attacking them. On the fourth shot, their attacker was knocked over, giving them vital seconds to increase the distance between the Thunderbird and their pursuer.

The T-Bird's rear wheels reached the road's blacktop.

Sam swung the wheel hard to the right. The tires screeched as the car spun around to a complete stop. He lifted the shift-o-matic up to first gear, and floored the pedal.

Sam glanced in his rear-view mirror at the mess of destruction they had caused. He grinned. "Now, this… my friend, Mike, is going to be pissed about."

He kept his foot to the floor until the T-Bird was cruising along at its top speed. Sam weaved his way through the residential streets and pulled out onto I-5 heading back into Portland.

Guinevere said, "What the hell was that?"

Sam shook his head. "That was Excalibur, wasn't it, Caliburn?"

The dog gave a sharp affirmative bark.

"Did you see how quickly it changed colors to match its background?" Guinevere asked.

"Yeah, they're called chromatophores," Sam said. "Little sacs in an animal's skin and hair follicles, filled with pigmentation, that erupt in response to external impulses in its nervous system. I know this because according to Aliana, Caliburn has the same unique mechanism, which he inherited from the DNA he shares with an octopus."

Guinevere looked around, still searching for the creature following her. "That explains how he could camouflage himself so perfectly. What about being bullet proof?"

"Maybe he was wearing a Kevlar vest?"

"I'm going to call BS on that one. For starters, no one wears a bullet proof vest all over their body and if he was wearing anything less than that, one of our shots would have connected with human flesh. Secondly, if he was wearing a Kevlar vest, his camouflage system wouldn't have worked so well – hence, he wasn't wearing anything."

Sam grimaced. "You're right. Which means he must share DNA with what... a Terminator?"

Guinevere said, "Yeah, I've never seen anything like it – and I've been to some rough parts of the world."

"Neither have I." Sam stared at the road ahead. It was filling up with morning traffic as they approached Portland. "We need to find another way out of Portland."

"Where do you want to go?"

The fog was lifting, and a thin ray of sun revealed the snow-capped peak of Mount Hood to the east. Sam said, "We need to get to my ship. It's the only place where I know we'll be safe until we can work out what's going on."

"That's great, but how do you plan to get there? Like you said, we've been targeted. People are watching the highways. What do you want to do, steal a car?"

"No." Sam grinned. "I have a plan."

"What's your plan?"

"You'll see." He opened his cell phone, despite being at the wheel, and scrolled down until he found a name – Terry Nelson – and pressed the call button.

Sally answered on the first ring. "Hello?"

"Sally. Is Terry around?"

"Is that you Sam?" Her tone was familiar, but there was an undertone of disapproval.

Sam held his breath. "Yeah, it's me Sally. I need help."

Sally didn't hide her displeasure. "All right, but Terry's not in that business anymore. I don't want you getting him into any trouble."

"No trouble, ma'am. I just need his help."

Sally didn't say good bye. She just handed the phone to Terry.

Sam said, "Terry. Do you still have access to the Shanghai tunnels?"

"Yeah. But I no longer do that sort of thing. I've come clean in life. I'm no longer in the trafficking business."

"Good for you!" Sam said. "Still, I'm going to need access to the tunnels and a boat – preferably something fast and full of fuel – at the other end."

There was a pause on the line.

"Terry. This is important. I wouldn't ask if I had another option. I'm being hunted by a really bad man."

Terry said, "All right. I'll leave the gate unlocked."

"What about a boat?"

Another pause.

"Yeah. I can get you one of those too. It's an ex-military patrol boat. Jet-powered. Should be fast and agile too. The only thing is, it doesn't belong to me. I can arrange to have it left on the dock for you, ready to go, but when the time comes, it will be up to you to secure it."

Sam glanced at Guinevere who was still holding the Remington shotgun as though she was about to shoot someone. His lips parted in a wry grin. "Okay. I think we can deal with that."

"That's it, Sam. After this, we're even."

"Thanks, Terry. Yep. After this, we're even."

Sam ended the call before his old friend could back out.

Guinevere said, "Well?"

"It's all right. My friend's going to secure us secret passage onto the Willamette River, where he's going to leave us a boat to steal."

"To steal? That's really nice of him."

"Hey. It's the best I could arrange at short notice."

In the middle of the bench seat, Caliburn started to bark loudly.

Guinevere patted him. "What is it, old boy?"

Caliburn didn't stop.

Sam glanced in his rear-view mirror.

A black Range Rover Sport was zigzagging in and out of traffic.

Sam cursed. "We've got company!"

Chapter Forty-Nine

"A Range Rover?" Sam asked. "Seriously? What is it with you guys and Range Rovers?"

Guinevere shrugged. "Call it British sentimentality."

Sam sped up, weaving through traffic. At the 405, he swung the cumbersome old Thunderbird into a hard right, down the exit ramp, into Downtown Portland. A quick glance in his rear-view mirror revealed that the Range Rover made the turn with ease, and was already accelerating out of the corner.

He swore. "Right now, let's call it a tank that handles better and accelerates harder than the T-Bird!"

"The escape tunnels..." Guinevere said, "Are we going to make it?"

Sam pulled the handbrake up and swung the wheel all the way to the left, sending the T-Bird sliding into West Burnside Street. "Of course we'll make it!"

He straightened up and reached down into the pocket in his jeans to retrieve his cell phone. His eyes darted between the oncoming traffic and his phone.

"Here, give me that!" Guinevere said, "What do you want me to do?"

Sam handed it to her. "Call Elise. There's only one in my contacts list."

Guinevere quickly found the contact and pressed call. "If she answers, what do you want me to say?"

"You'd better tell her we're going to be coming up the Columbia River shortly – and if I'm not mistaken, I'd say we're going to have some dangerous people in our pursuit."

"That's it?"

"Yeah. Tell her I'm going to need the Tahila to meet us there on the way – or we'll never reach them!"

"Okay, okay! I'll sort it out. You concentrate on not getting us killed in the process."

Sam nodded. He overtook the Streetcar, driving hard into Chinatown.

At NW 3rd Ave he chucked a left, and headed the wrong way down a one-way street. Oncoming cars kept honking their horns at him. He kept to the right, and to his relief, most cars tended to try and get out of his way.

Guinevere ended the call. "Hey! I thought you said you were going to try and not get us killed?"

Sam steered onto the footpath. "That might actually be harder than I led you to believe."

A big Peterbilt truck honked its horn.

Sam said, "See…"

Guinevere screamed. "Do you want me to drive?"

Sam ignored her jibe. Instead, he jammed on the brakes, coming to a complete stop in front of an old town grocery store.

"Everybody out!" he said.

A pedestrian in his eighties said, "Hey, you can't park there! That's a turning lane!"

Guinevere lifted the Remington 12-gauge shotgun. "I'd say our need is more important than their's."

The old man dipped his hat. "Right you are, ma'am. Right you are."

Sam opened the door and stepped into the old town grocery. Guinevere and Caliburn moved quickly.

A black Range Rover pulled up.

Sam shut the door, locking it behind him.

"Which way?" Guinevere asked.

Sam said, "Keep going. It's all the way at the back!"

Sam took the lead, guiding them past the Asian food section, deli, green grocer, and into the walk-in freezer.

Behind them, he heard the banging of someone breaking through the Plexiglas of the grocer's locked front door.

Sam continued past the first four deep-freezers.

At the fourth one, he stopped and opened it up. Instead of frozen goods, the freezer had a ladder inside that appeared to lead deep into the basement area below.

He said, "You go first!"

Guinevere didn't need to be told again. She climbed down the ladder at speed. Caliburn took more coaxing. The dog knew it was the only way out, but without thumbs it was pretty hard for a dog to climb down ladders.

The front door gave way.

Sam grabbed Caliburn. "I'm sorry, Cal… you need to get in there."

He lifted the dog up into the opening and passed him to Guinevere. An instant later, he climbed in and closed the door to the fake deep freezer.

Sam flicked on a small flashlight from his keychain.

It was a secret basement. To the south was another door, leading to the old grocer's neighbor's basement, and so on until the chain of basements formed a secret passageway all the way to the docks of the Willamette River to form the Old Portland Underground – better known locally as the Shanghai Tunnels.

They were originally built to move goods from the ships docked on the Willamette to the basement storage areas, allowing businesses to avoid streetcar and train traffic on the streets when delivering their goods.

Some believe that during Prohibition they were used by organized crime syndicates to move liquor, and even earlier still, they were used to Shanghai sailors.

Sam had no idea if any of the passageways' alleged illegal history was true, but he knew up until recently his good friend Terry had used the passageway in the transfer of illegal weapons into and out of the USA.

At the end of the Shanghai Tunnels, they reached a small dockyard beside the Burnside Bridge. Tied up to the jetty were high speed military jetboats. They looked like they were there for a demonstration and not for active duty.

A single Marine stood post and guarded the two vessels.

Guinevere said, "You didn't mention we needed to steal our getaway boat from the Navy!"

"I didn't know," Sam said. His eyes drifted to the last door, which opened up at the base of the Shanghai Tunnels. A camouflaged creature appeared to open it. "Time's up, Guinevere. We take that boat, or it's all over."

From the bridge, several men in balaclavas approached, each one carrying a machinegun. Most likely more mercenaries. Ex-special forces, the same as those who'd attacked them the day before at Powell's.

It was just the right amount of incentive to force them to steal an American Navy vessel and suffer the consequence.

Guinevere reached her decision first.

She brought the barrel of the Remington shotgun up to aim at the guard. "I'm sorry, but we're going to need to take your boat."

Chapter Fifty

Sam switched the twin jet engines on. They roared into life. Guinevere released the mooring lines, and Sam threw both throttles into the fully open position. Sam and Guinevere held on, as the jet propulsion system brought the fast attack boat up onto the aquaplane. He steered the boat north along the Willamette River, toward the Columbia junction.

Behind them, the camouflaged mercenaries jumped onto the second Navy vessel – a large inflatable boarding boat with oversized outboard motors – threw off its mooring lines, and raced after them. The black Range Rover took off again, its unseen driver heading north toward the Columbia River.

The two Navy boats were evenly matched in terms of speed. Both sat high up on the aquaplane, skimming the surface of the water.

Sam overtook a large cargo ship.

Behind them, the rat-a-tat-tat of machinegun fire confirmed that their pursuers had begun shooting at them. Their bullets raked the water several feet behind their stern. Their attackers quickly corrected their aim, and the rounds started to ineffectively rip into the jetboat's armored stern.

Sam drove on, swerving back and forth erratically, trying to make it difficult for their pursuers to get an accurate lock on them. He darted in between two cargo ships, one heading to port and one out to sea. He slipped into the narrow corridor, taking refuge in the lee of the inward bound cargo ship, and the shots from their attackers went quiet for a few minutes.

When they came out the opposite side of the cargo ship, their attackers were ready to greet them, firing another scattering of machinegun rounds into their hull.

They came out into the Columbia River, and turned south to head upriver.

Guinevere said, "You know this thing's designed for speed more than defense. Only its stern is well armored. A lucky shot here or there, and we're dead."

Sam nodded. "I know. You got a plan, Guinevere?"

"Yeah, as a matter of fact, I do," she replied. "Do you see that ship up ahead?"

Sam saw it. A slow-moving construction barge carrying concrete pylons stacked twenty feet into the air. "Yeah?"

"Do you think you could get to the left of it, and as soon as we're hidden from our attacker's view, circle round and come back the other way?"

Sam said, "I could do it. But I'm not sure why we'd want to. We don't want to head deeper into the Willamette River."

"That's my intention. I'm talking about getting behind our friends in that rubber boarding boat."

Sam grinned. "You want to hit them from behind?"

"Yes, I do."

"All right," Sam said. "I'm game if you are."

Caliburn barked.

Guinevere reloaded the Remington shotgun and took cover at the starboard passenger window, aiming outside.

Sam swung the jetboat to port, heading behind the barge. As soon as he was concealed by the massive concrete pylons, he swung the helm to full left wheel-lock. The jetboat turned sharply, like it was on the rails of a rollercoaster, centrifugal force jamming them into their seats, until they were pointing in the opposite direction.

He straightened the wheel, and the jetboat shot out behind the barge.

Guinevere pointed at the rubber boarding vessel up ahead. "Get me closer!"

Sam obliged, making a bee-line for the other Navy boat, closing the gap to just fifteen feet. The mercenaries turned to fire at them, but they were too late.

Guinevere fired all four shotgun rounds directly at their outboard motors. One connected with its fuel tank, and the back of the boat exploded in a ball of fire. The surviving mercenaries dived into the water. The burning debris that remained of the Navy boat skimmed across the river, before slamming into a café on Tomahawk Island.

Sam grinned as they sped away south along the Columbia River. "Nice shot!"

Guinevere said, "We might not be out of the woods yet!"

"Why?"

"I just spotted three of those soldiers climbing onto the dock at Tomahawk Island. They look like they haven't given up the fight."

"How?"

"They just stole some jet skis from X-treme Rentals!"

Chapter Fifty-One

Sam kept racing south, trying to put as much distance between him and the faster, more agile, high performance jet skis.

He overtook the *Columbia Gorge* – a recreated, historical, sternwheeler – packed to the brim with tourists who stood on its distinctive red, white, and blue tri-decks, reliving the Columbia River's rich history of paddle steamers.

As they reached the entrance to the Columbia Gorge, four jet skis split up to target them from four separate angles.

Sam glanced over his shoulder. "What do you want to do about them?"

Guinevere shrugged. "I don't know. We'll deal with it when they get closer."

"That won't be long."

"I know. But right now, we have big problems to deal with first."

"Really?" Sam asked, "Who?"

He glanced backward along the valley, watching stoically as two tiny black dots in the distance slowly grew into the recognizable shape of two military helicopters.

In the valley, the sound of the jet ski engines were suddenly overtaken by the downward *whoop, whoop* of two Sikorsky helicopters.

Sam cursed. His eyes searched the natural landscape as the Columbia flowed through the ancient gorge, looking for some sort of natural feature such as a cave or rock system in which to take cover.

Finding none, he said, "We're in big trouble. It's impossible to outrun those."

The sliding door of the first helicopter opened up and a single soldier started to fire rifle shots at them. They were difficult shots to take in a moving helicopter. Sam jolted the jetboat in sharp, irregular movements, adding to the sniper's difficulty. The shots went wide, but it wouldn't take much for them to get lucky.

Guinevere didn't give up so easily. "I'm going below decks to see if these guys have something we can use. Maybe we can set up a smoke screen for a bit of cover."

Sam said, "Good idea. Go!"

Guinevere came back up thirty seconds later, a big grin on her porcelain face. "This thing's equipped with an R2D2!"

Sam said, "You're kidding me!"

The Phalanx CIWS was a close-in weapon system for defense against anti-ship missiles, helicopters, and armored boats. It consisted of a radar-guided 20 mm Vulcan cannon mounted on a swiveling base. Because of its distinctive barrel-shaped radome, along with its automated nature of operation, the Phalanx CIWS units were nicknamed, "R2-D2" after the famous droid character from the Star Wars films.

The lines in Sam's face deepened and his piercing blue eyes seemed to darken. He spoke with unequivocal frankness. "You know those are US Navy choppers, we can't just shoot them down!"

Guinevere said, "It's going to be them or us, if we wait much longer."

He raced deeper into the narrowing gorge. To the right, Multnomah Falls came into view. It was the highest waterfall in the state of Oregon, its distinctive 620-foot waterfall spanning two tiers of basalt cliffs, and a large historic bridge in the middle.

Sam turned to face Guinevere and said, without hesitation, "Then, I'm afraid it's going to have to be us."

"All right, but I haven't come all this way just to get killed by our own people, so what are we going to do about it?"

"Hang on," he said. "Keep them distracted with a few warning shots. I've got to make another phone call."

Guinevere drew her Walther 99 handgun. It was unlikely to cause any damage to the military helicopter or its crew, but just in case, she still aimed wide.

Sam took his cell phone and called the Secretary of Defense.

The secretary picked up on the first ring. "Mr. Reilly?"

"Good morning, ma'am. I need your help."

The Secretary said, "What trouble have you gotten yourself into?"

"I stole a Navy jetboat on display in Portland, Oregon. I'm now racing up the Columbia River being pursued by a pair of Sikorsky helicopters, which keep shooting at me."

"What do you need?"

"Ma'am, I'd be really appreciative if you could contact the Navy and get them to call off their birds."

"Mr. Reilly, if you did indeed steal a US Navy rapid attack boat and the Navy sent two attack birds to get it back, you and I wouldn't be having this conversation."

"What are you saying, ma'am?"

"I'm saying, if Elise hadn't contacted me twenty minutes ago and informed me that you did something really stupid like steal one of the Navy's latest attack boats, the Navy wouldn't have sent two Sikorsky helicopters to take pot shots at you, they would have sent a pair of McDonnell Douglas F-15 Eagles from the Oregon 142nd Air National Guard – and they would have put a couple AIM-9 Sidewinders into you on sight – game over."

Sam lips curled upward with incredulity. "The two birds aren't our's?"

"No, Mr. Reilly. It looks like they're owned by your new-found friends."

Sam said, "I have your permission to take them out, ma'am?"

"Mr. Reilly, if someone is shooting on one of our Navy's attack boats, I see it not only as your right, but your duty to take them out!"

Sam grinned. "Yes, ma'am."

Guinevere exchanged glances with him. "What did she say?"

Sam grinned. "She says, they're not our birds, and you have her permission to destroy those helicopters."

Chapter Fifty-Two

Guinevere stared at the R2D2 unit.

The basis of the system was a 20 mm M61 Vulcan Gatling gun autocannon, linked to a Ku-band fire control radar system for acquiring and tracking targets. It also included one of the modern upgrades involving a FLIR – forward-looking infrared – sensor to make the weapon effective against surface targets. This proven system was combined with a purpose-made mounting, capable of fast elevation and traverse speeds, to track incoming targets. An entirely self-contained unit, the mounting houses the gun, an automated fire-control system and all other major components, enabling it to automatically search for, detect, track, engage, and confirm kills using its computer-controlled radar system.

She'd used the system on a British vessel years ago. It wasn't new, but the computer technology had been upgraded to the point where the weapon teetered tentatively close to AI territory, with the system performing every task, and the operator simply pressing the authority to kill button.

Guinevere didn't need to check with anyone.

She pressed the start button, and the R2D2 unit came alive. Its dome-shaped Ku-band fire control radar system rose out of the aft section of the attack boat.

It located two targets immediately.

The M61 Vulcan Gatling gun automatically altered its elevation, traversing slowly to track the first helicopter.

The R2D2 target monitor fixed on the first target.

CONFIRM TARGETS?

Guinevere pressed the confirm button.

DESTROY ACQUIRED TARGETS?

Guinevere didn't hesitate. She pressed the authorize- to-kill button, without which the weapon would have been classed as completely AI – Artificial Intelligence – the sort of weapon that frightened most civilized nations. Its implication was clear. You're ultimately delegating the decision to kill to a machine. A machine that doesn't have a measure of moral understanding or mercy.

An instant later, the machine came alive.

The 20 mm M61 Vulcan Gatling gun fired on the Sikorsky helicopter closest to them. 20 mm armor-piercing tungsten penetrator rounds left the autocannon's barrel at a speed of 3,600 feet per second, and at a rate of 3000 rounds per minute.

It fixed on the helicopter for just five seconds, sending a total of 250 rounds.

The Sikorsky's fuel tank was pierced and an instant later, the helicopter turned into a giant ball of fire, its rotors kept turning but, unable to maintain lift, the bird dropped into the river below.

The second helicopter banked hard, attempting to evade the attack its pilot knew was inevitable. R2D2 adjusted for the change in target's location, and fired another five second burst.

Guinevere watched as the second helicopter fell from the sky.

She returned to the armored pilothouse.

Sam glanced at her. "I see that's the end of that. How will that machine go against the jet skis?"

"Not so good. It was designed to take out large aircraft like bombers, not so useful against small surface-based targets."

"That's all right. They probably don't know that, and if they do, you're free to try and take them out anyway."

Guinevere said, "Sounds good. How much farther are we from the *Tahila*?"

"I don't know. We'll reach the Cascade Locks soon. If the *Tahila* isn't there, we're going to have trouble waiting for the water locks to rise before we get killed."

She took a deep breath and nodded. "Okay, we'll just have to deal with it when we get there."

Her eyes glanced at I-84 – the highway that ran alongside the Columbia River through the gorge – and she took a deep breath in. Her eyes narrowed.

Sam asked, "What is it?"

Guinevere swallowed hard. "There's a black Range Rover speeding along I-84."

Chapter Fifty-Three

Jason Faulkner drove hard along I-84.

The Range Rover hugged the blacktop as it followed the Columbia River Gorge, and wound its way westward through to the Cascade Range, which formed the boundary between the State of Washington to the north and Oregon to the south.

At the lowest elevations, there was a dense conifer forest of Douglas-fir, western red cedar, western hemlock, and grand fir, giving the mountainside an envelope of blue-green forestry. At the higher elevations along the mountain range, Silver fir, Sitka spruce, and Alaska-cedar dominated all but the highest peaks, which were snowcapped. Dense foliage of shrubs grew so exceptionally well that in many places the vegetation made the forest practically impenetrable.

Faulkner had lived in the region during the early projects at Camelot Weapons Industries. He knew the region well. Probably better than most locals. He thought about the region, about what he'd been trying to do, and how the human race has never known its true place in the world.

The gorge had supported human habitation for over 13,000 years. Evidence of the Folsom and Marmes people, who crossed the Bering land bridge from Asia, were found in archaeological digs. Excavations near Celilo Falls, a few miles east of The Dalles, showed that humans have occupied this salmon-fishing site for more than 10,000 years.

The gorge has provided a transportation corridor for thousands of years. Native Americans would travel through the Gorge to trade at Celilo Falls, both along the river and over Lolo Pass on the north side of Mount Hood. In 1805, the route was used by the Lewis and Clark Expedition to reach the Pacific. Early European and American settlers subsequently established steamboat lines and railroads through the gorge. Today, the BNSF Railway runs freights along the Washington side of the river, while its rival, the Union Pacific Railroad, runs freights along the Oregon shore.

The Columbia River Highway, built in the early 20th century, was the first major paved highway in the Pacific Northwest. Shipping was greatly simplified after Bonneville Dam and The Dalles Dam submerged the gorge's major rapids such as Celilo Falls, a major salmon fishing site for local Native Americans until the site's submergence in 1957. Native Indian petroglyphs were found in the Columbia River Gorge near The Dalles Dam.

Native Americans have lived in southeastern Oregon for at least 15,000 years, according to a 2012 find in the Paisley Caves. At that time, pluvial lakes filled many of the high desert basins. Little is known about the people who occupied the land at that time, except that they camped and hunted near the lakes. The earliest petroglyphs in southeastern Oregon may be as much as 15,000 years old, possibly much older.

In 1840, when the first white men came through southern Oregon, the Fort Bidwell Band and the Harney Valley Band of the Northern Paiute tribe lived in the southeastern part of Oregon around Greaser Canyon. However, given the age of the carvings, it is possible that the Northern Paiute people had nothing to do with their creation.

The meanings of the Greaser petroglyphs are not known. They may have been used in religious ceremonies or marked tribal ownership of territory. The designs may have been map directions or simply art created to tell a personal story.

No one knows.

Jason spotted the Cascade Locks up ahead.

The set of locks were built to improve navigation past the Cascades Rapids of the Columbia River. The U.S. federal government approved the plan for the locks in 1875, construction began in 1878, and the locks were completed on November 5, 1896. The locks were subsequently submerged in 1938, and replaced by Bonneville Lock and Dam.

He turned left onto the Bonneville Bridge. It was a steel truss cantilever bridge that spans the Columbia River between Cascade Locks, Oregon, and Washington state near North Bonneville approximately forty miles out of Portland.

Jason drove to the middle of the bridge and jammed on the brakes.

The Range Rover came to a complete stop. He pulled up the handbrake, and turned on the hazard lights.

Someone behind him honked.

It didn't bother Jason. Let them complain. It wouldn't make any difference. He wasn't moving his damned car.

He withdrew an M16 rifle, loaded a custom-made armor piercing bullet, and waited for his target to arrive.

Chapter Fifty-Four

The US Navy jetboat raced along the Columbia River.

Sam watched the four jet skis swerve ahead of them and to their sides, as they became increasingly brazen in an attempt to keep ahead of the R2D2's firing arc. The jet ski riders were carrying Uzi style submachineguns, and would intermittently fire a burst in their direction. Most times, the shots would fall short or wide, but occasionally they would rake the side of the jetboat's hull.

Guinevere, out of Remington shotgun shells, now waited until the riders got particularly close before firing with her Walther P99. They were nearly out of shots and the riders knew it. One rider came in close, assuming she was completely out. Guinevere waited until the rider was right up alongside them, before shooting the man dead.

That gave the remaining three riders a little pause, but soon, they started to work together to get closer, with all three riders taking turns to fire short bursts toward the jetboat.

It was working.

The riders were getting close to boarding the jetboat.

Guinevere fired her last two remaining shots. To Sam, she shouted, "I'm out!"

"We're nearly there," Sam replied. "Just keep them off the boat!"

He turned the jetboat in a sharp arc, sending large bow waves in an outward motion. The riders shifted their direction, two rode the bow wave with the agility of professional riders, while the third one got knocked off into the water.

Sam straightened up and kept heading west at full speed.

He picked up his cell phone and called Tom. "Tom! Tell me you're close!"

"Getting there. We're just about to enter the Bonneville locks. Can you hang in that long?"

"We'll do our best. We're out of shots and we still have two mercenaries on jet skis trying to board our boat."

"Okay, hang in there. Genevieve's in the armory finding a sniper rifle and we'll be there as soon as possible."

"All right, we'll see you soon."

Guinevere stepped into the pilot house. "They're trying to board again."

Sam shrugged. "So stop them."

"With what? I'm out of ammo."

"Find something!"

Guinevere ducked below, returning with a boat hook. It had a metal hook attached to a telescopic aluminum pole.

Sam glanced at her. "That's the best you can find?"

"This is it, unless you can work out how to increase the maximum traverse angle for the R2D2."

"All right. I'll try my best to keep them off the boat!"

Sam made another sharp turn, trying to shake their pursuers.

He came around the next corner and straightened up as he rounded the Bonneville Fish Hatchery. Robins Island came into view on his left, and the Cascade Locks to the far right.

The massive Cascade Locks opened up, to reveal a sleek, dark, vessel that looked like a predator.

Sam grinned. He'd never been so happy to see the *Tahila*.

He looked across his shoulder trying to find a sign of the two jet ski riders. He frowned. They had disappeared.

Behind them, both jet skis were floating in the water, without their riders.

Sam asked, "Where did they go?"

Guinevere lifted her finger to her lips to quiet him. She gripped the boat hook, like it was a spear, ready to take on the single boarder.

On the semi-armored deck above, she heard the movement of the boarders.

Sam held his breath, ready to change direction sharply, in the hope of knocking them off the boat. Guinevere readied herself to jab at the attacker's legs.

And in the distance, Sam heard the loud report of a sniper rifle being fired in rapid succession.

Chapter Fifty-Five

Sam slowly brought the Navy jetboat alongside the *Tahila*.

The two mercenaries who had tried to board their ship were now floating in the water. Both dead. Clean headshots.

Sam tied the Navy boat's mooring line to the *Tahila*. Genevieve and Tom came to greet them along the bow.

Genevieve was still holding an M24 sniper rifle.

Sam looked at her. "Thanks, Gen. Nice shooting."

"You're welcome."

Sam said, "Tom, Gen, this is Guinevere."

"Pleased to meet you," Tom and Gen said.

Genevieve glanced at the pole Guinevere still held like a weapon. Her brow furrowed with curiosity. "Just out of interest, what were you going to do with that?"

Guinevere made a coy grin. "I have no idea. But I'm glad we didn't have to find out."

Sam said, "I don't know. I still would have placed money on you with a boat hook over the mercenaries with Uzis…"

Caliburn wandered out of the Jetboat and gave a short bark.

Sam said, "And this is Caliburn. He's as smart as he is cute."

They helped lift Caliburn up onto the *Tahila's* deck.

Tom gave him a good pat and the dog mewled with pleasure at the attention. A moment later, the dog bared its teeth.

Sam said, "What is it, Caliburn?"

The hair on the dog's back spiked straight up. Caliburn barked ferociously. There was terror in his bark.

Its fur turned gunmetal gray to match the deck of the *Tahila*.

Sam swore.

And another sniper shot fired.

Chapter Fifty-Six

Everyone hit the deck hard.

Guinevere looked up, trying to gauge where the shot had come from. As soon as her head became visible, another shot fired.

She ducked back down.

Tom exchanged a glance with Sam. "Where are the shots coming from?"

Sam said, "I don't know. Not from the water. That was a downward shot."

Gen took a shooting position on her belly, searching the nearby landscape of Robins Island with its riflescope.

Sam asked, "You got anything?"

"Not yet," Gen said. "Wait. There's a man sitting inside that black Range Rover!"

"Can you take the shot?" Sam asked.

Gen shook her head. "Not from this position. It would be a lucky shot at best."

Guinevere shuffled back toward the US jetboat.

Sam said, "Where the hell are you going?"

"To get rid of the man in the Range Rover once and for all." Then, to Gen, she said, "Can you give me some cover fire until I get back in the jetboat?"

Gen nodded. "I've got it. Go!"

There's no time like the present. Guinevere slid to the side of the deck, and then jumped down onto the jetboat.

Gen opened fire at the Range Rover.

Guinevere climbed inside the jetboat, down into the aft weapons section.

The computer screen for the Phalanx CIWS had identified the black Range Rover as a threat. The monitor now flashed –

TARGET ACQUIRED.
CONFIRM KILL ORDER?

Guinevere hit the fire button.

The R2D2 system came alive, and the radar-guided 20 mm Vulcan autocannon swiveled into position, with the electric whiz of automated mechanisms.

It opened fire, sending more than six hundred rounds down its barrel in a matter of seconds, reducing the Range Rover to burning scrap metal and embers of molten steel.

Chapter Fifty-Seven

No one knew if Excalibur had survived the hit. From what Sam had seen of him when they were trying to escape Mike's house in Tualatin, Excalibur was barely slowed by multiple direct shotgun hits. He wasn't sure if anyone could have survived the damage done to the Range Rover, but nor could he imagine anything killing Excalibur.

Instead of waiting to find out, he ordered Matthew to navigate the *Tahila* downriver toward Portland. Let the local authorities investigate the wreckage. Excalibur wasn't after them. He was after Caliburn. That much was clear. Besides, they had a US Navy boat to return.

Sam stepped into the communications room on board the *Tahila*.

Elise looked up from her laptop. "You've been busy making friends again I hear."

Sam's lips curled upward. "Sometimes you just have to stand up to the bully in the playground."

"Rough playground."

"Yeah." He handed Elise the USB flash drive that he'd gotten from Caliburn's dog tag. "I've got a bet with Tom that you can crack this within an hour."

"What is it?"

"We found it on a stray dog's collar near where we were first attacked in the Tillamook State Forest. It has a military grade encryption code that I need you to crack. We're hoping it might have some answers about how to defeat whatever military experiment went wrong, leaving us with this incredibly violent and dangerous hunter."

Elise took it, inserted it into her laptop USB port, grinned, and said, "I'll see you in half an hour."

"I never doubt you, Elise. Never." Sam said, "There's one more thing I'd like you to run a search for while you wait for your program to break that code…"

"Sure, what is it?"

"Guinevere's brother left her a fairly cryptic message telling her to locate King Arthur's first sword, Caliburn. In his clue, he gave three locations – Glastonbury, England, Jerusalem, Israel, and the Dragon Breath Cave, Majorca. I need you to run a search, in all known archeology journals, and newspaper articles, to see if there's any connection with the fabled sword, and any of those places. I'm interested to see it, no matter how tenuous the connections."

"Okay. I'll get it to you shortly."

He sat down with Tom at the Round Table in the mission room. Tom brought him up to date with the Hanford Nuclear Site and the secret nuclear waste storage facility deep beneath the hills of Trinidad. The Secretary of Defense denied knowledge of the secret facility, dating back to the Manhattan Project, and the defense company *Camelot Weapons Industries*. An emergency response team from the Hanford Nuclear Site had been sent in to plug the tunnel.

It appeared that someone had recently dug the submerged underground tunnel to access a secure vault housed inside the Camelot Weapons Industries subterranean storage facility. Although what was stolen and what was originally stored there no one knows.

Sam said, "So we're done with the project?"

"We're done," Tom confirmed. "The Secretary of Defense has thanked us for our service, and advised that she will personally oversee the cleanup of spent nuclear waste, and the investigation into the secret nuclear storage facility and Camelot Weapons Industries. Now, do you want to fill me in on why everyone keeps wanting to kill you?"

Sam said, "I'm just one of those guys… that that sort of thing keeps happening to, I guess."

He then brought Tom up to speed with everything that had happened in the past few days. About the evil creature now known as Excalibur who was hunting them, as well as Caliburn, their highly intelligent dog, and their most likely history as military experiments into genetic development of hyper intelligent animals for war.

When Sam was finished, Tom said, "I don't get it."

Sam frowned. "What exactly don't you get?"

"What does any of this have to do with an old Arthurian Legend?"

"I have no idea. But I intend to find out."

"I mean, everything here is from an old Medieval legend."

Sam said, "Technically, if King Arthur existed, the legend originated during the Dark Ages."

Tom smiled at Sam's pedantic reference to the date surrounding a most likely fictional character who, despite his unending popularity, has no evidence of having ever existed. Tom said, "All right. Even so, look at this. You meet a beautiful woman named Guinevere three days ago…"

Sam lifted a hand to dismiss the coincidence. "She was backpacking in the Tillamook State Forest!"

"And yet, her brother was connected to the secret experiment, which involved forging new Arthurian weapons – Excalibur and Caliburn?"

Sam said, "I know, it looks kind of bad…"

"Forget bad. I just want to know what's going on. I mean, after all of that, I happen to find someone just days ago made a tunnel into limestone half a mile long to access a secret underground vault for a company called, Camelot Weapons Industries? I mean, come on, the coincidence is all too much. Next I'm expecting a wizard like Gandalf or Dumbledore to come along…"

"You mean Merlin?"

"Yeah, that's the one I was looking for."

Elise stepped into the room. Her eyes wide and a grin planted on her lips.

Sam looked at his watch. It had been fifteen minutes, probably too early for her to beat the encryption. "What is it?"

"It's done. I cracked the encryption code."

"Well done." His eyes exchanged a glance with Tom. "Looks like I win the bet." Then, to Elise, he asked, "What did you find?"

"Dr. Jim Patterson left a message for us," she said. "I know what we have to do, but you're not going to believe it."

Sam asked, "What did it say?"

Elise took a determined breath and said, "We need to find Merlin's SPELL book in order to defeat Excalibur."

Chapter Fifty-Eight

Sam studied Tom's face.

It was set with deep lines of incredulity.

Tom crossed his arms and said, "See. That's what I mean; this whole King Arthur legend thing has now gotten way out of hand!"

The creases in Sam's grin darkened. "Hey, I'll be honest, I'm pretty skeptical about finding Merlin's SPELL book too, and I've seen a lot of unbelievable things."

"Yeah, well, think what you like, but Dr. Jim Patterson certainly believed it was the only way to defeat Excalibur, and given what it says about Excalibur, I tend to believe him."

Sam asked, "What does it say about him?"

Elise said, "Excalibur and Caliburn were part of an extremely secret weapons development project that Dr. Patterson directed at Camelot Weapons Industries."

Tom shook his head. "The Secretary of Defense told me she'd never heard of the company, let alone any secret projects, or what they might have stored there."

Sam crossed his arms. "It wouldn't be the first time the Secretary of Defense has kept secrets from us when she believed that it was in the interest of national security. Or to avoid political backlash, for that matter."

"And burying nuclear weapons somewhere and then denying it until their waste products leak into North America's second largest river system, I tend to think would probably cause some serious political backlash," Tom added.

"Exactly," Elise said. "But in this case, I think you might be wrong."

Sam asked, "Why?"

"According to Dr. Patterson, Camelot Weapons Industries didn't have anything to do with nuclear weapons or the storage of nuclear waste products. In fact, they had been given the underground secret location to develop the King Arthur weapons based on Merlin's SPELL book."

"Why?"

"The same reason the location was used during the Manhattan Project to store deadly spent nuclear waste material…"

Sam said, "Because it was far enough away from anything and everything that, if things went wrong, they could contain it!"

Elise exhaled. "Exactly."

Sam asked, "But what happened to the project? And why was a British defense system being built in America?"

"According to Dr. Patterson, there was a problem roughly ten years ago with the program that was originally being developed by MI-6. Something to do with an internal ethics committee shutting them down."

"Experimenting on the blending of human DNA with a multitude of other animal species to develop the perfect fighting chimera… Gee…" Tom said, sarcastically, "it's hard to imagine why an ethics committee might have a problem with that."

Elise didn't bite with the ethics debate. Instead, she knew her job was to provide facts. "Upset by the loss of nearly a decade of research – both scientific and archeological – the original team of seven MI-6 operatives decided to defect to the US in exchange for the right to complete the project in secret, and sell its findings to our Department of Defense."

Sam said, "Well, that at least answers the question about motivation. If their project had scored a major defense contract it could have been worth millions."

Elise shook her head. "Not millions. It was going to be counted in billions. Over the course of its development, the project was estimated to eventually hit a trillion US dollars!"

Sam shook his head. "I don't understand. Developing super human soldiers is nothing new or extraordinary. Even the best soldiers – fast, strong, intelligent, resilient, you name it – wouldn't be worth a trillion dollars. So what was the program really about?"

"It all has to do with an end game..." Elise said.

"Which was?"

She said, "The development of an impenetrable new material."

Sam remembered how Guinevere's shotgun rounds didn't even give Excalibur pause. "They weren't just looking at protecting their soldiers, were they?"

"No. The contract's initial project was to develop a material that couldn't be damaged using traditional methods of warfare. The second part was to then mass-produce that material so that defensive shields on aircraft, tanks, APCs, helicopters, you name it, become invincible..."

"What was the third step?" Sam asked.

"To make missiles out of the same material."

"Why?" Tom and Sam said in unison.

"Because if you can protect your machinery and people with impenetrable armor, then why not utilize the same material to develop weapons that can penetrate everything."

"Use that to tip a nuclear ICBM and no country will ever be safe."

"Exactly. Russia builds a nuclear Intercontinental Ballistic Missile and we build the National Missile Defense System. Now everyone wants a weapon that can penetrate it."

Sam said, "Okay, now I see why our Defense Department was willing to gamble and spend big on the project, but what I don't understand is what any of this has to do with King Arthur and Merlin's SPELL book?"

Elise said, "Because Merlin was never a wizard."

Chapter Fifty-Nine

Sam had left Guinevere with Matthew to show her the Tahila while he, Tom, and Elise discussed the highly classified events of the leakage from the Hanford Nuclear Site. Now that the course of the conversation was returning specifically back to King Arthur and Merlin, he thought Guinevere had a right to know the truth.

He opened the door to the mission room and stepped out to find Guinevere at the command center. "Guinevere, you're going to want to hear this."

She followed him back to the mission room and sat down next to him.

Sam said, "Elise cracked the encryption to the USB flash drive found on Caliburn. The dog, and his owner, Dr. Jim Patterson – who we believe was killed by Excalibur in the Tillamook State Forest – were part of a scientific military experiment. In the notes, Dr. Patterson alludes to the fact that the entire project was developed based on Merlin's SPELL book that was first discovered after more than a decade of archeological research."

Guinevere's lips turned upward into a wry smile. "We now think Merlin's magic made Excalibur and Caliburn."

Sam sighed. "Sort of. Elise, do you want to explain?"

Elise nodded. "It was said that Merlin was lifetimes ahead of himself in terms of science and technology. Like Leonardo Da Vinci after him, he kept a book in which he drew detailed diagrams and mechanics of inventions that he knew wouldn't be built for hundreds of years after he had died."

Guinevere said, "We're putting together inventions that Merlin left for us?"

Elise shrugged. "Not necessarily for us, but yeah."

"But what could anyone from Merlin's era – whatever that era was – be useful to us now?"

"It's not that unbelievable," Sam said. "For example, Leonardo da Vinci drew working diagrams of the first helicopter, noting at the time that they had no means of producing enough power to turn its rotating blades fast enough to create adequate lift, but one day in the future, people would. His design was proven possible by Igor Sikorsky, on September 14, 1939, when the VS-300, the world's first practical helicopter, took flight at Stratford, Connecticut. That was hundreds of years after da Vinci died in 1519."

Guinevere arched her eyebrow. "And you believe Merlin was even more ahead of him?"

"It's not that unbelievable," Sam pointed out. "A true polymath, like da Vinci, and like Merlin, might only come around once every few hundred years. It seems unfortunate to waste that by having one born in the Dark Ages, before their knowledge and ability could really help drive humanity forward."

"What was Merlin?" Guinevere asked.

"He was a blacksmith," answered Elise. "But not just any blacksmith. He was so far ahead of his time he came to be known as a wizard."

Sam said to Tom, "See, he wasn't a wizard."

Tom said, "A great scientist with a SPELL book, he still sounds like a wizard to me."

Guinevere turned to Elise. "That's a good point. What spells did he cast, if he wasn't a magician?"

Elise said, "One of the areas of advanced research and technology development that Merlin was interested in was the area of SPELLs – which stood for Science, Physiologically Enhanced Level Locums."

Tom frowned. "Come again?"

"Merlin was using science to develop weapons that enhanced a person's physiological abilities by increasing its level locums."

"What's a level locum?" Sam asked.

Elise said, "The word *locum* these days means *something or someone that takes the place of another*. We often think of them as doctors who stand in while the normal doctor is away. But in Merlin's day, the Latin word, *locum tenens*, meant, *temporary place holder*. And in the days of King Arthur and the Round Table, his chivalrous knights were rated on their fighting ability in a series of combat levels. What Merlin aimed to do, was use SPELLs on a knight's armor, or weapons, to artificially place them at a higher combat level."

Guinevere smiled in disbelief. "Merlin was creating performance enhancing weapons and armor?"

Elise nodded. "It would appear so. What's more, he made two in particular, that we still hear about in legends today – Excalibur, the Sword in the Stone, and Caliburn, King Arthur's first sword that allowed him to single handedly defeat an invading Saxon army."

Sam frowned. "He was just a blacksmith?"

"Not just any blacksmith," Elise repeated. "He was a tinkerer and a scientist. But, yes, first and foremost he was a blacksmith, who became a legend, because he made King Arthur the greatest sword there ever was. What's more, even though he wasn't a wizard, he may as well have been. Some of the technology he wrote about in his SPELL book makes our engineers at DARPA look primitive."

Sam said, "He was that advanced?"

"You'd better believe it." Elise said, "The genetic engineering required to develop Excalibur and Caliburn were decades, if not more advanced than our top scientists today."

Sam said, "All right, does it say anything about how we're to use Merlin's SPELL book to destroy Excalibur?"

"Not really. Only that both Excalibur and Caliburn's skin is imbued by a powerful stone. It doesn't reference what the stone is made out of, only that such a stone exists and is extremely rare. The stone has an effect on every cell in their body, altering it at a cellular level…"

Guinevere asked, "To do what?"

Elise replied, "To make their skin impenetrable to any old or modern-day weapon."

Incredulous, Tom said, "You're saying Excalibur can't be killed with a modern bomb blast or armor penetrating bullets?"

"That's right," Elise said. "Only a weapon imbued by this ancient stone will be strong enough to penetrate their defensive skin."

Sam said, "But that can't be right. We took blood from Caliburn. The vet used a normal needle and syringe to draw blood. If Caliburn's skin was invincible, wouldn't the needle have just broken?"

"Not necessarily." Elise's purple eyes widened. "That's the unique wonder with this level of genetic engineering. Both weapons were developed to have some control over their defensive system. Think about it. We need our skin to breathe, to sweat. If our entire bodies were impenetrable, we would be inflexible."

Sam took a deep breath. "So, their skin hardens when they want to be protected?"

"Yeah, I think so," Elise said.

Guinevere said, "I don't even think it's a conscious decision on their part. I think the defensive thing happens in a microsecond, in response to an actual injury inducing attack, such as being struck by a bullet, or in response to adrenaline's release in a fight or flight response. Thinking back on it, Caliburn's skin took on a chameleon type of camouflage in response to a gunned attack at Powell's bookstore. It only settled down later, after we'd gotten away from the threat."

Tom said, "So, we need to locate Merlin's SPELL book to forge a new weapon to defeat Excalibur! Something that can pierce his skin, and kill him once and for all."

Elise nodded. "Or, you find one of the original swords."

"Excalibur and Caliburn?" Tom said, "Where would we even start a search for the two legendary weapons? People have researched their existence for more than a thousand years, and with the exception of what we've found on that USB flash drive, no one has been able to prove that the story of King Arthur belongs in the history books instead of mythology."

Sam thought back to the hidden messages for Guinevere inside the 830AD book, *Historia Brittonum*. He grinned. "We need to rejoin both shards of a fractured Caliburn. That's the weapon we'll use to kill Excalibur!"

Elise exchanged a slight glance with him, her eyes startled by his confidence. "How do you expect to find not just one, but both pieces of the ancient sword?"

Sam said, "Guinevere's brother, Patrick, who was involved in the program at *Camelot Weapons Industries*, left a cipher for her to use on the ninth century book, *Historia Brittonum* in the event that he died. What that secret message showed was a need to find Caliburn and have it forged back into one sword."

Tom asked, "Did he happen to mention where to find it?"

"Yeah, the cipher listed three locations. GLASTONBURY ABBEY, ENGLAND. JERUSALEM, ISRAEL, and the DRAGON BREATH CAVE – MAJORCA."

Elise thought about that for a moment, before she said, "King Arthur was said to have been buried in Glastonbury Abbey. Mordred was a Saxon King who was said to have beaten him in battle. What remained of King Arthur's sword was meant to have been buried with him. The other half… nobody knows, but if I was Mordred, I would have taken it."

Guinevere said, "According to legend, the mythical sword was broken in two during the battle of Camlann. Its supernatural powers were lost and King Arthur returned to Camelot with just one shard of the sword. It was assumed that King Arthur and King Mordred both died on that battlefield. But some accounts of the legend show that both kings survived. In King Arthur's case, he was taken to the Island of Avalon to be healed, and Merlin forged him a new sword, Excalibur."

Sam asked, "What about Mordred? Did he survive? And where did the other shard of Caliburn end up?"

"No one really knows. It was lost on the battlefield."

Sam said, "You mean, it might lay buried beneath a long since forgotten battlefield?"

Guinevere said, "It might. But I seriously doubt it."

Sam steepled his fingers. "Why?"

"King Arthur's sword was the source of all his power." Guinevere stared at the image of Caliburn that Elise had put up on the digital round table. It was a holographic projection. The sword itself looked more like a dagger than a broadsword. Her eyes idly stared at it. "Not just because of what it allowed him to do on the battlefield, but by the near mythical legends that surrounded it, each one seemingly more preposterous than the previous, all culminating in an enigmatic aura that placed Arthur on an insurmountable pedestal as a battlefield king."

A wry smile of understanding crossed Sam's lips. "You think Mordred, the Saxon king kept the remaining shard of the sword?"

Guinevere's eyes narrowed. "Wouldn't you?"

"Of course," Sam said. "Propaganda didn't just start during the second world war. People have been practicing the art of propaganda for centuries. And what's better than a sword with legendary powers? Mordred would have flaunted the fractured shard of Arthur's legendary sword to prove his own might in battle. So now, all we need to do now is locate Mordred's resting place to find his half of the sword?"

"Which we know ended up in Jerusalem," Guinevere pointed out. "Of course, how a sixth century legendary sword, stolen by a Saxon king should find its way into the heart of the Jewish Kingdom, I have no idea."

Elise said, "I think I can explain that."

"Really?" Sam asked.

"Yeah, I've got a wild theory. You want to hear it?"

They all nodded, their eyes wide with interest.

Elise said, "I believe Mordred used the other half of Caliburn to help Justinian the Great reclaim much of the Roman Empire."

Chapter Sixty

Sam turned his gaze to the holographic image of sixth century Europe.

Elise identified some of the important history to be taken from the 3D map, which showed a very different world than present day Europe. "When the Western Roman Empire ended in 476AD, it lost most of its land to various Germanic tribes. The Franks settled in Northern Gaul, The Visigoths in Hispania, and the Vandals in Africa. Only the Eastern Roman Empire survived. Then, in 527AD when Justinian the Great inherited the Byzantine Empire, he sought to revive the empire's greatness and reconquer the lost western half of the historical Roman Empire."

Sam, Guinevere, and Tom studied the map, trying to find out how a Welsh sword could become lost in a Byzantine Emperor's struggle to reclaim the Roman Empire.

"Are you with me?" Elise asked.

Sam nodded. "Not really… but do go on, I'll catch up."

"Good," Elise said, as she continued… "Justinian's rule constituted a distinct epoch in the history of the Later Roman Empire, and his reign is marked by the ambitious but only partly realized *Renovatio Imperii*, or 'Restoration of the Empire.'"

Elise swiped the holographic image of the sixth century European landscape to the left, and a new image came up, identifying the areas that the Byzantine Empire had reclaimed and now ruled.

She said, "Justinian had sweeping success with his restoration activities, making him known as the last Roman. His general, Belisarius, swiftly conquered the Vandal Kingdom in North Africa. Subsequently, Belisarius, Narses, and his other generals conquered the Ostrogothic kingdom, restoring Dalmatia, Sicily, Italy, and Rome to the empire after more than half a century of rule by the Ostrogoths. Justinian made a uniform rewriting of Roman Law, the *Corpus Juris Civilis*, which is still the basis of civil law in many modern states around the world. His reign also marked a blossoming of Byzantine culture, and his building program yielded such masterpieces as the church of *Hagia Sophia* in Constantinople, and the *Nea* in Jerusalem."

Sam's ears pricked up at the reference to Jerusalem. "What was the *Nea* in Jerusalem?"

Elise pulled the entire holographic European world map down from the Round Table and in its place retrieved an image of a massive church. "Justinian attempted to leave his imperial mark on Jerusalem by situating a building of unprecedented size and splendor, the *Nea*, within the context of Jerusalem's oldest and most sacred monuments. In Procopius's panegyric – that's a Roman word for a public record or speech – it can be seen that the architect developed a masterful work of propaganda. He was less concerned with extolling the greatness of the buildings that were constructed, and more so with celebrating the man who built them.

"So, in order to situate Justinian within the tradition of grand builders in Jerusalem, the architect modeled his account after the biblical narrative of Solomon's Temple. There are several literary parallels between the two accounts, the foremost being that, according to Procopius, both of the building projects were blessed by God. Furthermore, it seems beyond coincidence that the measurements of the *Nea* are roughly twice the size of the Temple. Like Herod's engineers, who had to extend the southern end of the Temple platform, so too did Justinian's architects; and just as Solomon imported cedars from Hiram of Tyre for the Temple's roofing, Justinian had cedars brought in from Lebanon."

Sam said, "What does any of this have to do with finding Mordred and his half of King Arthur's mythical sword?"

"I'm getting to that," Elise said. "Justinian had sweeping success in his achievements, mirroring those of King Arthur. He built a masterful kingdom, he implemented a new Roman law that was structured around making a more chivalrous and better kingdom for everyone, and his success on the battlefield was insurmountable, eventually increasing his Empire's total landmass by forty-five percent during his reign."

Sam's lips turned to a wry smile. "Are you trying to tell me Justinian was Mordred?"

"No. I'm telling you that his General, Belisarius, was widely accepted as a military genius after conquering the Vandal Kingdom of North Africa in the Vandalic War, followed by recapturing most of Italy from the Ostrogothic Kingdom in a series of sieges during the Gothic War. He was reputed to have a weapon so powerful during battle, that no army could defeat him. Who else do we know who had such power?"

Guinevere said, "King Arthur!"

Sam felt his heart race. If they could locate Belisarius's tomb, they might find the other half of King Arthur's sword. "Do we know what happened to the General?"

Elise said, "In 562, Belisarius stood trial in Constantinople on a charge of corruption. He was found guilty and imprisoned but not long after, Justinian pardoned him, ordered his release, and restored him to favor at the imperial court. In 565, Belisarius and Justinian, whose partnership had increased the size of the empire by 45 percent, died within a few months of each other. Nobody knows where he was buried, but some historians believe Belisarius had requested to be buried at a secret location within Jerusalem's most holy Temple Mount."

Sam grinned. "All right, so we know the general location where both pieces of King Arthur's sword might be found – the question is, how to close the gap, and find them?"

Guinevere closed her eyes for a moment and held her breath. When she opened them she said, "I have a solution!"

Sam said, "Don't keep us waiting. What have you got?"

"Elise, you said that Excalibur and Caliburn – the Arthurian swords – were intrinsically connected because they shared the same DNA?"

Elise nodded. "Yeah, but not necessarily DNA. The swords were said to share a particular ancient stone, presumably smelted into the original iron ore used in the foundry where Merlin forged them."

Guinevere beamed. "And consequently, both weapons were drawn together?"

"That's right. Dr. Patterson's notes refer to this strange connectivity between the weapons. Why?"

"Because, Caliburn – the dog, not the sword – knew when Excalibur was coming for him. It wasn't just a fear of the inevitable, the dog knew the morning that Excalibur arrived, he knew because he felt the other weapon in close proximity to him!"

Sam started to see where she was going. "You're right. I remember Caliburn telling us that he was frightened nearly half an hour before Excalibur attacked us at my friend's house in Tualatin. If the dog and Excalibur share the same stone material used in both ancient swords, perhaps, just maybe, all four weapons, separated by many centuries, are still connected."

Guinevere stood up. "We need to get Caliburn in here and find out!"

Sam stepped outside the mission room, and into the command center where the golden retriever was dozing.

The dog's ears pricked up, and he turned to greet Sam.

Sam said, "We need your help."

Caliburn followed him into the mission room. By now everyone had met the wonder dog. Guinevere laid out the SCRABBLE pieces on the Round Table. Next to it, she had a number of completed words for the dog's reference, like NO, YES, and WHY?

Sam said, "You knew that Excalibur was near before, didn't you?"

The dog gave a near silent whimper at Excalibur's name.

Sam took that as a yes. "You share a connection, don't you? You know when he's near and he knows when you're near, is that right?"

Caliburn nudged the word, YES.

Sam's eyes narrowed. "You apparently share some material used to build King Arthur's swords. Do you think you could find the remaining shards of King Arthur's sword? The first one. The one that shares your name, Caliburn?"

The dog nudged the word, NO.

Sam nodded. "Okay, I thought you had a connection. But I must have misunderstood."

Caliburn nudged the same word again. NO.

Sam leveled his eyes at the dog. "Are you saying that you do have a connection?"

This time the dog pointed to YES.

Sam grinned. "But you can't tell me where the fragment of the sword is?"

The dog barked a sharp affirmative.

"Is that because the connection isn't strong enough?"

Caliburn nudged, YES.

Sam thought about that for a moment. "What if I could get you close, say, the distance from here to the end of the boat, to the sword. Could you then find it for me?"

The dog barked excitedly and placed his paw on the note, YES.

Sam smiled. "All right Caliburn, you and Guinevere, Tom, and I are going on a flight to Glastonbury Abbey, England."

Guinevere said, "That's great, but how do you expect to take an unlicensed, non-microchipped dog on an international commercial flight?"

Sam grinned. "That's easy. I don't intend to fly commercial."

Chapter Sixty-One

Jason Faulkner picked up his cell phone.

The man at the other end answered. "What happened?"

"The dog got away."

"Again?" The man's voice was cold and hard. "How the hell did that happen?"

"He's not alone. He's got help."

"From who?"

"A marine biologist named Sam Reilly. His boat's gone. They boarded a private jet."

"Do you know where they're headed?"

"Yeah, my person at the airport said they registered a flight plan for Bristol International Airport, England. That's the closest airport to Glastonbury."

There was a long pause on the line.

Eventually the other man said, "They're going after the shards of Caliburn, aren't they?"

Jason grimaced. "It would appear so, but it beats me where they think they're going to find it. Our research never came close to finding it. One thing's for certain, it wasn't in fucking Glastonbury Abbey, where 12th century monks once duped an entire kingdom into believing that King Arthur's sacred tomb was interred, just to raise finances from the relic for pilgrimages."

"No. Maybe Sam Reilly knows something we don't?"

"I doubt it. From what I hear, he doesn't even believe in the Arthurian Legend."

"Yeah, well, we know the truth. And without that damned dog, we're in a world of trouble."

Jason agreed, keeping his sentiments to himself.

The man on the other end of the line, dissatisfied, said, "You know what will have to be done to complete the transaction and make this all right, Excalibur?"

Jason Faulkner took a deep sigh. "Yeah, I'm going to have to locate the original Sword in the goddamned Stone."

Chapter Sixty-Two

Glastonbury Abbey, England

The Gulfstream G650 flew into Bristol International Airport just after midday locally.

Sam borrowed a green Jaguar XF from the car pool at the private jet hangar. Guinevere was blown away at the concept that they just give Sam a luxury car while he's in town, but then Sam pointed out that the holding fees while his jet was at the private hangar would more than adequately make up for the sports car.

Sam, Guinevere, and Caliburn drove south along A39, while Tom and Genevieve took a commercial flight to Tel Aviv, where they would head to Jerusalem and start the difficult process of trying to locate where, if anywhere, Belisarius was entombed.

Sam said to Guinevere, "What makes Caliburn so valuable according to legend?"

He watched the dog in the mirror roll over in the back seat of the Jag, and give him a cursory bark.

Sam said, "It's all right. I'm talking about the swords, not you!"

Caliburn made a short whining sound and rolled back to sleep.

Guinevere said, "Apart from imbuing its owner, King Arthur, to rule any battlefield?"

"Yeah. I mean, what does the legend say about the sword?"

"How the hell should I know?" she replied.

Sam said, "You grew up over here. Your name's Guinevere and I have no doubt you were always a royal princess."

She smiled. "All right. There is that."

"So, tell me, what have you heard about the blade? What should we be looking for?"

"Legend has it King Arthur's sword was a giant broadsword. At its hilt was a single snake, which wrapped around itself, with two gems of gold for eyes. Rumor is those eyes were made of a bland, rudimentary pair of stones, but when Arthur entered a battlefield, they lit up, turning the sword to fire. That fire blinded his enemies, and was said to be one of the great sources of his power."

Sam said, "See, you did know the story. Great, so we're looking for a big sword with a snake, whose eyes turn the blade to fire and blind people?"

"That's about it."

Verdant rows of English countryside ran past their windows and the time disappeared quickly along the forty mile stretch to the historic town of Glastonbury.

Guinevere wore her hair in twin braids, somehow making her appear even more regal. Sam wasn't sure if she had meant to do it, or it just came naturally now that she was back in England.

She noticed him looking at her and smiled. "There's something I've been meaning to talk to you about, but… you know, it's never really been a good time, what with the whole being attacked by Excalibur thing and all."

Sam swallowed. He'd been waiting for this conversation. "You wanted to ask me something?"

Guinevere bit her lower lip as if judging whether now was the right time to have the conversation. It was probably the only sign of weakness he'd seen her openly display. She nodded. "Yeah…"

The golden retriever sat up and licked its lips, suddenly interested in the direction of their conversation.

Sam looked at her. "About the other night?"

"Yeah…" Guinevere paused. "No. What happened the other night?"

"I thought you wanted to talk about the fact we slept together. I wasn't sure…"

"Oh gosh, no. I'm nearly forty years old. If I can't sleep with someone at my age, when can I?"

Sam said, "So you're okay to leave it at that?"

"Yeah. Better than okay. It was a lot of fun."

Sam cringed. "What were you going to bring up?"

Guinevere smiled, her lips parting only slightly to reveal the tip of her tongue in a way that somehow showcased her mischievousness, and yet was intolerably sexy.

Sam said, "Come on… what is it? What did you want to know?"

"The crew on your ship, the *Tahila*… I asked them about the meaning of its name."

It was Sam's turn to grin. *So that's what this is about.* "What do you want to know?"

"It's a nice name…" Guinevere said, turning her head to meet his eyes directly. "Did you know your crew has a bet going on why you named it that?"

He placed his hand on his chin and mocked, "Do they really?"

Her eyes narrowed. "You knew?"

Sam shrugged. "I figured they would. They're an inquisitive bunch. *Tahila's* a unique name for a hundred million-dollar, state of the art, ocean salvage vessel. I wonder what the price will get to by the time someone cashes in on it. What do you think?"

She shook her head, her gaze drifting out toward the English countryside which was littered with green and yellow fields, like a giant puzzle. "I don't know."

"What do you think it means?"

"I don't know, really. Your ship… beautiful though she is, looks more like some sort of ocean predator. More like a nuclear attack submarine than a science and recovery vessel."

"You'd be surprised by what purposes she serves."

Guinevere persisted. "So what does the name mean?"

Sam said, "It's Tahitian, for the God of Wind…"

Guinevere met his eye, trying to discern whether he was serious or not. "And that's why you named it that?"

Sam laughed. "No. Truth is, in my early twenties I needed a break from life. I bought a little steel yacht named *Tahila*. It was one of the happiest times in my life, and I've never forgotten it."

She looked at him and knew at once that he was telling the truth. "That's a nice story."

Sam pulled the Jaguar XF up alongside a cobblestoned parking lot outside the historic ruins of Glastonbury Abbey.

He pressed the stop button on the Jag, and the engine died. "We're here."

Chapter Sixty-Three

Sam stared at the dilapidated ruins of the 7th century abbey.

The crumbling piles of stones, and fragile remains, were surrounded by a carpet of deep green grass, and a forest of giant oak trees.

Historians believed the abbey was built at the request of King Ine of Wessex, who enriched the endowment of the community of monks established at Glastonbury so that they could build a stone church in 712AD.

In 1184, a great fire at Glastonbury destroyed the monastic buildings. Reconstruction began almost immediately and the Lady Chapel, which includes the well, was consecrated in 1186. There is evidence that, in the 12th century, the ruined nave was renovated enough for services while the great new church was being constructed. Parts of the walls of the aisle and crossing were completed by 1189, but as was often the way at the time, funding ran out, and progress continued at a slow drizzle.

Pilgrim visits had fallen.

The monastery was getting desperate.

And then, in 1191 their prayers had been granted a miracle.

Two monks, who were digging to bury one of their brothers, found a grave with an oak coffin holding the remains of a gigantic man who had been severely wounded in the head. Buried beside him was a woman with a plait of golden hair.

Also found was an iron cross bearing the inscription, *Hic jacet sepultus inclitus rex Arthurus in insula Avalonia* – Here lies interred the famous King Arthur on the Isle of Avalon.

The monastery's abbot, Henry de Sully, argued that during the time of King Arthur's rule, the Glastonbury Abbey was surrounded by natural rivers, and a large lake, all of which had been buried and forgotten with the passing of centuries. But one thing they could be certain of was that there, in front of them, was the Tomb of King Arthur, buried on the Isle of Avalon.

The discovery of King Arthur and Queen Guinevere's tomb in the ancient cemetery provided fresh impetus for visiting Glastonbury. The pilgrims flocked, the coffers grew, and the Glastonbury Abbey became one of the wealthiest monasteries in England.

That was, until the Dissolution of the Monasteries occurred and King Henry VIII disbanded monasteries, priories, convents and friaries in England, Wales and Ireland, appropriated their income, disposed of their assets, and went to war. At the start of the Dissolution of the Monasteries in 1536, there were over 850 monasteries, nunneries and friaries in England. By 1541, there were none. More than 15,000 monks and nuns had been dispersed and the buildings had been seized by the Crown to be sold off or leased to new lay occupiers. Glastonbury Abbey was reviewed as having significant amounts of silver and gold as well as its attached lands. In September 1539, the abbey was visited by representatives of the King, who arrived there without warning on the orders of Thomas Cromwell. The abbey was stripped of its valuables and Abbot Richard Whiting, who had been a signatory to the Act of Supremacy that made Henry VIII the head of the church, resisted and was hanged, drawn and quartered as a traitor on Glastonbury Tor.

Sam and Guinevere wandered through the old ruins. Caliburn sniffed the air, scratched the grass, and played like an ordinary dog, but he didn't find any sign of King Arthur's first sword.

Sam took the retriever to the site of King Arthur and Queen Guinevere's purported tomb beneath the high altar of the Lady's Chapel. A large plaque noted the burial site of the legendary king of Camelot and his queen.

He said to Caliburn, "What do you think, is it all pretend, or did the monks of Glastonbury really find King Arthur's tomb?"

Caliburn sniffed some more, and pawed at the ground where King Arthur was meant to have been buried.

The dog mewled, and started to walk away in disinterest.

Sam looked at Guinevere, "I'll take that as a no."

Guinevere smiled. Sam thought she always looked beautiful when she smiled, and she smiled all the time.

She said, "I guess not."

A moment later, Caliburn barked, and headed off at a run.

The dog crossed the road to Abbey House, a 19th century gentleman's residence that now ran as a bed and breakfast.

Sam's eyes narrowed. "What the hell's gotten into him?"

Guinevere said, "I don't know, but we'd better go find out."

Caliburn stopped in the middle of a field directly in front of the Abbey House and started to dig with his paws, his tail wagging with almost as much enthusiasm.

Sam came up to him and gave him a good pat. "You found it?"

Caliburn barked, in an eager note of confirmation.

"Well done," Guinevere said. Then, glancing at the large windows of the occupied bed and breakfast at the Abbey House, she said, "I think we'd better wait until nightfall before we go any further."

Sam nodded. "I think you're right. Come on, let's find a hardware store and buy some shovels and a pry bar in case we get lucky. Then we'll find somewhere to have dinner and wait until it gets dark."

They waited until nine p.m. before they started to dig.

At ten-thirty, one of their shovels hit something made of stone. Sam went back to the Jaguar and retrieved a long, heavy, steel prybar.

It took another half an hour before he and Guinevere could muster enough leverage to remove the stone cover, and lay it on the side of the gravesite.

Sam shined his flashlight into the hole, just three feet deep.

Inside, were the bony remains of a single skeleton and the fractured shard of a single sword. There was no name on the tomb, and no shield, which would have been unusual during the time when burying an Anglo-Saxon king.

Guinevere said, "What do you think?"

Sam stared at the rusty weapon's hilt. "It doesn't look like much, but you've got to think, if it isn't King Arthur's first sword, *Caliburn*, then it's one hell of a coincidence."

"I agree. So, now what? Do we just take it?"

"Yeah, we didn't come all this way to leave it here. That's for sure." Sam climbed down and removed the rusty hilt and shard of a sword. "I'm sorry King Arthur. I'm afraid the world needs your sword more than you right now, but if we make it through this alive, I promise to return her to you, all mended."

"He's been dead for nearly fifteen hundred years!" Guinevere said, "Come on, before someone comes!"

Sam climbed out of the pit.

He fixed his flashlight on the remnants of a badly weathered iron sword.

It really wasn't much to look at. The hilt had no name on it, but a carefully defined snake engraving was wrapped around the hilt. At the very top, the snake's head stood out emphatically, with two holes where the eyes appeared to be missing.

From the distance, a bright spotlight fixed on them.

A man shouted, "What in God's name do you think you're doing!"

Chapter Sixty-Four

Sam squinted through the beam of the man's flashlight.

The man wore the dark robes of a monk, but in his right hand was a Walther P99 handgun. The same weapon used by the men who had attacked them at Powell's back in Portland.

The man fixed his beam on the remnants of *Caliburn* in Sam's hand. The weapon looked like nothing more than a rusty shard of iron, with a small hilt, but the stranger's eyes went wide at the sight of it.

"So you've come for King Arthur's sword, have you?"

"Is that what this rusty thing is?" Sam asked. "I was kind of expecting something more… I don't know, grandiose or something? Nothing about this explains how it helped King Arthur defeat the Saxons."

The stranger eyes filled with mirth. "You don't expect me to believe that, do you? You've come here to the exact position, in the middle of a field nowhere near the location where King Arthur was said to have been buried, and just happened to stumble upon the greatest swords that ever existed."

Sam shrugged. "What I can say, I'm just lucky."

Guinevere faced their attacker. "What do you want with us?"

The robed man said, "Isn't it obvious. I'm going to have to kill you and bury you with the sword you so desire."

"Why?" She persisted, her voice showed an inflection of curiosity rather than fear. "What makes it so important to you?"

"Not me. I don't want the god forsaken weapon. My job is to make sure you don't unite both shards of *Caliburn* and condemn us all to hell."

At the sound of his name, Caliburn jumped up from the grass in the distance, where he'd been sleeping, and ran toward their attacker.

The attacker instinctively turned the Walther P99 on the dog.

Sam shouted, "Caliburn no!"

The robed stranger stopped. His previously solemn face turned to joy. His lips beamed with pleasure. And the man said, "Caliburn! Is that you, old boy?"

Chapter Sixty-Five

Dexter pulled back his robes to reveal a hard face, filled with scars.

He leaned down and gave Caliburn a big hug. "I can't believe you're still alive!"

The man with the Arthurian relic and the woman looked at him with incredulity. "You know Caliburn?"

"Know him?" Dexter said. "Hell, I knew him before his treatment."

Guinevere said, "He's your dog?"

"No. He was originally Dr. Jim Patterson's dog. Jim brought him onto the team for the first genetic modification program, using Merlin's technology."

The man with the dagger stepped closer, but Dexter aimed his handgun at him. "Not so fast. Who are you and how did you end up with our dog?"

"My name's Sam Reilly." He gestured toward his friend. "This is Guinevere Jenkins."

Dexter studied the woman like a scientist might a specimen. It was the eyes. Liquid jade. And the crown of dark red hair that made him believe. "My god! You're Patrick's twin sister!"

"That's right," she said. "You knew my brother?"

"Yes. My name's Dexter Cunningham. I worked with your brother at MI-6, in the project code named King Arthur. He was a good man, despite his flaws."

"Thank you," she said.

Dexter remembered how much Patrick liked to kill. He had often wondered if the man hadn't entered MI-6 how long it would have taken him to commit murder and end up spending the rest of his life, wasting away, in a high security prison.

"If I recall correctly, you were at MI-6 too. If you're anything like your brother I guess you're pretty dangerous."

Sam said, "You'd better believe it. We were attacked a few days ago, and she got rid of five elite soldiers like they weren't there."

Dexter breathed heavily. "They would have been working for Excalibur, paid mercenaries, deadly and committed to the highest bidder."

"Dexter Cunningham!" Sam grinned as though suddenly recognizing his name. "Your name's Dexter!"

"Yeah?"

"You were one of the seven members of the original team from MI-6 who went to work for *Camelot Weapons Industries* in Oregon!"

Dexter arched an eyebrow. "That's right. How do you know about that?"

Sam said, "Because I examined the wreckage of the *Hoshi Maru*. On the bulkhead, where Excalibur slept for nearly seven years while he was trapped on board the drifting wreck, there were seven names. Four had already been crossed out – presumably killed – but your name and two others were still there."

"I take it Dr. Jim Patterson was on the list of people still alive?"

Sam nodded.

Dexter said, "He's not anymore."

"We know. He left a USB flash drive hidden on Caliburn's dog tag. It outlined the King Arthur project and advised the only way to defeat Excalibur now was to locate Merlin's SPELL book. Of course, not knowing where to find it…"

"You're going to try and fix *Caliburn* so that you can kill Excalibur."

"That's right," Sam said. "The question is will it work?"

Dexter thought about it for a moment. "If you can find the second piece, and somehow join the two shards together I believe you have a chance. The thing is a mended sword is never the same as one that hasn't been broken."

Sam said, "It doesn't need to be great. Just sharp and strong enough to penetrate Excalibur's defensive skin."

"Do you know where the second piece of the sword is?"

Sam said, "We have a lead that it was buried with Mordred – AKA General Belisarius – somewhere in Jerusalem."

Dexter nodded. "That's what we heard, too. But we never found it."

Sam shrugged. "You never found King Arthur's tomb, either."

"You're right. You got one step further than us." Thinking of their next immediate problem, Dexter asked, "Do you know where the forge is?"

"We know Merlin's cave was somewhere in Majorca, Spain. But like here, we only have a rough idea, and nothing solid."

Dexter said, "That's right. The entrance is somewhere inside the Dragon Breath Cave in Majorca. It's well-hidden and below the water line. You could easily miss it even if you knew it was there. I'm not even certain I could find it again, much less work out how to enter it."

"The thing is blocked?"

"Yes. An ancient stone mechanism that Merlin crafted himself to protect his magic grotto from intruders. It's said to be the source of his wealth. The ore he mined there was used to imbue his SPELLs with unimaginable powers."

Sam asked, "Do you want to come with us? We could use your help."

Dexter shook his head emphatically. "No. I don't. I haven't stayed alive all these years by trying to challenge Excalibur. I'm going to return to a monastery, where I'll remain in hiding for the remainder of my days."

Sam frowned. "It doesn't sound like much of a life for a professional soldier. Isn't it worth facing your fears and helping us defeat Excalibur?"

Dexter exhaled slowly through pursed lips. "You don't get it, do you? Excalibur likes his new found powers. When they experimented on him, the SPELL changed him in ways you can't imagine. The very same SPELL that worked on Caliburn's innate goodness, and strengthened it, latched onto Excalibur's evil side – making it flourish, and turning him into a monster so far removed from the man he once was, to make him unrecognizable as human."

"He's that bad?" Sam asked.

Dexter nodded. "There are worse things than dying. You'll know that if you meet Excalibur without Caliburn in your hand."

Sam said, "All right. If that's the case, we'd better get going. Thanks for your help."

"You're welcome. I'll rebury King Arthur's tomb. The last thing we want is for Excalibur to know that you're making progress." Dexter met Sam and Guinevere's eyes, holding their gaze for a moment. He said, "Good luck."

Chapter Sixty-Six

Old City – Jerusalem, Israel

Sam rented a Fiat 500, the tiny Italian two door car that blended in with every other small rental car at Ben Gurion airport in Tel Aviv. He figured it was better to rent something that didn't stand out for what they were doing. It might take them a while to find the second piece of *Caliburn* and the last thing they needed was for people to be asking questions about who they were.

They took Israel Highway One southeast into Jerusalem.

By 8 a.m. they reached the Old City of Jerusalem and first set their eyes on the ancient walled city, which had been occupied for more than three thousand years. Sun struck the ancient stone wall turning it a golden bronze.

They parked the car, and lined up with a throng of people to enter the Old City of Jerusalem through the Damascus Gates.

Sam stared at the massive wall.

It was built in 1535, when Jerusalem was part of the Ottoman Empire. Its sultan, Suleiman the Magnificent ordered the ruined city walls to be rebuilt even higher. Under his rule, 2.5 miles of the stone walls were lifted to an average height of forty feet, with a thickness of eight feet. The walls contained thirty-four watchtowers and seven main gates open for traffic, with two minor gates reopened by archaeologists.

The wall protected a wealth of historical and religious sites of major significance after the region had witnessed nearly four thousand years of brutal exchanges of ownership. In the present day, the Old City had been divided into four uneven quarters. Moving in a counterclockwise direction from the northeastern corner, was the Muslim Quarter, Christian Quarter, Armenian Quarter and Jewish Quarter.

Some of the greatest religious sites were located within the monumental walls. Temple Mount and Western Wall were sacred to the Jews, the Church of the Holy Sepulchre for Christians and the Dome of the Rock for Muslims. The Dome of the Rock, a gold-domed Islamic shrine, was built on the site of the destroyed Jewish Temples in Jerusalem. The Dome, located on the Temple Mount, was built by Caliph Abd al-Malik. It's the oldest surviving Islamic building and was constructed at the very site where Muslims believe Muhammad ascended to heaven. Next to it, was the Church of the Holy Sepulchre in the Christian Quarter of the Old City of Jerusalem. The church contains, according to traditions dating back to at least the fourth century, the two holiest sites in Christianity: the site where Jesus of Nazareth was crucified, at a place known as Golgotha, and Jesus' empty tomb, where he is said to have been buried and resurrected. The tomb is enclosed by the 19th-century shrine called the Aedicule.

Sam, Guinevere, and Caliburn gave the border guard his paperwork for Caliburn that showed the dog was a specially trained archeology dog, who had been granted approval to visit the Old City to assist with a current archeological project. Elise had hacked the official Israeli Customs Office, and issued the pass for Caliburn – making the pass technically legal, but the documented archeological dig was fictional, and Sam just hoped the border guard didn't have time to check.

The border guard glanced at their papers, and nodded them through.

They headed down Via Dolorosa into the Muslim Quarter, and met up with Tom and Genevieve who were waiting for them in the Austrian Hospice Café. It was a Viennese-style cafe renowned as being able to deliver a splendid combination of class, ambience, and delectable food.

A man greeted them at the door, and said, "You must be Mr. Reilly and Mrs. Jenkins?"

Sam nodded. "That's right. How did you know?"

"Your dog," the waiter replied. "A Mr. Tom Bower told me that you would be arriving shortly and asked me to send you up onto the private rooftop. I was told that I would recognize you easily as soon as you arrived, because you would be traveling with a golden retriever."

Sam met his eye, the crease of a suppressed smile forming on his lips. "That's right. He's a specialist archeology dog, trained to search for certain scents centuries old."

The waiter seemed uninterested by their story, his expression neither accepting or dismissing their ruse. The man nodded. "If you will come with me, I'll take you to meet your friends."

They followed the waiter through the garden terrace, and up three flights of masonry stairs, onto the rooftop, from which, Sam could see the outcrops of the ancient city. Behind them, and to their south, stood the golden dome of Dome of the Rock, Jerusalem's most prominent feature of its Old City landscape. In the opposite direction Sam's eyes spotted the Western Wall – AKA the Wailing Wall – and the Resurrection Rotunda in the Church of the Holy Sepulchre.

Sitting, drinking Arabic tea at the other end of the rooftop, was Tom and Genevieve.

Tom stood up to greet them. "Ah, Sam... you made it. I hope you're hungry."

The dog tilted his head to greet them and mewled eagerly.

"It's all right, Caliburn, we've already got food waiting for you," Tom said, as he pointed to a bowl of water and cooked lamb beneath the table.

Sam looked at the food on the table. It was enough to feed an army. A rich combination of Viennese and Arabic food adorned the table, from goulash soup, schnitzel, sacher-torte, through to baklava.

All four of them sat down at the table, while Caliburn scoffed his brunch, and Tom brought them up to speed with their research trying to locate the burial site of Belisarius.

Tom said, "The good news is we've located in the archives a story about a grand marble tomb being built and an unnamed person being buried within it on the 4th of April, 565AD."

Sam said, "That's within a week of Belisarius's death!"

Tom suppressed a smile. "Exactly. That's what we thought, too."

Sam put his Arabic tea down. "There can't be that many grand burials in marble tombs during that period?"

"None quite that extravagant for the year."

"But there was no record of his name?"

"No. According to the historical archives, the person had served Justinian the Great, but there had been a problem – something that had tarnished their friendship or soured the political relationship – either way, Justinian had refused to acknowledge the person's friendship but had offered to pay for the tomb and burial. Shortly after that, Justinian died, and so whatever the secret, it died with him."

"Where was the burial site?" Sam asked.

Tom replied, "A private necropolis near the Nea Church. It's two blocks away."

Guinevere said, "That's got to be Belisarius! I mean, everything matches up perfectly. The secret friendship. Belisarius was tried by Rome, and sentenced to death, but Justinian the Great pardoned him out of respect for his battle achievements, but this in itself had caused political upheaval for Justinian. The time of the burial matches. Also, the fact that it came out in the region near the Nea Church, which Belisarius sponsored."

Sam beamed with pleasure. "That's great, let's go there, and check it out now with Caliburn!"

"That might be a bit difficult. We have a sketch of the building, but most of the city was destroyed during the Siege of Jerusalem in 612AD. So, unless you happen to have a magic map, depicting the topographic regions and buildings around that time period, I think we're all out of luck."

Sam grinned. "Actually, there is. It's called the Madaba Map."

Chapter Sixty-Seven

Dexter Cunningham met his attacker with the unique dignity of someone resigned to die. After seven years of running, a certain calm came over him once he knew it was finally over.

"It's been a while, Excalibur." Dexter grinned. "I can't say the years have been kind to you."

Excalibur ignored his attempt to brush off the abject terror of meeting him in the Glastonbury Abbey. "I've heard it's not how good you look over the years, but the amount of years you have... or something like that... I don't know... but what I do know is soon, you'll be dead, and I'll still keep on doing what I've always done."

Dexter said, "That's not what I heard. I heard someone was coming for you."

He threw his Walther P99 handgun into the nearby lake to stop Excalibur using his own handgun to kill him. Excalibur wasn't even carrying a weapon. He knew he didn't have to. The bullets couldn't harm Excalibur, but they would end up killing Dexter.

Excalibur grinned wickedly. "Who tracked you down?"

"A man. His name was Sam Reilly. He said he was looking to find and rebuild Caliburn so that he could defeat you."

Excalibur grinned. "Is it possible? Could Caliburn be put back together again?"

"Sure. But you would need to locate both shards of the sword."

"If he does that... how would he fuse them together again?"

Dexter grinned. "You're asking if a steel forge could join two of the hardest pieces of weaponry together?"

Excalibur nodded. "Can it be done?"

"No."

"So, they're on a fool's errand?"

Dexter said, "No. There is a way."

"How?"

"Why should I tell you?" Dexter asked, defiance trying to overcome the tension in his voice. "We both know you're going to kill me, anyway?"

Excalibur bared his teeth in a Machiavellian grin. "Because I can kill you quickly or I can take my time and keep you alive for weeks. I have the time. My internal clock's not ticking along like yours. I would do that, if you don't tell me what I want to know."

Dexter sighed.

There was no point considering if Excalibur was telling the truth. The evil had risen in him like a cancer. He'd tortured people when he was with MI-6, justifying the need to perform it secretly despite being against the Geneva Convention, but it didn't take long for him to develop a liking for it, and like a drug, he soon became addicted. There was no doubt in his mind, since he'd undertaken the genetic procedure, he had become worse.

Dexter said, "There are two stones."

"The serpent's eyes," Excalibur said, reverently.

"Yes. According to the legend, the stones belong in the hilt of the weapon, and are said to be the source of the sword's power."

Excalibur said, "But I heard the serpent's stones were broken from Caliburn's hilt during the battle of Camlann?"

"It was."

"So, they're lost for eternity. Probably buried under hundreds of tons of concrete and modern infrastructure by now."

Dexter said, "You're wrong."

"Really? What happened to them."

"Merlin found them. He took them back to his cave, and secured them in the eyes of the serpent once more."

"So they're lost."

Dexter grinned.

It was a fraction of pleasure, but he held onto it, like a child with candy. He knew he was about to die, but there wasn't a hope in hell Excalibur would ever see Caliburn fused together once more. And without one of the two ancient relics from King Arthur's reign, he was bound to die, also.

Dexter said, "Unless, you happen to know where to find Merlin's Cave… and a truly righteous person to extract the eyes from the serpent."

"I agree that might be difficult."

"Or you might get lucky… and draw Excalibur from the stone."

That made Excalibur laugh. Dr. Jim Patterson had intentionally returned the blade of Excalibur to the stone, where no one in present day could remove it. Merlin had designed it specifically to meet Arthur's genes. So that no one else could wield the weapon.

Unless he happened to locate one of Arthur's descendants.

Excalibur stopped laughing.

There was no more that Dexter could offer him. He would have liked to make the man suffer, but as Dexter had pointed out, he would be wiser to spend that time working to locate the serpent's eyes.

A moment later, he drew a dagger from his belt, and lunged. Dexter didn't move. He didn't try to fight. Like a king that had been checkmated, he simply waited to die.

The blade struck the base of his neck, slicing straight through – and sending him to a permanent darkness.

Chapter Sixty-Eight

Excalibur picked up his cell phone and dialed a private number.

A man answered on the first ring, and simply said, "Yes."

Excalibur said, "They're in the Old City of Jerusalem."

"Good. Well done. I'll send someone to go pick them up immediately."

Chapter Sixty-Nine

Muslim Quarters, Jerusalem

Sam Reilly said, "The Madaba Map preserves a sixth-century perception of the topography, cities, and monuments of the Mediterranean. The mosaic was discovered on the floor of the Church of St. George in Madaba, Jordan, and has been dated from 560–565, less than twenty years after the inauguration of the Nea in 543, and it is the oldest surviving cartographic representation of the Holy Land."

"How far does it cover?" Tom asked.

"The map depicts the Mediterranean world from Lebanon in the North to the Nile Delta in the South, and from the Mediterranean Sea in the west to the Eastern Desert. The city of Jerusalem is given prominence by its size and the mosaicists' devotion to the detail of its monuments. No city represented in the map is larger. The central location of Jerusalem in the mosaic further supports Jerusalem's importance in the minds of the map's creators."

Guinevere asked, "Where do we find the map?"

"The floor mosaic is located in the apse of the church of Saint George at Madaba."

"Great. So now we're off to Jordan?"

Sam shook his head. "No. I can download an in-depth digitization of the ancient map."

"All right, let's do that and see if we're in luck," Tom said. "Hopefully it captures part of the region near the private necropolis two blocks from the Nea Church."

Sam pulled out a laptop from his backpack. He switched it on and synched it wirelessly to his satellite phone. A few minutes later he managed to download the digitized archive of the ancient mosaic of the Madaba Map.

He brought the image up onto his computer screen.

Guinevere sat next to him, while Tom and Genevieve stood behind them and leaned in to examine the image.

Sam said, "You'll notice that the map isn't oriented to the north, like modern maps. Instead, it faces east, toward the altar in such a fashion that the position of places on the map coincides with the actual compass directions. Originally, it measured 68 feet by 23 feet, and contained over two million tesserae. But nearly forty percent has been lost over time."

Tom said, "Let's hope the part we need wasn't in that section of the map."

Sam stared at the map.

The mosaic depicted an area from Lebanon in the north to the Nile Delta in the south, and from the Mediterranean Sea in the west to the Eastern Desert. Among other features, it showed the Dead Sea with two fishing boats, a variety of bridges linking the banks of the Jordan, fish swimming in the river and receding from the Dead Sea.

To the bottom right, was a lion hunting a gazelle in the Moab desert, a palm covered Jericho, Bethlehem and other biblical-Christian sites, although some of the images had been rendered nearly unrecognizable by the insertion of random tesserae during a period of iconoclasm. Some historians believed the map may have once served to facilitate pilgrims' orientation in the Holy Land. All landscape units are labelled with explanations in Greek. A combination of folding perspective and aerial view depicts about one hundred and fifty towns and villages, all of them labelled.

Tom said, "Where's the Nea Church located on this map?"

Sam pointed to the southeast of the Old City, just outside the walls of Jerusalem. "Right there. Southeast of the base of Mount Zion."

Genevieve said, "According to the archives, Mount Zion was not a new site in Jerusalem for Christian patrons to erect their monuments, and as a result of past projects, monasteries, churches, and cult sites already existed there. Consequently, the highest available spot for the Nea to be constructed was on the southeastern slope of the hill, a fair way down from the hegemonic vistas afforded to the Basilica of Hagia Sion that perched on the mount's peak. Yet by choosing this site, Justinian was attempting to position the Nea within the hierarchical power structure that was connected to the topographical highpoints of Jerusalem."

Tom studied the map. "So therefore, if Belisarius's tomb and necropolis is meant to be about three blocks to the northeast of the Nea Church, it puts it somewhere over here, next to the Garden Tomb?"

Genevieve frowned. "It's hard to believe that the Tomb of Jesus is meant to be Belisarius's secret tomb?"

Sam said, "There's been some debate over this since medieval Christianity. According to the Bible, Jesus was crucified very near the city of Jerusalem. Some have taken that to mean the Garden Tomb, while others believe it was merely a better representative of the Bible's description of where Jesus was crucified and then resurrected. In contradistinction to this modern identification, the traditional site where the death and resurrection of Christ are believed to have occurred has been the Church of the Holy Sepulchre at least since the fourth century."

Tom said, "My mother taught me to never start a religious geography debate in Jerusalem, but it still doesn't explain why there's no signs of the stone walls and distinctive roofline of the wealthy, private, necropolis."

Sam stared at the map. "I see what's happened. You're looking at the map wrong."

Tom bit his lower lip. "You think I can't read a map?"

"No. I know you can read a map. But Madaba Map is aligned toward east – not north."

Tom's eyes widened. "That's right. If that's the case, then it would put it here, somewhere to the west of the Damascus Gates."

Genevieve held out an image of a sketch of the private necropolis. "I don't see anything like this on the Madaba Map."

Guinevere glanced over Sam's shoulder. "No. It's right there."

"Then we're in trouble because that whole region was demolished and is now full of stone pavers that make up Beit HaBad Street," Tom said, pointing to the street. He looked at Sam and said, "Unless you have another idea?"

Sam thought about it and grinned. "As a matter of fact, I do. We only need to get close to the burial site and Caliburn will get us the rest of the way. Why don't we go beneath Beit HaBad Street?"

Tom said, "How?"

"Through Zedekiah's Cave."

Chapter Seventy

Zedekiah's Cave was also referred to as Solomon's Quarries.

It was a five-acre underground meleke limestone quarry that runs the length of five city blocks under the Muslim Quarter of the Old City of Jerusalem. It was carved over a period of a thousand years and is a remnant of the largest quarry in Jerusalem, stretching from Jeremiah's Grotto and the Garden Tomb to the walls of the Old City.

The entrance to Zedekiah's Cave is just beneath the Old City wall, between the Damascus and Herod Gates. Only the mouth of Zedekiah's cave is a natural phenomenon. The cavern and miles upon miles of passageways were carved by slave laborers over thousands of years. Herod the Great used the main quarry at Zedekiah's Cave for building blocks in the renovation of the Temple and its retaining walls, including what is known today as the Western – Wailing – Wall.

From the entrance to the farthest point, the cave extends about 650 feet. Its maximum width is about 330 feet and its depth was generally about thirty feet below the street level of the Muslim Quarter, although there are several lower levels and blocked tunnels too, where few have ever explored.

Sam Reilly waited until five p.m. to meet Tom, Genevieve, Guinevere, and Caliburn at the mouth of the cave, matching their arrival with the nightly closure of the ancient cave and quarry system.

They bribed a local guard to leave the external gate open for them to have a private viewing for two hours. They then switched on their flashlights, stepped through the narrow entrance, and followed the cave as it sloped down into a vast three-hundred-foot chamber.

Drops of water, known locally as "Zedekiah's tears," trickled through the ceiling on them as they walked.

They passed through the auditorium, heading south, through a series of artificial galleries hewn by ancient stonecutters into strange patterns and formations.

Sam checked his computer tablet.

On it, he had superimposed an image of the known Zedekiah's Cave map with the modern-day map, and the presumed site of Belisarius's secret tomb marked on the Madaba Map.

Using the three linked maps, Sam headed down the southern path deeper into the quarry system. Chisel marks were visible along the walls where slaves once cut away the stones that masons once used to build much of the Old City of Jerusalem. They passed a large gallery in which hundreds of nearly finished building blocks made out of meleke – the lithologic type of white, coarsely-crystalline, thickly bedded-limestone used throughout the Old City – which were once destined for some long-ago structures, are locked into the rock where the stonecutters left them centuries ago.

Sam glanced at the dog. "Are you sensing anything?"

Caliburn gave a disinterested bark.

Sam said, "All right, let's keep going."

Tom laughed and asked, "How do you know that was a no and not a yes?"

A moment later, Caliburn ran forward barking excitedly.

Sam grinned. "Because that's what he does when he says yes!"

Chapter Seventy-One

A massive chockstone blocked an ancient passageway.

Caliburn barked wildly, as though his complaints might encourage the massive stone to make way for them. Sam checked his map of the quarry system. It showed the chockstone, but not the passageway beyond.

Sam studied the massive piece of stone wedged between two edges of a passage. It was similar to the ones he had seen in Derinkuyu, an underground city in Turkey. The wedge was nearly impossible to open from the outside, yet easily able to be shifted from the inside.

There was nothing they could do. No amount of leverage would allow them to get through it. They would need to head off and try again tomorrow with some sort of drilling equipment.

Sam said, "We'll try again tomorrow."

Genevieve met his gaze and said, "That's it?"

"Yeah, unless you happened to bring dynamite, I think we'll have to call it a night."

Genevieve shrugged. "No dynamite, but enough C4 to blast a hole through this edge here."

Sam met her eye. His eyebrows arched with disbelief. "You brought C4 into the Old City of Jerusalem?"

Genevieve nodded. "Among other things... hey I thought it might come in handy."

Sam said, "How did you even get away with that? The security in Jerusalem is tighter than Fort Knox!"

Genevieve made a teasing smile and bit her lower lip. "I spent my youth working for my father, who was the boss of the Russian Mafia. I still have connections with some... bad people around the world. And some of them still owe me favors."

Sam said, "All right. Do you think you can blast the edge of this stone wedge like a pair of masonry hinges?"

"No problem."

Tom asked, "Won't the guards hear you outside?"

Genevieve answered immediately. "No. We're a quarter of a mile down here. It will be an isolated explosion. If the guards hear it at all, they won't necessarily identify it as being down here. Besides, remember, we just paid them to look the other way. The last thing they're going to want to do is keep an ear out for any explosions we might cause."

"They might wonder?" Sam said.

"Sure. But it's not like there's meant to be anything valuable down here. It's a quarry dug out over thousands of years. Anything of value that could be removed, had been centuries ago."

Sam glanced at the rest of the team. "What do you think? Do we take the risk?"

Caliburn barked excitedly, his tail wagging fast. Tom, Genevieve, and Guinevere all followed with their agreement.

Sam said, "All right, set the C4 – let's blast this thing."

Chapter Seventy-Two

The blast from the C4 shook the cavern.

Its sound echoing throughout the ancient passageways of the quarry. Sam waited for the dust to settle and then examined the damage. The meleke limestone cracked under the explosion, leaving a jagged crack running along the side of the wedged stone, from the edge all the way to the center, like a giant scar.

He pressed his hand against the stone.

It didn't budge.

He looked at Genevieve. "Any chance you brought some more of that stuff?"

She grinned. "You bet there is. I was just trying to avoid causing too much of a ruckus aboveground."

Sam turned his eyes back to the door. The crack in the middle appears to be splintering outward. Like glass, the first crack is the hardest to produce. A second one might just cause the entire thing to shatter.

He said to Genevieve, "Why don't you put it right there, smack bang in the middle of the door?"

She nodded. "All right. I'll put it in the crack. How much do you want?"

Sam set his jaw firm. "As much as you've got."

She nodded and emptied the contents of her backpack into the crack at the center of the door. She then turned to face the rest of the group. "You might all want to take a farther step back this time."

No one needed to be told twice.

The group took cover in the vaulted room adjacent to the passageway.

Genevieve depressed the detonator.

This time, their whole world shook.

Sam didn't wait for the dust to settle. A blast that size might just have notified half the world above them. If they were going to get answers, now was going to have to be the time. He stepped through the thick layer of limestone powder that wafted through the passageway.

He shined his flashlight at the chockstone, but none of it remained.

Sam stepped through the new opening, into a narrow passage, and a moment later, Caliburn passed him, barking as he led the way.

They all followed the retriever.

Caliburn took them to a large vaulted room. Like an old catacomb, there were rows and rows of tombs scattered throughout each end of the vault.

Sam said, "Which one, Caliburn?"

The dog ran toward a big one at the end, and simply placed one of his paws up on it.

There was no fancy inscription or anything on the tomb to identify the person inside, but it was the grandest one inside the private necropolis.

An old iron bar, once used in the lowering of the tomb's cover, was used to pry it open again.

Inside they found what they believed to be the skeletal remains of Belisarius and a single shard of a sword. At a glance, it matched the other side of *Caliburn*. Next to it was a book made of vellum. Sam picked it up and fixed his flashlight on its pages.

The writing was almost illegible, but there was no mistaking the title – *King Arthur of Camelot*.

Guinevere was the first to make the connection. She said, "Could it be?"

"Could what be?" Sam asked.

She took a reverent breath. "That here lies King Arthur!"

"What?" Sam and Tom replied.

"Think about it. All this time, we've assumed that the story of King Arthur was set in England, but what if we were wrong?"

"I'm not following you," Sam said. "The story of King Arthur was set in England. Besides, if this is King Arthur, who's dead in that secret grave we found in Glastonbury?"

"That was Mordred, an Anglo who tried to fight off a young Saxon named Belisarius in the sixth century. We knew the General had come from Germany, which at the time was part of the Roman Empire."

"Okay," Sam said. "I'll take the bait. If that's the case where did King Arthur come from? And Camelot?"

Guinevere shook her head. "You're missing it. King Arthur never existed. Nor did Camelot. Belisarius did and so did Merlin. Think about it. If Merlin was from Britain, why was his forge supposed to be in a grotto in Majorca?"

Sam grinned. "Because it was under the Byzantine Empire at the time."

"Exactly."

Sam frowned. "But what of this book?"

"*King Arthur of Camelot?*"

Sam gave a puzzled nod. "Yeah."

"It was an ideal. Belisarius fought for Justinian the Great because he believed in what the man was trying to achieve. Not only did the Eastern Roman Emperor restore nearly 45 percent of the Roman Empire in his life, but he was determined to set about creating a new order of rules that was just and fair for everyone within his kingdom. You said it yourself, that his *Corpus Juris* is still used today in law systems around the civilized world."

Sam smiled. "And so, Belisarius, wrote about Camelot – the perfect kingdom – with a Round Table, where everyone had a place, where knights were chivalrous, and the kingdom was ruled in peace..."

Genevieve interrupted his thoughts, and said, "The one thing I don't understand is how did anyone ever hear about King Arthur if the only book has remained buried here all this time?"

Sam said, "After failing to bring order to the Anglos in Briton, a young Belisarius joined Justinian's campaign to reclaim the Roman Empire. During the campaign, he wrote stories to remind him what he was fighting for."

"About the perfect civilization?"

"Yes. A perfect empire, inspired by the notion of all that was good and just in Camelot. But he soon learned that any real change took centuries, and the people to make it. A king, no matter how good their ideals were, needed time and for the people to make the difference. As a deeply religious man, he was buried nearby the supposed burial site of Jesus and the Resurrection. His book was left in his tomb – for an honest knight to come along."

"Galahad?" Guinevere asked.

Sam shook his head. "No. The man's name was Geoffrey of Monmouth and he was in the process of ransacking Jerusalem in the name of the First Crusades."

Guinevere said, "Belisarius knew his tomb would be pillaged one day?"

Sam nodded. "I believe so. And when Geoffrey found the book during the 11ᵗʰ century he instantly saw the benefit that his kings might have in his new book, *Historia Regum Britanniae* – which would place England's kings as the rightful rulers."

Caliburn barked loudly and bared his teeth.

All eyes turned to the passageway – where three heavily bearded men, their faces covered with Arabic keffiyehs, and holding Israeli Uzis had arrived.

Chapter Seventy-Three

They were all herded out of the Zedekiah's Cave at gunpoint.

Sam noticed as they passed the mouth of the quarry that the two guards, they had bribed to enter the ancient cavern were dead – their throats cut.

They were taken outside the Damascus Gates, where a helicopter was waiting for them. Any thoughts of escaping while they were still within the Old City were quickly discarded when one of the men mentioned that they had been paid to steal a dog, and they didn't care less if they had to shoot any of the people with the dog.

Tom and Genevieve were the first to be put into the AH-1 Cobra helicopter.

Next went one of their captors, who pointed his handgun – a 9mm Jericho 941 pistol – at Genevieve's head. The man said, "If anyone plays badly, I will shoot her in the head. Understood?"

There was a general murmur of agreement.

Caliburn was then lifted into the helicopter. The dog's eyes were somber as he moved with his tail resting between his legs, until he was all the way at the back of the helicopter.

Sam and Guinevere were pushed into the back of the helicopter next, and the man who appeared to be in charge climbed in last.

The third captor climbed into the pilot's seat in the cockpit. He switched the helicopter's engines on, and they were in the air within minutes.

Sam said, "Where are you taking us?"

The captor in charge said, "Into Jordan."

"Why?"

"Because it's easier for the man who pays our wages to meet you there…" The man tilted his head and made a half-grin. "Well, not you, the dog…"

Sam said, "Someone must really like dogs?"

"Not all dogs. Only this one."

"Who?"

"I don't know the man's name. Only that he goes by the codename of Excalibur and that he's offered a princely sum for the return of a very specific dog – a golden retriever, who has the unique ability to change the color of its fur to hide into its surroundings."

Sam said, "So then, if it's not personal, and you've been hired to get the dog, why take us?"

"Excalibur doesn't care whether you live or die. But I know a man in Jordan who would pay a high price for captured tourists – particularly Americans…"

"What will he do with us?" Guinevere asked.

The man shrugged. "I don't know and I don't care. Does the farmer ask what the butcher is going to do with his animals?"

Guinevere turned away, so that he couldn't see her fear.

The man said, "Ah, you are very beautiful. You can guess what such a man would do with you? No? Maybe, I should keep you as my own slave? Or one of my wives? The other wives will be pissed by your beauty, but what can they do about it?"

Sam met Guinevere's steely gaze. Neither said anything. They didn't have to.

Guinevere smiled lasciviously at her captor.

The man smiled back, revealing missing teeth. "Good girl… I'm going to enjoy…"

He didn't get to finish his sentiment.

Instead, Guinevere struck him in the throat in a sharp, jabbing motion with her fingers rigid. The force was strong enough to crush his windpipe.

The man gasped for air.

Guinevere launched herself at his Uzi.

The man squeezed the trigger, in a desperate attempt to gain control, despite being unable to breathe and having no more than a few minutes to live without immediate medical interventions. The Uzi fired wildly, raking the side of the helicopter with peppered bullet holes.

Guinevere gripped his forearm with both hands and slammed the arm down on her knee, shattering his elbow, and introducing him to two new, and very unnatural, ranges of motion in his arm.

The second captor responded quickly, turning his 9mm Jericho 941 pistol from Genevieve's head to Guinevere's.

But then Tom, seeing a solution, threw his entire 240-pound weight into the man.

The 9mm Jericho 941 pistol fell and Genevieve, Tom, and their captor all dived to get it. Against all odds, their captor was the first to reach the trigger. Genevieve hit him in the face, and then stuffed her fingers into his eye sockets.

The man screamed in agony, and began firing wildly.

A rogue shot hit the pilot in the head.

Guinevere grabbed the now flaccid arm of her captor in her hand, and turned the Uzi on her captor – putting several bullets in his head before he realized she was twisting his arm backward.

With the pilot dead and no one at the controls, the helicopter started to spin wildly. The blinded captor was thrown out of the AH-1 Cobra.

Genevieve and Tom pulled the pilot out of the seat, and together regained control of the helicopter.

Guinevere unceremoniously dropped the dead pilot and the captor who was in charge out the helicopter's open side door.

Tom looked back over his shoulder and said, "Now where do you want to go?"

Sam grinned. "To find Merlin's Cave so we can forge this sword back together and kill Excalibur."

"Great. Any idea where that is?"

"Not really. But I've been told to look within the Dragon Breath Cave, in Majorca."

Chapter Seventy-Four

Dragon Caves – Majorca, Spain

Majorca was one of Spain's Balearic Islands in the Mediterranean.

Having landed at the Palma de Mallorca Airport with a budget airline commercial carrier, and driven east along the Ma-15 in a rental to Manacor, Sam felt his two most recent locations couldn't be in any more of a direct contrast to one another. Where Jerusalem was a melting pot of religion and culture, forced together out of necessity, and guarded with a not so small army, Majorca was a resort location, where vacationers could ease out of their stress filled lives and into the careful, Spanish, resort world, known for its beaches, sheltered coves, limestone mountains, and some historic Roman and Moorish remains.

They arrived at the caves shortly after six p.m. when the security guards were securing the gates. In keeping with their counterparts in Jerusalem, the guards who locked the entrance to the Dragon Caves in Manacor, happily took the bribes they were offered, so that Sam, Tom, Genevieve, Guinevere, and Caliburn could take a private tour of the cave system in a little wooden rowboat.

The Dragon Caves were four majestic caves, interconnected. Discovered in medieval times, they are located in Manacor, near the locality of Porto Cristo. The caves extend to a depth of eighty-two feet and reach approximately two and a half miles in length. The four caves are called Black Cave, White Cave, Cave of Luis Salvador, and Cave of the French, and are all connected to each other.

The caves were formed by water being forced through the entrance from the Mediterranean Sea, and some researchers think the formation may date back to the Miocene Epoch. There is an underground lake situated in the caves called Martel Lake, which is about 377 feet in length and 100 wide, with an average depth of twelve to forty feet. It was named after the French explorer and scientist Édouard-Alfred Martel, who is considered the founding father of speleology. He was invited to explore the cave in 1896. A German cave explorer, M.F. Will, had mapped the White and Black cave in 1880. Martel found two more caves, as well as the underground lake.

The Dragon Caves have been known since the medieval times. Legends were passed around for long times about pirates and Templars hiding their treasures here and how a dragon guarded them. In 1339 some soldiers were sent into the caves to retrieve the treasures and this marks the beginning of the exploration of the caves.

They headed down the boardwalk descending into the limestone cave system. Spectacular stalactite formations and intricate canopies drip dramatically from the vaulted ceilings while descended nearly a hundred feet below the surface through four enormous interconnected chambers. Sam glanced at the Lakes of Diana, a crystalline blue lake that looked magical. If Merlin really did cast SPELLs in an underground divine grotto, this certainly looked like the place to do it.

The temperature remained a constant 70 degrees Fahrenheit all year round.

At the fourth chamber, a large wooden rowboat had been pulled up alongside the boardwalk next to Lake Martel, one of the largest subterranean lakes in Europe. During normal visiting hours, tourists are guided through the lake with a floodlit, floating violin concert at the end of the chamber.

Caliburn leaned into the edge of the lake and began licking and drinking the salty water.

Sam grimaced and pulled the dog back from the water's edge. "What is wrong with you? That's saltwater. It will make you sick!"

Caliburn tilted his head, and made an apologetic groan, his eyes staring up at him, somber and forlorn.

Sam gave him a good pat. "It's okay, Caliburn. I just want you to stay safe, that's all."

The dog barked in acknowledgement, like a child who knew that he had been scolded out of love by a parent.

Tom climbed onto the boat first and Sam held it steady. The two girls climbed in next, carrying two large backpacks with an array of floating bathymetric surveying equipment. Sam stepped on board, and Caliburn jumped in after.

Sam carefully set up the array of floating sonar transducers and his laptop. The system worked by taking multiple images of the lakebed from a variety of angles in order to determine the depths and detailed delineations of the chamber.

Tom picked up the oars. "Is everyone ready?"

Sam and the girls said, "Ready."

Caliburn barked.

And Tom rowed.

It took nearly two hours to row across the two-and-a-half-mile lake, while the computer took in the sonar data and developed a detailed bathymetric map of the surface below the water. Caliburn didn't show any sign of interest, never barking, or looking eagerly toward some distant, or hidden vault, where Merlin's forge might have once burned with magical fire.

They extracted their equipment and came out the other side of the chamber.

Sam paid the security guards an additional tip – if there is such a thing as tipping with a bribe – and climbed back into their hire car.

He said, "I don't get it. I was certain this was the right place."

Tom said, "I didn't see any hidden passages, or even locations which might have once been the entrance to a secret tunnel."

"All right. We'll talk to some local guides in the morning and see if they know of any other nearby caves or grottos."

Guinevere said, "Until then, we have another problem to deal with."

Sam frowned. "What?"

Caliburn whimpered.

And Guinevere said, "Caliburn's sick."

Chapter Seventy-Five

Sam drove fast.

They were heading into Palma to find a veterinarian clinic to help Caliburn.

By the time they had reached the animal hospital, the retriever had vomited twice, and then became lethargic, before drifting into unconsciousness.

Guinevere said, "Sam! This won't work."

"It will work!" Sam said, his voice hard and emphatic. "Tom's found a place that's open. We'll be there in a few minutes!"

"No," Guinevere said. "I'm saying what do we do if he needs an operation?"

Sam said, "Then we pay for the operation. We're not going to let him die!"

"Can he be operated on?"

"Sure he can. Why not?"

Guinevere pursed her lips. "Because Caliburn shares the same defensive system as Excalibur."

Sam thought back to the time the vet at Cannon Beach drew blood from the dog. "His defensive system only engages when he's threatened."

"What does that mean if he's unconscious?" she asked.

Sam said, "I have no idea."

He pulled up in front of the vet clinic. A doctor was just closing up. Sam shifted the car into park, got out, and picked up Caliburn in his arms.

"Wait!" he shouted to the doctor.

The doctor took the dog in with a glance. He grimaced and unlocked the door again. "All right, let's get him inside."

Sam carried Caliburn through the door.

The vet asked, "What happened?"

"I don't know. He was well a few hours ago, then he just started to get sick. He vomited a couple times, became lethargic, and has now been unconscious for about ten minutes."

The doctor frowned. "Has he eaten anything strange today?"

Sam thought about the saltwater that Caliburn was interested in. The lines on his face deepened. He said, "He drank from the Dragon Caves. I stopped him, but he'd already had a good drink."

The vet bit his lower lip. "Look. There's a lot of bacteria in that water, as well as plenty of fungal runoff from the limestone stalactites."

"That's bad?" Sam asked.

"It isn't good," the doctor said. He started tapping the dog using downward pressure on his fingers, and listening to the corresponding resonance. Organs that are hollow make a different sound then those that are solid. If something's inflamed, it will make a different sound. The vet stopped and met Sam's eye. "This dog's appendix is inflamed."

Sam said, "Can you fix it?"

"Maybe. Probably not though. If he's already unconscious it means his appendix has most likely burst, and he's now become septic. We'll need to start him on intravenous antibiotics immediately, and operate. Is that what you want?"

Sam didn't hesitate. "Yes. Do whatever it takes."

The doctor looked like he was going to discuss his fees and risk, but one glance at Sam's hardened face, and he simply said, "I'll call one of the clinic nurses to come in immediately to assist with the operation."

They all waited until the nurse arrived and Caliburn was under anesthetic before they left. Sam gave his cell phone number to the doctor and asked to be called as soon as they knew anything.

Sam stepped out of the vet clinic.

He felt the full force of fatigue grip his body.

Guinevere said, "Are you okay?"

Sam shook his head. "I don't know. I will be when Caliburn pulls through."

Tom handed him his cell phone. "Sorry, Sam, Elise says she's been trying to call you for the last hour."

Sam took the phone. "What have you got?"

Without preamble, Elise said, "I found the last person on Excalibur's kill list."

Sam was still dazed by the events with Caliburn. "Sorry, what, Elise?"

"You found a list of names on board the *Hoshi Maru*. You dubbed them Excalibur's kill list because each name represented one of the seven initial members of the King Arthur research team, who went on to work for Camelot Weapons Industries. There were only two members who were potentially still alive on that list. The first was Dexter Cunningham, who you met in Glastonbury, and the second was Jason Faulkner."

"That's right. We assumed he was dead?" Sam's heart jumped. "Tell me he's still alive!"

"He's alive. And what's more, he's currently living in a villa in Porto Cristo."

Sam said, "That's close."

"Yeah, maybe too close."

"How did you find him?"

"He used his credit card to buy dinner."

"And that worries you?"

"Yeah." Elise said, "Here's a man who's managed to stay completely under the radar for more than seven years and now he slips up?"

"After seven years, maybe he's entitled to make a few mistakes?"

"No. It's not that. I mean, if he was smart enough to reveal no digital trace in all that time, why all of a sudden use an old bankcard to access money."

"Maybe he thought after all this time, Excalibur had finally stopped pursuing him?"

Elise shrugged. "I don't know. Maybe you're right. I have an address where he's staying. Do you want to go speak to him?"

"Yes. Definitely. I can be there in under an hour."

Elise said, "Just be careful, okay?"

Sam grinned. "Thanks Elise. I will."

Chapter Seventy-Six

Sam knocked on the door of the small red bricked Spanish villa.

A big man opened the door with a warm and gregarious smile on his face. The man spoke in perfect Spanish, and asked, "Hello, may I help you?"

Sam frowned. "No hablo mucho espanol."

The man smiled. "You're American?"

"That's right," Sam replied, happy to at least be passed the first hurdle of language.

The man's eyes narrowed, and he gave a cursory glance outside the front yard, as though searching for others. "What can I do for you, sir?"

"This is going to sound strange, but is your name, Jason Faulkner?"

The man's jaw stiffened. His eyes hooded over. "Who are you?"

"My name's Sam Reilly."

"Should I know who you are?"

"No."

The man frowned. "Then why do you know who I am?"

Sam said, "Because, I believe we're both being hunted by Excalibur."

Jason waited for a long time, before taking another glance outside his house. Satisfied they were alone, he opened his front door, and said, "You'd better come inside and tell me what you know about that abomination."

Sam quickly brought Jason up to speed about the death list they'd found on board the *Hoshi Maru* and about the history of the King Arthur program.

When he was finished, Sam asked, "Will you join us?"

Faulkner crossed his arms. "To do what?"

"We want to destroy Excalibur once and for all."

"I don't know if Excalibur can be destroyed. According to the scientists who made him, they utilized some sort of stone that alters a person's strength and toughness at a cellular level."

"That's why we're putting Caliburn back together."

"You've located Caliburn?"

"Yes."

"Both shards?"

"Both shards. But we still have to find the twin stones that belong in its hilt, known as the…"

"Serpent's eyes!"

"You've heard about them?"

"What's more… I know where to find them!"

Sam asked, "Where?"

"Inside the Dragon Caves."

Sam frowned. "We've already searched the cave. There wasn't anything to be found. Maybe after all these years, it's been destroyed?"

Jason shook his head. "Of course not. Merlin was too smart for that. He wouldn't let strangers accidentally walk into his magical grotto. He put a near magical lock on his grotto. You know it was where he mined the rare element used to imbue his weapons with SPELLS, don't you?"

Sam nodded. "I guessed that might be the case. What else do you know about Merlin?"

Faulkner said, "Merlin was originally a blacksmith, but so much smarter than those that he served that he was said to have been born in the completely wrong time altogether. He built weapons that no one could defeat. But weapons weren't the only thing he built. He was more of an engineer. He'd tinker. He'd design and build complex machines. In fact, he was so good at it, he developed the nickname of, Master Builder."

"What did you say?" Sam asked.

"He was so ahead of himself that he developed the nickname of Master Builder."

"Could it be possible?" Sam asked to himself. "Merlin was a Master Builder?"

"Yeah, that's what I said." Jason stared at him. "Are you all right, you look like you've seen a ghost."

"It's nothing," Sam said. "What were you saying?"

Jason smiled, as though he was enjoying himself. "Merlin wouldn't let any strangers accidentally walk into his most precious grotto."

Sam asked, "How did Merlin keep it so well hidden all these years?"

"The same way anyone keeps treasure hidden."

"And what's that?"

"He keeps the entrance secured under lock and key, making it impossible to access."

Sam frowned. "Great. So, we're back to finding an ancient key?"

Jason shook his head and revealed an enigmatic key carved out of a piece of black obsidian. His face was lit up with enjoyment at Sam's reaction.

Jason grinned. "Fortunately, I have the key."

Chapter Seventy-Seven

Merlin's Cave, Majorca

Sam introduced Jason to Tom, Genevieve, and Guinevere.

They retrieved dive equipment and returned to the gates to the Dragon Caves. Genevieve made short work of picking the locks.

They headed down into the enormous cavern, past the flag-shaped stalactite, the snow-covered stalagmite, the deep blue Lakes of Diana, and down to the end of the path, where the boardwalk turned into the jetty of Martel's Lake.

All five of them donned their SCUBA equipment. According to Jason it was only a short tunnel. They could probably swim through holding their breaths once the keystone was removed, but the SCUBA gear made it easier and safer.

They then rowed along the underground lake.

About a mile in Jason said, "Stop. Here."

Sam looked at him. "What's here?"

"The keystone."

Tom asked, "How does it work?"

"Like any other key." Jason handed him the strange stone key.

Tom took it. The key had been intricately carved into the shape of an ornamental key. Only in this case it was made of obsidian. Tom said, "It doesn't feel very strong. Are you sure it won't break as soon as we try and turn it?"

"None of us are strong enough to snap that key," Jason assured him.

Tom handed the key back to him. "I'll let you do the honors."

They tied the rowboat to a large stalagmite, and one by one, dropped backward into the crystal-clear waters of the Martel Lake.

Jason led the way.

They reached a natural crevasse where two independent pieces of limestone formed a bridge together. At the far end there was a slight crease in the stone. The only sign of previous chisels used in the area.

Sam fixed his flashlight on the keyhole.

Jason inserted the obsidian key.

He turned it to the right and backed away.

A moment later, the stone on top floated to the surface.

It wasn't limestone as it appeared to be. Instead, it was a thoroughly porous form of pumice, which was naturally buoyant. The stone had been weighted down using rocks, and the obsidian key merely released their grip on the giant pumice stone.

With the larger stone removed, it revealed a narrow passageway.

All five of them swam through the opening, coming out into a large grotto on the other side. Sam surfaced. A faint blue glow resonated through the grotto giving it a mysterious and almost magical feel. It was bright enough that they were able to switch off their flashlights.

A set of obsidian stairs climbed onto a small island at the center of the grotto.

Sam took those to the top.

Out of the water, he removed his SCUBA gear and swept his new environment with his eyes. The place seemed mostly innocuous.

A stone pedestal adorned the center of the island. Upon the top was a large papyrus book. Sam took in a deep breath, reverently.

It was Merlin's SPELL book.

He turned to Jason. "Is that what I think it is?"

Jason grinned, his eyes wide. "Yes. Merlin's SPELL book."

"If your team has been here before, why didn't you take the book?"

"We did."

Sam face twisted into a wry expression. "And then you returned it again?"

Jason nodded. "Yes. The SPELL book only works while it's in here. It has something to do with the natural glow from the ceiling."

Sam stared at the speckled blue stars and smiled. "They're glow worms?"

"Yes, but not natural. Not the kind you find in Australia or New Zealand. These are chimeras, genetically engineered by Merlin, to develop a very specific type of bioluminescent light. Without that light, no words are visible on the book, and no SPELLS can be cast."

Guinevere gasped.

Sam asked, "What is it?"

"Look at that!" she said.

Sam shifted his gaze to the bottom of the stone stairs inside the underground lake. There was a stone on the lakebed. He switched his flashlight on and focused it on the stone.

The rusty hilt of a sword hung from the stone, its blade permanently sealed inside.

Sam said, "That's Excalibur?"

"Yeah," Jason confirmed. "I bet you were expecting something… shinier?"

Sam nodded. "I suppose so. In the medieval legends, the sword is supposed to glow like fire and be a radiant beacon of the king's power."

Jason nodded, knowingly. "Yeah. I was surprised, too, the first time I saw it."

"But?"

"According to Merlin's SPELL book, when the sword is withdrawn from the stone, it begins to glow. The rust disappears, and the weapon becomes one of the greatest powers on Earth."

"So why don't we just pull it from the stone?"

Jason rolled his eyes with incredulity. "You think any one of us have the strength to draw that sword?"

Sam made a half-grin. "Are you telling me, when the best minds of MI-6 explored this cave, no one was able to engineer a mechanical device to extract the sword?"

Jason laughed. "You have no idea what we're dealing with here, do you?"

"Not really," Sam admitted. "But I guessed that it couldn't take that much to draw a thousand plus year old sword from a stone. I mean, why not remove the stone from the cave, then in an engineer workshop somewhere, use a diamond tipped drill – the same sort of thing they use in the mining industry – to remove the stone."

"First off, that stone's not going anywhere. It's fused with the grotto's floor. And second, we've already tried diamond tipped drills. More than twenty-four hours, and it didn't even leave a scratch."

"Wow. All right. Then how do you suggest we fuse King Arthur's original sword?"

Jason said, "With the Serpent's eyes."

Chapter Seventy-Eight

Sam stood next to Merlin's SPELL book, where it rested on the stone pedestal.

Jason Faulkner quickly flicked through an array of unique weapon designs, science experiments, and prototypes. The entire book reminded Sam of reading Leonardo da Vinci's Engineering Journals. There were engineering designs for weapons and machines that reigned throughout the ages, including weapons that weren't developed until centuries after Merlin had died, with some still unachieved.

Merlin must have known that it would be more than a thousand years before general technologies had advanced to the point where some of his machines could be developed. The genetic engineering that produced Caliburn and Excalibur, using modern day CRISPR DNA snipping technology, was more than a thousand years ahead of his lifetime. Like Leonardo da Vinci, who designed the "Flying Screw," thought to be the first design of a modern helicopter, Merlin had engineering diagrams of interstellar rockets and quadcopter drones.

Jason continued flicking until he was far back in the earlier sections of the SPELL book. He stopped and grinned.

All four of them stared at the page.

It depicted a short sword. Nothing grand like a broadsword. More of an enlarged dagger. By now, that wasn't much of a surprise. Sam was already in possession of both shards of the ancient sword. He knew how small the weapon was. But even seeing it in Merlin's diagrams and schematics, the weapon looked small and unassuming.

The blade appeared to glow.

And at its hilt, a single snake, wrapped itself around – and in its eyes were stones that glowed like fire.

Next to the drawing were the words, Serpent's eyes.

"This is it!" Jason shouted.

Sam said, "That's great but those are small stones. They could have been lost anywhere."

"No. After the battle of Camlann, Merlin retrieved the stones, and hid them in here."

"Where?"

"Like the hilt, he hid them inside the eyes of a serpent."

Chapter Seventy-Nine

Emilee Gebhart stared at the video image she had been sent from the CCTV.

It captured a man coming up onto the road, off the beach where the shipwreck of the *Hoshi Maru* had landed on the beach. The man was completely naked, but his body seemed to be a camouflaged blur. At first, she thought it was a problem with the CCTV, but then she realized the rest of the screen seemed to be in perfect focus.

The stranger walked across the road, making the conscious decision to step out of the way of the CCTV cameras along the main strip of the small coastal town of Cannon Beach.

The CCTV had lost him.

But the recording kept playing.

There was a flash as the image skipped to another viewpoint. This one focused on the back of a bank. It was privately owned by the bank, and only ever reviewed if there was a problem, giving an explanation as to why she was only just seeing it now for the first time.

At first, she thought it was just a blank recording, but then she spotted it. The stranger. He appeared to be wearing clothes, but they didn't quite fit him right. Not just that, they weren't in the right spots. She paused the image, and stared more closely at it.

Her lips twisted into a wry expression of bizarre confusion.

The man wasn't wearing clothes. Instead, they were somehow part of him. Like a tattoo imbedded in his skin, only just not quite right.

What is that?

A moment later, another man entered the frame. A soldier, wearing the uniform of an Army Ranger.

The man spoke to him. Everything seemed fine, and then in a split second, the strange man spun around with a straight razor. The weapon struck his opponent's throat, slicing through it cleanly. The stranger picked up the dead man like it was a carcass and threw him into the trunk of the man's car.

The murderer picked up the soldier's duffel bag, removed a uniform from it, and got dressed.

He climbed into the car.

At the last moment, the stranger looked up at the CCTV – his eyes on the camera with defiant arrogance.

Emilee swallowed hard.

It was the same man she had met at the road block in the Tillamook State Forest.

What did he say his name was?

Jason Faulkner.

She picked up her cell phone and called the FBI agent who was leading the investigation. She quickly explained the CCTV video and gave the agent the name of the suspected perpetrator. But the agent told her to forget about it. The whole thing was no longer her problem. Not her case. She was to go home, delete the record of the CCTV, and forget she ever saw it.

Emilee tried to argue her case, but the agent cut her off.

She glanced through her Sheriff's logbook and searched for the phone number that the other person had given her that night.

In her own handwriting she spotted the name and read her notes.

Sam Reilly.

Piercing deep blue eyes. Intelligent. Good looking. Dangerous. Physically capable of committing murder. Unlikely to have motive. Seems nice.

She picked up her cell phone and called the number he had left her.

The number went to voice mail.

Emilee said, "Mr. Reilly. This is Sheriff Gebhart from Tillamook. I have reason to believe the person who tried to kill you is named Jason Faulkner. He can kill with his hands and a razor blade. Call me as soon as you get this."

Chapter Eighty

Guinevere said, "Merlin kept a snake pit?"

Jason nodded. "Yep. Serpents. Come with me I'll show you."

They all followed Jason across a stone bridge that led off the island into a small carving into the side of the grotto, where more than a thousand snakes slithered at the bottom of a pit.

Guinevere was curious. "What keeps them there?"

"The walls I assume…" Jason said.

"Then you assume wrong," she said. "Snakes are animals and animals need to eat. Thus, they need to be fed." She fixed the beam of her flashlight down the bottom of the well. "There, see! Those little holes lead out somewhere, most likely where they can feast on rodents that enjoy the food left here by the ubiquitous tourists."

Sam said, "I think you're right. The question is, what makes them come back?"

Guinevere took a deep breath. "Its warmer here. The snakes are attracted to the warmth. There must be some sort of underground spring that runs beneath the well. As it does so, it warms the cobblestones, and warms the snakes, making them happy to keep coming back."

Sam said, "This is fascinating, but Jason, where's the snake with the gems from Caliburn's eyes?"

Jason stared at the throng of slithering snakes. "It will be down there."

Guinevere was incredulous. "After all this time?"

"Yes. You see, the rare element that Merlin mined here, and in which he imbued powerful SPELLs to his weapons, not only strengthened the user of the sword with great strength, impenetrable skin, and deadly speed – but it also triggered a unique change at a cellular level, preventing disrepair."

Guinevere said, "Are you telling me, Merlin hid two of these rare elemental gems inside a snake's gouged eyes, and that the blind snake has been wandering this pit for more than a thousand years?"

Jason shrugged. "Afraid so. But you have to admit, Merlin was nothing, if he was not ingenuous and cool with his tricks. No one would ever imagine the lost serpent eyes from Caliburn would be inside a real snake, trapped in a snake pit for all eternity."

She said, "That's horrible. That poor creature!"

Sam said, "The real question now, is how do we entice it to come here?"

Guinevere said, "I can do it."

"Really?" Sam, Tom, and Jason said together.

"Sure. I practice Reiki. It has to do with energy fields and vibrations. Animals are incredibly susceptible to it. A snake like that must be terribly tired after all these years. It will come to me."

Sam said, "And when it does, we'll kill it."

Jason shook his head. "Haven't you heard a word I said, Mr. Reilly. The serpent has been imbued with the SPELL powers of the two rare earth elements."

"You're saying its scales are impenetrable?" Sam asked.

"Sure are."

Sam asked, "Then how do we get those stones?"

Guinevere said, "I know. He has to willingly give up the stones."

Chapter Eighty-One

Guinevere performed what the other three people in the room feared was nothing more than an attempt at magic. But she knew that the ancient Reiki practice worked. She could offer the snake kindness and relief from the burden it had carried all these years.

She altered the surrounding energy around the pit. At first nothing happened, but soon the snakes became livelier, slithering around and shifting their positions within the pit.

Sam held his breath.

Tom looked incredulous.

Genevieve gripped the handgun she had kept, and threatened to shoot any snake that threatened to leave the pit.

And Jason looked bewildered and thrilled.

Guinevere continued to work her magic.

A single snake, with glowing eyes, like fire, made its way to the top of the snake pit, and slithered to greet her.

Sam and Tom took a step back.

Genevieve took a step forward and aimed her weapon.

Sam placed his hand in front of her, warning her not to interrupt.

And Jason remained transfixed as if by magic.

Guinevere spoke softly. "It's all right. I'm going to take those painful things from you."

The snake didn't make a sound. Guinevere moved her hand tentatively closer to the snake, and the snake didn't try to back away. Nor did it try and bite her.

She forced herself to examine the eyes that burned like fire. Then, taking a deep breath, she reached forward and removed the two stones.

The snake appeared disoriented for a moment.

She held her breath.

And the snake quickly slithered away to the corner above the snake pit. She watched as it wrapped its scaly body in on itself, almost appreciative at having relinquished its ancient burden. It seemed to suddenly age quickly and die.

Sam removed both parts of Caliburn so that he could hold them both in his hands. "Now what do we do?"

Jason said, "Hold them together, while Guinevere places the two rare earth elements into the tiny eyes of the serpent at the sword's hilt."

Sam held the two shards of the ancient Arthurian relic. Guinevere placed the stones in the snake's sockets. The sword glowed bright, sending a blinding ray of heat outward, like the force of a sun coming out from behind an eclipse.

Guinevere squinted.

Jason gripped the hilt of the sword, raising it upward.

He began to laugh. It was a big, boisterous laugh.

Guinevere had heard that laugh before – in the Tillamook State Forest – when she was being attacked by something truly evil.

She said, "He's Excalibur!"

Jason grinned. "Guilty as charged!"

Sam tried to knock the sword out of his hand, but the sword and its wearer had fused together, in an impenetrable shield.

Genevieve opened fire with the Uzi she'd taken from their captors in Jerusalem.

She put nearly twenty rounds into Excalibur, but none of them penetrated his body.

Jason grinned. "Hey, that wasn't nice!"

He turned and swung Caliburn around in a quick, striking motion.

Everyone dived back into the underground lagoon.

Guinevere swam downward, until she reached the rusty remains of Excalibur, the Sword in the Stone.

Her hands tightened on its hilt.

The sword turned red with fire and slipped free from the confines of the rare earth element stone.

Chapter Eighty-Two

Excalibur caught Sam Reilly.

He said, "It almost feels wrong to kill you, my friend. After all you have done for me. You see, my own internal stone doesn't last forever. Unlike these rare elements that Merlin mined, the ones that Caliburn and I were fused with were synthetic. If I hadn't found a sword, I too would lose my powers soon, and then, well… we can only imagine what some people might have wanted to do with me."

Sam said, "You have the sword. You may as well go. There's nothing we can do to you, and like you said, you owe us, without us, the sword would never have been forged together once more!"

Excalibur nodded. "You're right. Unfortunately, I can't leave anyone here to know the truth. It's nothing personal, I hope you understand."

He held Sam by his throat, enjoying the pleasure of power once more. It would feel good to kill again. He'd been working so hard to suppress the urge while he hunted for the weapon. Now he could let himself go free.

Sam said, "Does it hurt?"

Excalibur grinned. "Why Mr. Reilly, are you afraid of death?"

Sam motioned for him to come closer.

Excalibur's eyes narrowed. "What is it?"

Sam moved close to his ear and whispered, "Welcome to hell, Excalibur!"

Excalibur gasped.

The pain was unfamiliar and foreign to him, that at first, he couldn't even imagine what had caused it.

His eyes drifted downward.

At the impossible.

The shaft of the ancient sword blade pierced through his chest.

Behind him, Guinevere heaved the blade hard, until the hilt of the weapon became jammed into the back of his chest.

Excalibur tried to take a step forward.

He tried to move.

But all energy was drifting from his body.

He fell backward, into the cool waters of Merlin's grotto.

And sank to the bottom.

He'd always been a strong swimmer. But his arms and legs no longer obeyed his command. He kept his mouth shut, until his lungs burned, and he involuntarily took in a deep breath of cold water.

Excalibur looked up, but his open eyes saw nothing but darkness.

Chapter Eighty-Three

Sam Reilly made his way down to the Majorca docks, where the *Tahila* was waiting for him.

Guinevere greeted him at the side of the jetty.

Sam and Tom had stayed behind inside Merlin's grotto to return both swords to their rightful place inside the ancient stone at the bottom of the lagoon.

He met Guinevere's eyes. "Is Caliburn all right?"

She grinned. "I'll let him tell you himself."

From inside the *Tahila*, Caliburn barked.

Matthew followed him onto the deck. "That reminds me. Now that you're back, what are we going to do with Caliburn. I mean, it's not like he's going to want to live here, with us?"

Sam's lips parted in a wry smile. "That's a good question. Caliburn, what do you say, do you get sea sick?"

The dog barked.

"I'll take that as a no. Welcome aboard the team."

Sam turned to Guinevere. "What about you? Any idea where you'll go?"

"I don't know…" She closed her eyes, grinned, and opened them again. "I might just return to the Oregon Coast. Something about the weather reminded me of home."

Sam met her eyes, they were dry, but somber. "So this is good bye?"

She nodded. "I've lived in the world that you live in. If I had met you years earlier, I might just have decided to run off and join your crusade, but I've been there, and lived that life, I'm ready for a quieter time. But thank you for the time we spent together. It was nice."

Sam stepped closer to her, took her hands in his and then kissed her lips. "Good bye, Guinevere."

Chapter Eighty-Four

Office of the Secretary of Defense, Pentagon

The Secretary of Defense finished hearing the highly unlikely, yet incredibly accurate theory of Jason Faulkner being the deadly beast that went on a killing spree along the Oregon Coast. She listened and waited until the highly intelligent and extremely capable Sheriff of Tillamook finished her assessment.

Emilee Gebhart sat on the couch, her posture simultaneously poised and relaxed. She finished her spiel and then said, "Madam Secretary, I originally took my findings to the FBI agent dealing with this problem. When he refused to speak to me, I went straight to the director of the FBI."

The Secretary grinned. "And when he refused to speak to you, you went straight to me."

Her lips pursed as she exhaled, but she met the Secretary's eye with defiance. "Yes, ma'am."

The Secretary unfolded her arms. Smiled. And said, "All right. I'm going to level with you, because you're obviously an intelligent person who knows when they're being given the run around, and when to keep pushing."

Emilee held her breath, feeling her heart hammer in her chest. "Thank you, ma'am."

"Don't thank me yet," the Secretary replied, her voice cold and hard. "Jason Faulkner was a highly trained killing machine with the British Intelligence Agency, MI-6. After being discharged, he came to Oregon to undergo a highly unethical, genetic experiment aimed at changing his physiology to make him a better soldier. The project worked. He became a deadlier weapon. But we lost complete control of him. You have my word that the project has now been shut down – and with it, all evidence of its existence permanently deleted."

Emilee Gebhart studied her for a moment. Nodded. "All right. That's it then."

"That's it." The Secretary dismissed her. "Thank you for your service."

She watched Gebhart leave. The Tillamook sheriff was tall, and lithe, and quite beautiful, but there was a distinct determination and purposeful movement in her stride.

The Secretary stopped her. "Gebhart…"

"Yes, ma'am?"

The Secretary's scowl twisted into the briefest of smiles. "You were right to bring this to the top. We did the wrong thing here. We're not perfect, you know that, don't you? In our ongoing attempt to keep America safe, we make mistakes. Governing parties change. The course of duty, honor, and rightfulness alters alongside history. With each generation, we strive to form a better Union, a more noble society, where everyone gets a decent seat at the table. Lessons have been learned over the course of this project, mistakes were made, but we will do better."

The sheriff nodded. "Thank you, ma'am, but crimes have been committed."

"I know. And people will be punished."

Gebhart's eyes narrowed. "There should be a public hearing."

"Probably. But there won't be." The Secretary's voice was emphatic. "I made sure of that."

Gebhart avoided her scrutinizing gaze. "Is there anything else I can do for you, Madam Secretary?"

The Secretary of Defense smiled at Gebhart's righteousness. She had been Secretary of Defense long enough to know that there was a great big expanse of gray between right and wrong. Her job was to help steer America on the right side of the line, but sometimes in the name of defense that line needed to be crossed. This was one of those times. If they hadn't authorized the experiment, it was only a matter of time before someone else did.

She said, "Emilee. I read your file. I know you've been striving to overcome the challenges of living up to your father's tremendous achievements nearly all your life. That, even today, there are some people who believe you were awarded the position of Tillamook sheriff because of his achievements."

Gebhart crossed her arms, and met her gaze.

The Secretary said, "I believe you've already proven your worth. One day you'll lead this country in ways you can't even imagine. And I hope to see you when you do. Good luck."

"Thank you, Madam Secretary."

The Secretary watched her leave.

When the door was firmly closed, she picked up her cell phone and dialed a number that she had used multiple times in the past two weeks.

A man answered. "Madam Secretary..."

"Arthur..." The Secretary interrupted him. "The King Arthur project has been permanently shut down as a failure. *Camelot Weapons Industries* will be liquidated and absorbed by the Department of Defense."

Arthur said, "Just one more week. I told you I could get Excalibur to come back."

The Secretary grinned. "You haven't heard?"

"Heard what?"

"Your precious little weapon was broken. A girl with a kind heart withdrew the Sword in the Stone, and killed Jason Faulkner."

The phone line went silent.

"Arthur?"

"Merlin forged that sword with King Arthur's DNA! No one else could draw the sword!"

The Secretary shrugged. "Oh well, you might be right there. So, with a noble heart, and DNA she shared with her ancestor, Guinevere withdrew the Sword from the Stone and ended your little experiment."

"This can't finish like this!"

"But it already has, Arthur. It already has."

The End

Printed in Great Britain
by Amazon